Provenance

ACCRUE'S END : BOOK TWO

PROVENANCE

E.R. SMO

Dark Tempest Press, LLC.

ISBN: 979-8-9871898-2-5

Cover by J Caleb Design
Instagram: @jcalebdesign

Chapter 1

How could a hard-fought victory fill Kyo with such an overbearing sense of weakness and failure? Holding off an army of skeletons and preventing Sybilla from turning every citizen of Oasis into raging shades should have boosted his confidence to tremendous heights. He fought alongside the Aurora, as if he'd truly followed in his parents' footsteps. After surviving numerous life-threatening situations, he deserved to consider himself an honorary member of that elite group of mages.

A particularly weak one in comparison. It made his stomach sink whenever he thought too hard about it.

With an aggravated shout, Kyo thrust his palm against the solid rockface that stretched high above the city of Oasis, flinging pebbles in every direction. His wind spell rotated furiously like a drill, condensing as he pushed his hand forward, but he stopped before it exploded. Wiping sweat from his forehead, he admired the wide hole he'd created, minuscule compared to the whole of the cliff, but at least no one would notice.He couldn't help but grin as he stared at his hand and flexed his fingers. Though it still required some focus, he could perform the spell successfully with each attempt, getting closer to becoming second nature. A positive step forward.

But it was small in the grand scheme of his desire to be as powerful as his parents. Even with this spell officially added to his arsenal, it hadn't been enough to deal with Sybilla, not without the added power of the accrue stone. He had a long way to go before he could truly stand side by side with the likes of the true Aurora.

Kyo exhaled slowly, arms slumping and easing the tension from his body and closed his eyes, only to be greeted by an image of one of Blanq's undead flashing in his mind.

He gasped and his eyes shot open. With a sigh, he ran his hand over his face. Being like the Aurora included more mental strength too apparently. Nearly every time he closed his eyes, either Blanq's skeletons or Sybilla's maniacal face appeared.

With the sun resting high in the sky and greater heat accompanying it, Kyo decided it'd be best to leave the remote corner of Oasis and head back to the inn, or risk being left behind when the airship arrived to take them to Alderdeem. He was nearly as excited as Rosette when Krysta said an airship would be coming to get them. What better way was there to travel across the continent?

The excitement dwindled when his mind turned to home and Alden. Even the chancellors had been split on whether to consider him a willing accomplice to Sybilla and Blanq's actions or a victim forced to aid them. Krysta vocally sided with the former, which made his brow crease whenever he thought of it. He had to resist the urge to slap some sense into Her Highness. Still, when the time came, he'd defend his godfather as best he could and make sure he returned home.

Yet a tiny voice in the back of his mind echoed sentiments of Alden truly being an enemy. The friendly, loving godfather merely an act until the time came to enact their plans. Kyo clenched his eyes and shook his head, burying these thoughts under years of happy memories.

He jumped atop the nearest rooftop, propelled by wind from his feet, jogging and leaping from one to the other. While his eyes shifted between the glittering, multicolored sea stones that adorned the roofs and the vast ocean to his right, his mind remained fixed on Alden. Despite what *Her Highness* may think, Kyo believed in his godfather. His explanation about the connection between the accrue stones and his parents' deaths, as well as Sybilla and Blanq's overwhelming power—what choice did he have but to cooperate to further his goal of destroying those stones for good?

Kyo entered the inn and found his party sitting in chairs in front of the hearth, though it remained dark and unlit. In a desert city like this, it only made sense to light a fire at night when the temperature dropped significantly. A few other patrons sat alone or in small groups, chatting away. Once Kyo claimed an empty chair, Krysta raised her palms and released a burst of ice magic, cooling the air around him.

"Thanks." Kyo slumped in his seat and smiled.

"How much longer until the airship gets here?" Rosette asked, sitting on the arm of Roland's armchair, bouncing in place.

"Be patient, kiddo. It'll come, and you'll get your first airship ride." Roland turned to Krysta. "We owe you a lot. Even trying to get us a home in Alderdeem is more than we deserve. Not that we want you to change your mind, of course."

Krysta smiled. "Don't say that. You two deserve it for helping take down Sybilla. Even if you felt you didn't have a choice."

Her smile turned to a frown, meeting Kyo's eyes who motioned with his hands for another burst of cool air. Rolling her eyes, she obliged.

"If I may ask, did communication with your uncle go well? I imagine he misses you quite a bit," Marsh said.

Krysta shook some of her emerald hair from her face. "Well, after he got over the initial shock of hearing from me, which may or may not have resulted in him falling off his throne, he agreed to send for me immediately. Though I could tell he struggled to decide between happy and angry. I did wander off without telling anyone months ago, after all."

"I'm sure you won't be the only one getting a lecture from His Majesty," Estella said as she approached them. The Aurora's cleric and conjurer grabbed a chair from a nearby table and pulled it toward the group, taking a seat. "We did keep your presence here from him so things didn't become more complicated. We were afraid he'd send some of his royal guard, and doing so might have caused Sybilla and Blanq to rethink their plans and go who knows where."

"Where are Cedric and Garret?" Kyo asked.

"Those two didn't want to waste time in further investigating the source of the corruption, so they're off to follow a few leads. I'll be dealing with His Majesty myself it seems." Estella ran her fingers over her brunette curls. "So much for that vacation Garret wanted. It sounded so nice too."

Marsh sat up straight, keeping his gaze on Estella. "They have leads? Anything worthwhile?"

Estella shrugged. "We'll see. Among other things, they want to help transport any corrupted to Spellnix Hold to be cured by Blanq. Many towns and cities don't have easy access to airships. What's worse, people well to the west may simply be too far away to make the journey before they turn. Sadly, Blanq's willingness to cure them isn't viable for everyone."

"If only we could find out where the two of them learned their teleportation spells. That would certainly make things easier," Marsh mused, rubbing his chin.

"It would," Estella agreed, "but I have a feeling we won't get an answer. And we couldn't attempt to force the information from them if we want Blanq's continued cooperation. Regardless, these aren't details you all need to concern yourself with. Even you, Your Highness. You've all done more than enough. Take the time to relax."

Kyo leaned back in his chair, staring at the ceiling. "You won't get any argument from me. I'll gladly do nothing and sleep as much as I can. Between eating and training of course."

"After what we've been through, I honestly can't even argue," Krysta said.

Estella turned in her chair to face Krysta. "On second thought, Your Highness, there is something I'd ask of you."

"Please stop calling me that."

Estella didn't acknowledge her request. "You could help me convince your uncle to loan out his airship fleet to towns and cities across the continent. Without them, I couldn't begin to imagine the number of people who would have no hope of being cured once they become corrupted."

"That will be a tough sell. I can try, but I don't see it going well. As caring a ruler as he is, that benevolence is limited to Alderdeem and the region it sits in. Politics and all." Krysta's eyes met Estella's. "Still, I will do what I can."

"That would be appreciated. Now, for the real reason I came to find you. How are you doing?" Estella asked, her eyes drifting across the five mages seated near her.

Kyo rotated his right shoulder. "Still sore but otherwise okay."

"I know how you are physically." Estella leaned forward, staring with intense concern. "Shades, Sybilla, Blanq…the loss of ones close to you. In barely a week, you all have been through so much, more than some experience in their lifetimes. And unlike us, you have not had time to grow used to it. So again, I ask, how are you?"

Silence fell upon the party. Kyo kept his gaze on the floor for several seconds, and when he glanced up, he noticed no one else made eye contact with Estella either.

How *was* he? Alive at least, so how could he complain? He still breathed, Sybilla and Blanq were in Spellnix Hold, and he could leave the corruption to the Aurora to investigate. Sure, Sybilla haunted his dreams, the loss of Ruby, and Alden refusing to come home tore at Kyo's heart, but what sort of Aurora in the making would he be if he couldn't handle that on his own?

"Sometimes, I hear something far away and am afraid it's a shade," Rosette confessed, her eyes glued to her lap and fingers gripping her dress.

Marsh nodded in agreement. "There had been a case for me where children were screaming while playing outside." He inhaled deeply and blinked hard. "And for a brief second, I thought it could have been a shade's screech."

Estella offered a warm smile. "Shades are terrifying creatures. Horrible to say, given what they once were, but your reaction is understandable and expected. Do not think it's abnormal."

Roland grabbed the flask from within his coat and took a swig. "Have to admit, even I get a bit unnerved when I think back to fighting Sybilla and how unhinged she became by the end. Silver lining, I learned my Rosette is even tougher than I thought." He smiled at his adoptive daughter, who did the same in return. "Maybe I can ease up on how protective I am of her." He raised his hand, the tips of his thumb and index finger barely separated. "Just a little."

Krysta shook her head, rubbing her eyes. "I see Layla whenever I close my eyes. And I'll have to break the news to my family as well." She barely held in a sob with the last few words.

"I can take on that burden if you'd prefer, Your Highness," Estella offered.

"No. I let her go. I failed to see what she was planning to do. I'll take responsibility."

Estella left her chair and approached Krysta, gently pulling her to her feet and embracing her. "I wasn't there, but you mustn't blame yourself." Estella turned to look at the others. "I know you will find a cleric or two in the palace, but while I'm there, you may come to me if you need to talk. It's part of what we as clerics do, easing your minds as well as your bodies."

Krysta released deep, shaky breaths as she buried her face against Estella's shoulder.

Kyo remained silent, but when Estella's eyes met his, he nodded. He had no intention of taking her up on her offer, but avoiding confrontation was best.

"Though I am still new to the clergy, you may come to me as well," Marsh said.

"Probably not the best idea, kid." Roland lifted Rosette from one arm of the chair and set her down on the other so he could look at Marsh. "You've got just as much going on in that head of yours as the rest of us. I doubt you're in a headspace to be able to help when you're trying to deal with it yourself."

Marsh frowned. "As a cleric, it is my duty to—"

Roland held his hand up, and Marsh quieted. "You need to be able to help yourself before you can help others. This doesn't just apply to clerics but to everyone. Sometimes you need to take a backseat and recognize when something should be handled by someone else. Something I wish we were better at putting into practice, honestly. When you don't need counseling yourself, that's when you can try your hand at it."

Marsh stared at Roland, pursing his lips. "I suppose you are correct."

"Of course I am. I am older and wiser," Roland teased, grinning.

"Old man." Rosette giggled.

"Hey, not *that* old, shrimp."

"Take it easy, geezer," Kyo teased.

Estella took her place back in her chair after Krysta calmed down. "I hope you all get along as well while living together for a while in the palace."

"I have to admit I am excited." A smile returned to Marsh's face. "I have never been to Alderdeem. And being invited into a royal palace has me a bit intimidated. Though I would also like to visit the cleric chapels as well."

"I'm sure the palace is nice and all, but seeing that big tree the city is built around is going to be crazy." Kyo had seen drawings in textbooks, but to see something of such a scale in person—he could hardly imagine it.

"That 'big tree' is called The Ancient," Krysta said.

Kyo sensed a history lesson coming on but couldn't speak up in time to stop it.

"The space between each pair of roots houses a different district of the city. The leaves that fall from The Ancient are used to create all sorts of goods, most notably skin revitalizing cream and other beauty products." Krysta gently ran her hand along her cheek. "I'm an avid user of such things. And it's part of why Alderdeem is the wealthiest city in the world."

Kyo rolled his eyes so hard he thought he'd catch a glimpse of his brain. "Someone sure is full of themselves. If I go to Alderdeem, will I be beautiful too?" He removed his hair tie, letting his silver hair fall free. He ran his fingers through it, performing a few poses, which sent Rosette into a giggle fit and even got a chuckle from Marsh.

"You could surely use it. Your skin is dry as Blanq's skeletons, and don't get me started on your hair." Krysta turned her head, letting her long ponytail flick in the air. "You're just jealous."

"There are more important things than having the smoothest skin and silkiest hair, *Your Highness*," Kyo said, putting the hair tie back to re-form his low ponytail, which reached between his shoulder blades.

Estella giggled. "You two get along so well. I'm sort of jealous."

"I think we have very different ideas of what 'getting along well' means," Kyo grumbled.

The door to the inn opened, and a tall man walked in, the embroidered insignia of a deciduous tree on the left breast of his robes and a shield surrounded in flame on the right. His robes were faded crimson, with gold trim like a cleric's. While the man had several small scars on his right cheek and above his eyes and more wrinkles than Roland, there wasn't a single gray strand in the man's short-cropped chestnut hair.

When Krysta approached him, the man knelt on one knee, keeping his eyes to the floor. "Your Highness, it is good to see you again. We can depart to Alderdeem when you're ready."

Krysta crossed her arms over her chest. "My uncle isn't here, Hayner. You needn't be so formal."

Hayner rose and grinned slightly. "Sorry, a force of habit." He opened his arms, and Krysta melted into them, embracing him tightly. "It really is wonderful to see you again. We were all so worried about you" His arms squeezed tighter, and he raised her off her feet, getting a yelp and giggle out of her before being set down.

"I know," Krysta muttered. "I'm sorry to worry you all. I just…"

"You don't need to explain to me, Your Highness. I understand full well why you did so. Your uncle has been irritable to say the least since you've been gone though. It will be nice to see him calm again." Hayner looked past her. "Is this the party you mentioned?"

"That's right." Krysta held out her hand toward Kyo and the others. "You of course know Estella already."

Estella stood. "Good to see you again, Hayner."

Hayner placed his fist on his chest and bowed his head. "You as well, Estella."

"Then we have Kyo Sonata, Marsh Umbrafin, Roland Strattner, and his daughter Rosette Strattner," Krysta said, pointing to each respectively." She motioned to Hayner. "And this is Hayner, one of my father's royal guard and also his advisor, when he needs a second opinion."

"A pleasure to meet you all," Hayner greeted with a bow of his head. "I'm sure I'll get the details soon enough, but thank you so much for taking good care of Her Highness while she's been away from home."

Kyo waved his hand dismissively. "Don't thank us too much. Honestly, we've only known her for a week or so. Before that, she was on her own."

Marsh stood from his chair. "We should also be thanking you and everyone at the palace for agreeing to host us. It is truly an honor."

"Not at all," Hayner said. "If you're ready, we can head to the airship immediately and begin the trip home."

Once everyone stood, Hayner and Krysta led the way from the inn.

"Your parents will have opinions on your choice of dress, Your Highness," Hayner commented.

"Oh, don't I know it," she replied. "I hope to change before I see them."

"Good luck with that." Hayner gently nudged her side.

A smidge of jealousy hit Kyo as he watched those two interact, similar to how he and Alden acted together. And she had parents to return to. From what Kyo had gathered, those at the palace seemed nice and friendly, especially toward her. She had said she loved her parents but they were overbearing. How bad must it have been for her to run off for half a year?

Either way, he had other things to focus on. He wouldn't sit idle while in Alderdeem. Increasing his internal magic pool and learning new spells and swordplay were at the top of his agenda. Hopefully, he'd be able to make use of the palace's resources, whether tomes or people.

Chapter 2

Bones of the long deceased littered the outskirts of Oasis. Kyo watched as enforcers and civilians alike brought mostly intact skeletons back to the tomb beneath the city, while disposing of lone bones. A few mages used earth magic to control the sand to transport large numbers of bones together, but even so, cleanup would take time.

Blanq had gone through all of that as a mere distraction.

Since she and Sybilla were locked away, it shouldn't matter anymore, but the lengths they went to for something so evil made him shiver.

"It's time to go home," Krysta said softly.

Kyo stopped walking and turned his attention toward the airship towering over them. He'd never seen one up close. It didn't look much different from a large ocean ship by design and with a wooden finish. He broke from the group to get a view of the airship from behind, staring in awe at the two massive magic-tech engines built into the stern. They propelled the ship with wind spells, while the two he couldn't see underneath the hull kept it afloat with gravity spells. His heart pounded, excitement and fear fighting for dominance at the prospect of flying for the first time.

"Hey, Kyo. Let's get moving," Roland called.

"Yeah, yeah." Kyo jogged toward his party and followed them up the gangplank to the deck.

"We will depart in a moment." Hayner approached a small cabin, speaking a few silent words to the pilot, whose hands were already on the helm. Hayner then headed below deck.

"We're actually going to fly on an airship!" Rosette shouted, beaming. She ran to the railing to look over the edge, but Roland followed close behind and pulled her away.

"Whoa there, kiddo. Wait until we're in the air. And be careful near that railing."

Marsh rested his hand over his lips and chin but couldn't hide his smile. "This will be my first time as well. It is sure to be quite an experience."

"Not to mention meeting royalty in a palace," Kyo added.

Krysta glared. "Excuse me, you've already met royalty."

Kyo waved his hand dismissively. "You don't count."

Her jaw hanging open brought a grin to his face, but it faded as the airship shook beneath them. The engines roared as the airship lifted from the ground, and Oasis became smaller by the second. He'd jumped from a spire mere days ago, so this shouldn't be too intimidating…he hoped. Rosette broke from Roland's grip to peek through the railing, and Kyo followed, watching the ground grow more distant with wide eyes as the wind blew through his hair and licked at his face. The airship rotated to face the northeast, then the wind engines kicked in, propelling them forward.

The only thing keeping him from smiling was Alden's absence. He should have been here with them. Knowing him, he would try to sell his enchanting services to the king. Instead, that stubborn ass ran off to who-knew-where. Though it left a lonely gap in his heart, Kyo also felt pride for his godfather and his determination to do the right thing. Wherever he had disappeared to, Kyo hoped Alden was safe.

Hayner returned and struck up a conversation with Krysta, so Kyo kept his attention on the swift-moving desert beneath them. Best to block out her summarization of events. Hearing her recount her loss would bring his own to the forefront of his mind, and he didn't need that. Instead, he focused his thoughts on their destination. A massive city to explore, nestled among the roots of a mountainous tree. His grip tightened on the railing, excitement flowing through him. More than anything else, he hoped to convince one of Krysta's royal guards to teach him a thing or two. If he'd learned anything over the past week or so, it was coming to terms with the reality of his own weakness. Something he had to change.

Marsh apparently had the same idea, engaging in conversation with Estella. While Kyo couldn't hear what they said, Marsh's hand motions made it clear they were discussing spells. The desire to open his spell tome pulled at Kyo, but he ignored it for the time being. He had made great progress with his spellcasting recently, but his swordplay suffered, having been useful against the skeletal army but completely ineffective against Blanq and Sybilla. Perhaps that was where his focus should be for the near future, as well as combining his weapons and magic.

Kyo sighed and sat against the railing. He shouldn't be letting his mind become overwhelmed with so much. After all they'd been through, he needed to relax. No reason to rush. He repeated this in his head. With Sybilla and Blanq locked away, he had plenty of time to hone his crafts. The first few days at the palace should be spent doing nothing important. He had earned the right to be a freeloader for a short time.

As time passed, the dry, dull desert gave way to a rocky landscape littered with lush green grass and plants. And eventually, they flew over what was called the Infinite Farmstead. An exaggerated name of course, but even from their current altitude, Kyo couldn't see where it ended. From wheat and corn to fruits and vegetables, workers harvested the food grown below and exported them across the continent and even to Kattelink Island.

"Hello there, Kyo."

The voice shook him from his trance. Kyo turned to see Hayner standing before him. He rose and met the man's eyes.

"First and foremost, I would again like to thank you for being by Her Highness's side during the recent troubles," Hayner said. "I'm glad she found such capable allies. Though I suppose the son of two Aurora couldn't be anything else." A slight grin spread across his lips.

Kyo's eyes shifted to the side, and he released an unenthusiastic chuckle. "Please. If anything, we learned we are far from capable. The only reason we're still here is more due to luck than anything else."

Hayner placed a hand on Kyo's shoulder. "And yet here you stand, all five of you. Sometimes, it's not all about power but determination and, yes, luck as well. Regardless of how you perceive it, you have my gratitude."

"Well, you're welcome, I guess. So, since you're a royal guard, and I figure you occasionally see the Aurora, did you ever meet my parents?" Kyo asked.

"Oh yes. They were skilled mages and took most things seriously. Though no one could escape them recounting stories about their baby boy. My condolences. But if your goal is to follow in their footsteps, I'd say you are well on your way. Including making friends in high places." Hayner retracted his hand and placed both behind his back.

"Friend" may be pushing it, but Kyo figured it best not to say that out loud. "Appreciate it. But hopefully next time I get involved in some insane situation, I'll be ready for it. I'll be sure to relax, but I plan to spend some time in Alderdeem getting stronger."

Hayner nodded. "That is a good mentality to have. Despite what you've all been through, you haven't let it deter you from your goals. Not everyone can say the same." He turned his head, eyeing the others enjoying the view or engaging in conversation. "Perhaps it's fate that Her Highness came across such wonderful people."

"I guess she's more to you than just someone you are charged with protecting, huh?"

"Indeed so." He turned back to meet Kyo's eyes. "My parents were royal guards as well. They raised me to eventually follow them and serve the royal family, which I didn't mind, as they treated us well. Though we have a small age gap, Her Highness and I grew up together, and so I see her as something like a younger sister. I would give my life to protect her. Not because of duty but because I care for her well-being. I could only hope any allies she makes would feel the same."

Give his life to protect Krysta's? Fighting alongside each other was one thing, but that might be going too far. Then again, would he do that for any of the others? They hadn't known each other long. It'd be silly to even consider it, right? Hopefully, they'd never find themselves in a situation like that. For all Kyo knew, they'd never have to fight side by side again.

"If she doesn't go running off again," Kyo replied, "then it might not be a concern, right?"

Hayner smirked. "True enough. Though it's difficult to suppress a strong will like hers." His gaze shifted, falling onto Rosette. "The young girl there. She's a summoner, correct?"

"Yeah, she's just a kid but she was very helpful. Not sure we'd be here without her. But I feel bad about her having to fight like that to begin with. Why? You're not going to give her trouble, are you?"

"I don't intend to, so long as she doesn't cause us any."

Kyo narrowed his eyes. "She's a good kid, so don't give her a reason to be upset."

"I'm sure she is. It's like dealing with a saber. They are often cute and friendly, and you love them. You want to hug and pet them. One day, one bites you. It doesn't stop you from loving them and wanting to pet them, but you're going to be more cautious around them going forward because you recognize the potential danger. It only takes one bad decision. There's nothing wrong with being vigilant." Hayner strolled toward Roland and Rosette.

Kyo sighed and turned his attention beyond the railing. A cheerful kid like Rosette wouldn't summon a Relinquished knowing the death and destruction they could cause. The possibility wasn't even worth thinking about. She only seemed to care about summoning Altruists to help her.

Hours passed, conversations came and went, food consumed — or in Kyo's case inhaled — and overall, he found it more enjoyable traveling via air compared to sea. Though that may have been because he'd never experienced it before. The views changed over time, allowing them to see towns, rivers, and hills from high above. He wondered if it were possible to obtain such mastery over wind spells that he could fly like this through magic alone. That may have been asking too much, but he could dream.

"Come look at this," Estella called out.

Kyo joined her, and the others followed suit. The airship approached The Barrier Peaks, the mountain range separating the region of Alderdeem from the remainder of the continent, stretching from north to south. His gaze followed her pointed finger to a cliff where a massive bird with deep onyx feathers sat in an equally enormous nest. Kyo's eyes widened at the scale. If it flew to the nearest town, it could easily crush houses beneath its talons.

"It's a zu," Roland said to Rosette, who sat atop his shoulders.

"How is it so big?" Rosette asked with a gasp.

"Because it eats all of its vegetables." Roland laughed as she pinched and tugged on his cheek in response.

The zu turned its head to follow the airship passing by but otherwise made no move.

Kyo wondered if it sat on an egg. Even a newly hatched chick would be enormous. "What does something like that even eat?"

"Nearly any creature large enough to satisfy it," Estella said. "It's not unusual to find cockatrice at the foot of the mountain, or oversized creepy crawlies within the rocks. There's plenty among The Barrier Peaks to keep it away from humans. Unless humans venture too close of course." Her finger lowered toward a forest growing within a narrow gap within the mountain range. "The Living Forest is the most direct route through, but as cheesy as its name is, it is also accurate. The ferals and plant life within that forest are one and the same and rather hostile."

"Which is why a mutually beneficial deal was made between Alderdeem and towns on the west side of the mountain," Krysta said matter-of-factly. "Approved merchants can take an airship to and from Alderdeem to bypass the danger or otherwise take an ocean vessel. There has been a significant drop in vendors being attacked or killed since that was put into place. Well before I was born of course."

Ugh, another history lesson from Her Highness. And he bet there would be plenty more once they were at the palace.

"It is dismal to think that in every town we have flown across, there are bound to be at least a few corrupted people who may not make it to Spellnix Hold to be cured," Marsh said, gripping the railing. "Where did it come from? How does it spread? Is there a source, or is it simply a part of this world now like any other sickness?"

"Hey, come on, bedhead. You're going to drive yourself crazy thinking like that." Kyo rested his hand on his back. "Right now is a time for us to relax."

"Kyo is right," Estella added. "Those questions are exactly what we Aurora are hoping to answer. Cedric and Garret are out there looking for answers as we speak. But you mustn't let your mind dwell on what you can't change. Surely, you've been told that during your time as a cleric, haven't you? That doesn't only apply to when you are attempting to heal others."

Marsh nodded. "Yes, I am aware. And do not misunderstand—I do wish to see Feracael be rid of the corruption, but with those feelings also comes a morbid fascination. To me, it is something that should not exist and yet does. And I would welcome the chance to learn more."

"When all of this has passed, I wouldn't mind sitting down with you and explaining what we've found," Estella smiled at Marsh, who returned the gesture.

"If you all look very closely toward the bow of the ship, you can make out The Ancient." Krysta said. "But don't let it fool you. We're not going to reach Alderdeem until morning. That shows you how enormous it truly is."

She was right. Kyo could barely make out what appeared to be a bundle of greenery on the dark horizon. He couldn't wait to see it up close. Aside from that, he'd soon have an entire city to explore—restaurants to try, tomes to purchase, and cryst to earn to afford both. So long as they didn't force him to dress in fancy, stiff clothes around the palace, he expected to enjoy his time there.

Chapter 3

Kyo stared in awe at the trunk of The Ancient, the airship flying around it like an insect buzzing around an average tree in Mistwell's park. High above, the canopy of green leaves stretched well beyond the city's limits. Even so high in the air he couldn't make out the top. Below them sat Alderdeem, a circular, three-tiered city separated into districts by the massive roots of The Ancient. The internal tiers sat at higher elevations, looking similar to the sections of a wedding cake.

How did anyone navigate a city like this? He'd for sure get lost for hours if he wasn't careful. Oasis seemed like a small village in comparison. The sheer size made him curious what sorts of shops, restaurants, and other businesses he'd find. He glanced over at Rosette hopping up and down as she stared at the city below, Roland close behind her. Going from no home to settling down in a place like this would be a huge change for them but hopefully for the best.

"Do you think we're allowed to climb the roots?" Rosette asked without taking her eyes off the scenery below.

"Those roots are a lot bigger than they look from up here, kiddo. Not so sure that'd be an easy thing to do," Roland said, a smile on his lips. A wider smile than Kyo had seen on him yet.

Krysta and Marsh stepped toward the railing to join them.

Krysta stared upward. "The canopy is its own ecosystem. I've never been, but those who have say there are ferals that have made a home up there. Mostly the avian type. I can't say how those that can't fly made their way up there in the first place."

"Nature always finds a way to do surprising things. It is a part of what makes it so fascinating." Marsh's attention turned to the bow of the airship as they rounded the trunk. "Is that the palace down there?"

Kyo followed his gaze to find a magnificent structure, one he'd seen drawings of in history books. Massive stone walls cornered by rounded towers topped with azure roofs, a lush green garden on the western side, and more windows than he could count. Forget the city proper—he'd get lost trying to navigate the palace.

"That's right. The palace houses the royal family of Alderdeem, as well as some palace workers and the royal guard," Krysta said proudly.

"I might die of starvation trying to find a kitchen in that place," Kyo groaned.

Krysta clicked her tongue and shook her head. "Don't be so dramatic. It isn't so bad once you get used to it."

"I can't imagine how long that would take," Kyo mumbled.

The airship passed by the palace, descending toward the base of The Ancient, a growth from the trunk wide enough to have nearly a dozen airships docked. Metal beams and plates were under construction, vaguely taking the shape of what would eventually be a dome to cover the entire dock, though it appeared far from finished. Workers used their magic to transport, cut, and weld the metal into the appropriate sizes and shapes.

Kyo raised a foot onto the railing, but Krysta pulled him back by his hoodie. "Oh no you don't. Not this time. We will be going straight to the palace, so you need to reach deep, grab whatever minute sense of manners and etiquette you can find, and apply it." She released his hoodie and glared. "Better yet, maybe it's best you don't speak."

Kyo rolled his eyes. "Relax. I was just going to—"

"We have arrived," Hayner announced then bowed, right arm extended to his side. "Your Highness, if you would."

Krysta nodded and motioned for everyone to follow. They descended below deck and left the airship, Hayner at the head of the group.

A chilly breeze wafted through, Kyo immediately zipping his hoodie for extra warmth. He expected the extra chill after having traveled so far north, though the constant shade provided by The Ancient didn't help. "So, does the city not get enough sunlight or what? Must be gloomy always being in shade."

"Originally, that was the case," Hayner said while keeping his eyes staring straight ahead. "However, it didn't take long after the establishment of Alderdeem for the queen of that time, Queen Myra Alexandra, to see the detriment of their situation. Therefore, she initiated a project to adjust the direction of the branches and leaves in such a way that the city below could receive ample sunlight. The project lasted well after her reign and life. Naturally, not all of the city can escape the shade, but many areas, with particular focus on the residential districts, receive proper sunlight."

"I am sure they used magic to aid them in that project. A mixture of spells and physical means to adjust the direction of the branches?" Marsh asked, staring up at the canopy.

"Correct. Every so often slight adjustments are needed, but the majority of effort spent above is for gathering leaves and plants for medicinal and commercial use, as well as studying the ferals that have made The Ancient their home." A grin spread across Hayner's lips. "On that note, do be careful. As rare as it may be, bird droppings have been known to slip between the many branches and onto an unfortunate civilian's head from time to time."

Rosette burst into giggles. "Raining bird poop."

Roland pulled a fluffy purple jacket from the enchanted travel pouch on his hip and helped Rosette slip it on.

The walk to the palace took nearly thirty minutes, the paved path lined with lush green trees, their thin pink petals beginning to sprout. They passed through multiple iron gates with a pair of guards at each, who bowed to Krysta upon seeing her.

Kyo never thought much about the clothes he wore, but as he stared down at his boots with a layer of dry mud and his shorts fraying in places, it dawned on him he may be underdressed for entering a royal palace. Oh well, too late to do anything about it. A couple years ago he'd been escorted through Mistwell by Ruby and Ren in his pajamas without embarrassment, so why care about what royals he'd never met before think? The memory sent a pang of sorrow and guilt through him. If it had meant Ruby surviving, he'd gladly let her and Ren be as much of a pain in the ass as they pleased.

The front doors of the palace opened, a pristine red carpet welcoming them inside. On either side sat trophies and relics, some in glass cases combined with magic barriers, others uncovered. To Kyo, it looked more like a museum than what he expected from a palace entrance. A golden goblet adorned with shimmering jewels. A slightly curled piece of yellowed parchment he didn't have enough time to read. Though his steps paused at the authentic dragon skull mounted to the wall. Who would have gone all the way to the Southern Continent, Morterra, to battle and manage to kill a dragon? Marsh and Roland also gazed around with wide eyes and slack jaws, the latter having to pull on Rosette's coat to keep her from running from the party. Roland would have his hands full keeping her excitement in check.

Hallway after hallway, they passed by countless rooms, framed paintings lining the wall, and the occasional encased treasure on display. Finally, they found themselves in front of a pair of tall, crimson-painted iron doors. Krysta pushed them open, revealing a massive rotunda, the far side lined with bay windows reaching the ceiling and two thrones, only one occupied. There sat who Kyo could only assume was the King of Alderdeem, a hefty man with a bushy black beard, equally bushy eyebrows, a golden crown atop his head, and a robe patterned similarly to Hayner's with the addition of fluffy white trim.

The second they entered, the king stood and descended the few steps from his throne, marching toward them. Hayner approached and opened his mouth, but the king sidestepped him without a word, closing in on Krysta before embracing her tightly.

"You…you absolute dalcop. How dare you worry your family like that." The trembling in the king's deep voice revealed more relief than anger.

Krysta returned the embrace, burying her face in his shoulder. "I do not regret my actions, but I am sorry to have worried you, Uncle."

Kyo stood awkwardly, not sure where to place his hands as their hug dragged on. Clearly being referred to as stupid by doting family member, or in her case "dull head," wasn't unique to Alden and him. Estella stood at attention, seemingly unbothered, but the others glanced this way and that, Rosette rocking on her feet.

The king pulled from Krysta and cupped her face. "I have missed you so much and worried every day. And to find out what has been going on this past week, I could hardly sleep!" He took a moment to look her up and down. "Well, I do rather like the green hair. Though I doubt my sister will agree," he said with a soft smile.

Krysta chuckled. "Thank you. I do hope to change before I see them. But for now…" She turned to face the group, extending a hand to her uncle. "This is King Richard Rose, ruler of Alderdeem and my uncle."

While Roland the others bowed with an arm over their stomachs, Kyo did so with both hands at his sides, traditional for those from the western regions of Terrorigo like his father. Krysta then introduced each of them by name.

"Good to see you again, Your Majesty," Estella said with a smile.

"And you as well, Estella. The report I was given stated you were working with Cedric and Garret, is that right?"

Esella nodded. "Yes. Though I'm not against waiting for you to finish your reunion with Her Highness. I can give you an update on what the Aurora has been doing afterwards."

King Richard nodded. "Very well. If you could please stay here until then. Hayner, I expect you to be present during the debriefing as well."

"Yes, Your Majesty," Hayner said with a bow.

The king put his fist before his lips and cleared his throat, keeping his other arm wrapped around Krysta, as if she might run off again if he let her go. "Now then, before anything else, I want to thank you all for accompanying my niece during the recent dangers she's faced. I fear what may have been if she hadn't found you, and I am extremely curious to hear in detail what you all have gone through. I do, however, know some of the basics: Sybilla, Blanq, and the accrue stone." His gaze shifted from one to the other. "Oh, excuse me. Please, feel at ease. Don't worry about how you move or speak. I want to know my niece's new friends and allies for who they are."

Kyo sighed and let his shoulders slump. "Good, I don't think I can stand so straight all day." He rotated his shoulders, still a bit sore from his fight two days ago. "I guess I should start, huh?"

They took turns recounting the events that took place, this time not holding back any details. Each member of the group chimed in when appropriate. There was a pause when Krysta mentioned Layla's fate, a few tears and another embrace before the story continued. When Kyo described his conversation with Alden in Oasis, Krysta butted in her theory of him being a willing accomplice. Kyo fired back, and Roland had to step between them to keep an argument from erupting. By the time the story had ended, the king sat in his chair again, face in his hands.

"I hadn't thought you were so directly involved, Krysta, fighting against a shade, Sybilla twice. And Layla. She deserved better." King Richard took a deep breath then slapped his knees. "All of you have been through much. And you have my thanks. Kyo Sonata, my condolences for Ruby, as well as your parents. Those two were remarkable, if a bit unpredictable."

"Thank you, Your Majesty." Kyo clenched his jaw, Ruby's death too fresh to not have sadness well up at the mention of it.

"Uncle, I'd like to request Roland and Rosette be given a home here in Alderdeem, since they currently have none. After all their help, I feel they deserve that much," Krysta said.

King Richard shifted his attention to Roland and Rosette then nodded. "I gathered as much from their part of the story, and I agree. I will see to it that preparations begin as soon as possible."

Rosette squealed, jumping in place before leaping into Roland's arms, who hugged her closely and smiled wide. "Thank you so much, Your Majesty," Roland said. "I can't tell you how much we appreciate this."

The king waved his hand dismissively. "Not at all. And until then, you are all welcome to make yourselves at home here in the palace. Krysta has never brought friends here before. It does my heart good to see her meeting new people of her own volition and not as part of her royal duties."

"As if I ever had time to go out and make friends," Krysta grumbled.

King Richard laughed nervously. "The fault of that lies more with your parents than anything, unfortunately."

"Where is she?" a feminine voice cried from beyond the doors behind them. "Move aside."

Krysta pinched the bridge of her nose. "Speak of the Relinquished."

The doors burst open, a woman in a flowing scarlet gown exposing her shoulders and her raven hair in a bun stormed into the throne room. Behind her trailed a man with signs of gray in his otherwise short chestnut hair, wearing a gold-trimmed cerulean suit. Together, they approached Krysta and embraced her, though she made no move to do the same.

"My poor, poor dear! You're finally home. We've been terribly worried about you." The woman sobbed against Krysta's shoulder.

"How could you run off like that, and without saying anything?" the man asked, his pronunciation overly regal. "We've hardly been able to sleep for the past half a year. Although I must admit, your ability to evade detection from anyone sent to retrieve you is impressive."

The woman slapped the man's arm. "Arthur, do not be impressed with her running away."

"Apologies, dear," Krysta's father muttered, rubbing his arm.

"I'm sorry, but I needed space. I needed to get away from the palace," Krysta said. She moved her hand toward her mother's back, but her mother pulled away before she could.

"What have you done to your beautiful black hair?" her mother asked, face scrunched in disgust. "And this outfit, oh it's so dirty and… Where is the fashion sense in this?"

Her father also took in Krysta's appearance. "Charlotte, dear, she was likely attempting to fit in with the common people."

"Even so, did she have to pick an outfit that showed off so much of her legs?" her mother asked, attempting to pull Krysta's shorts lower.

Krysta swatted her hand away. "My clothes and my hair are just fine. Would you stop?"

Her mother finally glanced past Krysta, her gaze falling on Kyo and the others. "Krysta, dear, are these friends of yours?"

"Yes, they are," Krysta started. "This is—"

But her mother interrupted. "How utterly drab. They really came to the palace looking like this?"

"Mother!" Krysta shouted.

Kyo stood wide-eyed, not sure what to do or say. All he could manage was a side glance at Marsh, who glanced back with equally wide eyes and tight lips, silently saying he didn't know what to do either.

"What? Sorry, was that rude? We could always offer them more suitable clothes," her mother suggested with a quirked brow. "Speaking of, we need to get you out of these rags and into something more fitting. Arthur, let's see what she currently has in her closet."

"Charlotte, this is hardly the time," the king said in a firm tone. "Come back after we've—"

"Come now, this is our dear daughter's homecoming." Arthur rubbed his chin, he and his wife acting as if the king wasn't there. "We should have something newly created for her. I will let the seamstress know she has work to do. Oh, perhaps something slim, yet elegant with—"

"Enough!" Krysta's voice echoed throughout the throne room. "Stop, I don't want to hear another word. This is exactly why I left in the first place. Always trying to control everything, day in and day out. I want you both to leave. Go."

Her parents shrank back a bit, frowning. They exchanged looks, like sad saber pups.

"I'm sorry, I'm simply trying to—" her mother started.

Krysta silently pointed toward the door.

"Come along, Charlotte. Let's give her some space," Arthur said, gently pulling his wife back.

She nodded. "We're glad that you're safe, Krysta. We love you."

Krysta groaned loudly, gripping her hair. "I love you too. I do. Just…please leave. I'll come find you later, I promise." Once the two had gone, her body slumped. "I'm already exhausted."

"That went about as I expected. I'm sorry about my sister. Krysta, why don't you show your friends where they can rest, and you do the same. And do not hesitate to ask any of those under the palace's employ if you need anything at all." The king adjusted himself to sit up straight in his throne. "Estella, Hayner, let's get to business, shall we?"

As the two approached the king, Krysta sauntered toward the doors, silently motioning for the others to follow.

"I think I get why she ran off now," Kyo whispered to Marsh, who nodded in agreement.

Chapter 4

Mischief came naturally to Kyo, a byproduct of his parent's love of the same. While certainly not on the level of Marsh, given his past, Kyo had a history of sneaking around and acting natural while doing something he shouldn't. Though it inevitably failed more often than not. In this case, his goal was the training grounds outside the west wing of the palace he may or may not have had permission to use. He could always ask, but that risked being told no. Better to find out after getting some use out of them. Within the palace walls, he was out of his element. The royal guard, maids, and others who worked for the royal family already eyed him with curiosity whenever he passed, making getting away with anything difficult.

Adding to the challenge, he had to navigate this labyrinth of a palace. Simple two-story homes, chancellor offices, clerical chapels—he could manage those easily. But this…his best strategy had been to figure out which direction was west and keep going until he found himself outside. On his way, he passed workers dusting tapestries, cleaning glass cases, and speaking in hushed conversations. He tried to keep his eyes forward but ears open as he heard a royal guard nervously flirting with one of the ladies dusting a painting, mentally wishing him luck.

Kyo gave a smile or a simple nod to those he passed, hoping he hadn't wandered into a wing of the palace he didn't have permission to enter. After their meeting with the king yesterday, a member of the royal guard whose name escaped him explained some basic ground rules, as well as listed off places they did not have permission to go. Some were obvious, like other people's bedrooms, the throne room unless given special permission. Then came more surprising examples, such as the old prison far beneath the palace. Rosette had to be reassured that no direct path existed from the prison to the palace.

Finally, he saw the wooden-framed glass doors that led outside. After turning his head to ensure no one was watching, Kyo made his way outside to an overcast sky.

As he walked down the gray stone path leading to the training grounds, practice dummies came into view, a row of ten on the right and the same on the left. Beyond them was a short set of stairs leading to a massive circular area with stone walls about as tall as an average adult. He suspected this was for training with other people, but he had no use for it. At least not at the moment.

He turned and approached the nearest target dummy. It and its parallel behind him had the shape of a human, all limbs included. Down the line, each pair took a different form: a blob, a zu, a long thick worm, and others with enough space between for trainees to make use of all sides of their target. For him, the human one would do. Though Sybilla and Blanq were incarcerated, shades still remained a constant threat. He ran his fingers along the slightly rough canvas material, feeling the bumps of straw underneath. While staring at the dummy, he pictured Sybilla's face, grinning at him and daring him to strike.

One of his black-bladed short swords materialized in his right hand, and Kyo slashed at the dummy's left hip. On impact, the dummy shimmered in a multicolored light, rippling from the impact spot on the hip a palm's width before vanishing. He swung his arm to the right then slashed again with more strength. This time the ripples of light spread a bit farther before they disappeared. The protective spell on the dummy not only ensured it remained intact but also showed the potential damage a strike could cause by how far the spell's lights spread. And given how powerful the royal guards must be, he bet the spell could withstand a lot of punishment.

Perfect. He wished he had something like this at home.

Kyo summoned his other sword in his left hand and inhaled deeply. Magic energy from within his body traveled down his arms and his hands, filling them with the slightest warmth then into the blades. Wind whirled around the blades, flattening the grass around him, his unzipped hoodie billowing slightly. He doubted it'd have nearly the effect of when the spear on Roland's polearm glowed, giving his weapon increased durability and sharpness. Sometime soon, he'd ask Roland to teach him how to perform that spell. The excitement of training with real dummies and adding new spells to his repertoire had Kyo bouncing on the balls of his feet.

His movements started simply, slashing his target with purposeful aim, targeting critical spots on the body like the throat and heart. As he continued, he shifted right and left, ducked and jumped to avoid imaginary attacks. After about ten minutes, he performed acrobatic moves, using wind from his feet to flip over the dummy, strike it from behind, keeping a focus on using his blades but occasionally throwing in a kick or body check. He stopped briefly to remove his hoodie and tie it around his waist then continued.

This went on for about half an hour before he stopped, his swords vanishing. Panting, he wiped what little sweat there was from his brow, the chilly northern air keeping him cool despite the frenzied activity. During his solo training, he came to an undeniable conclusion. Training like this—against an enemy that couldn't fight back and without new techniques to learn and master—would offer minimal advancement. Though it did help release pent-up energy and frustration.

With a loud grunt, he punched the dummy in the chest and glared while continuing to press his fist against the protective spell. "You'd better rot in Spellnix Hold for the rest of your lives. Both of you."

Releasing a breath, he pulled his fist away. So long as Blanq and Sybilla remained incarcerated, Alden would have less to worry about while he hunted for the other accrue stones. The sooner he finished his search, the sooner they could go back to living a normal life.

The life of luxury wasn't going to sway him into being lazy.

He headed back inside to plot out his training. One positive thing came from his time out here. No one berated him for using the training grounds. Though he hadn't used them for long, someone must have noticed. Even so, he'd stick with using them only when they were unoccupied.

Although he hadn't sweat much during his mini training session, he still felt the need for a hot shower. It might not be desperately needed now, but it likely would be by the time he found his room again, assuming he found it before nightfall. He swore he'd never get used to such a massive place.

Farther down the hall, he saw a familiar set of white robes and messy blonde hair enter a doorway. Curious, he decided to trail his cleric friend to see how he was spending his time. He entered the doorway and paused, eyes wide as he took in a massive library. Shelves upon shelves stretched to the ceiling of the first floor, and so many he couldn't see the far side of the library. To his right past a librarian desk were even more shelves lined with books thick and thin. And up a wide set of spiral stairs was an entire second story.

"Geez. I wonder if they have any spell tomes at least." Hopefully, they weren't all boring historical books. He spied the tail of Marsh's robes disappear behind a bookshelf and took off after him.

But after a few steps, a voice called out. "Do not run in the library."

Kyo turned to see an old man behind the librarian's desk glaring at him. He gave a toothy smile and nervous laugh in return and opted to walk with long strides instead, following the trail of Marsh's robes. Which wouldn't have taken so long if he could have run after him. After the accidental game of coeurl and mouse, he saw Marsh set a pile of books onto a table and take a seat.

"What are you doing, bedhead? Studying some new spells?" Kyo asked.

A loud shush rushed through the library like a wave, making him cringe. How could that old man even hear him from back here?

Marsh looked up to Kyo and smiled then shook his head. "No. At least not at the moment," he said in a hushed voice. "I am simply doing my part in the corruption investigation."

Kyo pulled out the chair next to him and took a seat. "You think you're going to find something in here? It'd take forever to search all these books."

"Yes, well, there are of course certain literary sections that could be omitted. I am keeping my search in the non-fiction section. Which does not make the task any less daunting, honestly."

"No kidding," Kyo muttered, looking around at the many shelves and countless books within eyesight alone. "But what do you think you'll find? The corruption is a new thing. I doubt there's any books written on it already."

"I am attempting to keep all possibilities open. What if it comes from a feral that has recently reappeared? Or what if it is the result of an experimental spell gone wrong, the attempts documented in one of these books?" Marsh asked, gently patting the book on top of the pile. "This is too important to make assumptions that could cause us to overlook something crucial."

Kyo sighed and eyed the pile of books. "I guess you're right. I'm not telling you not to do it. But I sure hope these books have some sort of index or something." He gently patted Marsh's back. "But with any luck, the Aurora will find something any day, and we'll be one step closer to a cure that doesn't require Blanq's cooperation."

"Or preferably, a way to stop the spread altogether. Spending my time using these vast resources to find a solution is the least I can do."

"No wonder you became a cleric. You just can't stop helping people huh? Well, don't overdo it, okay? If you're going to be doing this and training to become a better cleric, make sure you get plenty of rest. When in doubt, nap it out." Kyo grabbed the book atop the pile and opened it, flipping through the pages to get an idea of what Marsh was in for. No pictures, small print. At least the back had a glossary, but that itself could have been its own book. "Are we going to find you dead at this table later?"

Marsh chuckled. "I doubt it. I will be careful and get plenty of rest, I promise." The cleric took the next book from the pile and opened it. "An infection of magic itself. It sounds impossible, yet we've seen it for ourselves. That narrows down my research but also makes it difficult to know where to start. How does one look for an impossible thing?"

"In the place you'd least expect?" Kyo continued to flip through the pages but put no focus on anything written within.

This corruption was like a specter that followed every person, every second of the day, and could strike at any time. For all he knew, he could wake up corrupted tomorrow with no way to prevent it. And how shameful would it be to have to be taken to Blanq so she could cure him?

The clicking of heels hitting the hardwood floor sounded and stopped beside them. "Marsh I can see reading a book, but you? I'm honestly surprised. Or have you already overworked your brain from trying?"

Sighing, Kyo turned toward Krysta's familiar voice but paused. While still emerald green, her hair had been done in a braid circling her head, and the rest had been given a wavy texture, cascading down her back. She wore subtle makeup on her lips, cheeks, and eyelids, as if she were ready for a date. Her dress was crimson with thin straps on the shoulders, reaching the floor with a slit on the right side to her thigh.

"Who knew you could actually look pretty?" Kyo scoffed.

"Excuse you! I am always a beauty and take good care of myself, thank you," Krysta snapped.

The echoing shush sounded again, her already blushing cheeks turning even redder.

"You do look lovely, Krysta," Marsh said. "I am not used to seeing you dressed so elegantly, but I suppose we will be seeing more of it now that we are here. It suits you."

Krysta's shoulders slumped and she smiled. "Thank you, Marsh." She turned to Kyo. "See, *that* is how you give someone a compliment. Learn that, and perhaps a girl will give you the time of day."

Kyo rolled his eyes. "Maybe someday. I have more important things to worry about."

"So I've heard. Did you like using our training grounds?"

"Uh…yeah, they're pretty nice. They could be useful."

"Well, of course. I've used them plenty of times, and I plan to go back to it soon. I suspect we all will after what we've been through. It'd be foolish not to." Krysta ruffled Marsh's already messy hair. He pretended not to notice. "When you're ready, come find me and I'll introduce you to a member of the royal guard who I think will be great to teach you."

"Of course. Thank you, Krysta." Marsh smiled at her before returning to the pages of the book, leaving his hair messier than before.

"As for you," Krysta said, pointing to Kyo, "I doubt you're actually busy reading, so come with me." She turned, her heels clacking against the hardwood floor as she walked away, not checking to ensure he followed.

Kyo glanced between her and Marsh before rising from his chair. "Guess I'll see you later." He again walked in long strides until he caught up to Krysta but didn't speak until they were out of the library, lest he incur the wrath of the librarian again. "So, where are we going?"

"To find Hayner. I think he would be best suited to teach you. He should be patrolling the upper west wing around this time." She led him to the nearest stairs to the third floor and turned left, seeming to lose her balance more than once. They maneuvered several more hallways, spotting Hayner who turned and focused his eyes on them.

"Your Highness." Hayner knelt down on one knee and bowed his head. "How may I be of service?"

Krysta sighed. "Please stand. I doubt my uncle is peeking from around the corner."

Hayner stood and nodded then asked with a knowing grin, "How does it feel to be back in the expensive dresses and intricate hairstyles?"

"I'm struggling to walk in these heels after so long, the dress is too tight, and the braid is squeezing my head. How do you think it feels?" Krysta groaned.

"Home sweet home, huh? It's still good to have you back." He then turned to Kyo. "Was there something I could help you with?"

"Yes, actually," Krysta said. "I want you to help train Kyo to become a stronger mage. Guide him, oversee him using the training grounds, whatever you feel is effective."

Hayner cocked a brow. "While I'm capable of teaching someone, is that how I should best use my time? I have no shortage of important duties."

"I know. Consider it a personal favor to me." Krysta kept her eyes straight ahead as she spoke. "As much of a dunce as he may be, he has a good heart and was crucial in defeating Sybilla and Blanq. I think it would be beneficial to many if he were to become a more effective and knowledgeable mage."

Kyo didn't know whether to focus more on her compliment or insult. Though her words did fill him with a bit of pride. It almost felt like he was being treated like a true Aurora would be.

Hayner looked between the two before bowing his head. "Very well. If that's what you wish, then I'll help him how I can."

"Thanks, Hayner." Krysta smiled wide and embraced him briefly.

"The things I do for the brat princess," Hayner teased.

"Hey!" They both laughed before Krysta turned to Kyo. "There you are. Don't cause him any trouble, got it? He's also my uncle's advisor remember, so he's a busy man." She turned to walk back down the hall, stumbling again and mumbling about stupid heels.

"Okay then. I guess you'll be teaching me, so thanks. I appreciate it," Kyo said.

"Don't thank me yet. Even if it's a personal favor to Her Highness, I won't bother with someone who will only waste my time." Hayner studied Kyo up and down. "She stated you favor wind spells, correct? I don't use them myself, but I don't think that will be a problem. Actually, I think that's perfect. You're going to show me what you can do right here and now."

Kyo's eyes widened, looking around. Sure, the hallway was wide, but this hardly seemed like a place to cast spells or fight. "Are you sure about that?"

"Don't argue. Hold out your hand, palm up. Cast a spell, focus the wind into one spot. Condense it as much as you can and don't hold back."

Kyo exhaled and did as asked. Wind gathered in his palm, growing more violent by the second. His hoodie flapped around his waist, loose strands of hair whipped about wildly, and he was sure his feet were what kept the unsecured gold-trimmed scarlet carpet in place. Hayner's robes flapped about, and he squinted to protect his eyes. If Kyo had to do this as some sort of test, he may as well impress his new teacher.

The wind continued to condense and take the shape of a drill, wide base against his palm and narrow tip pointing straight up.

"I sent Sybilla flying with this spell," Kyo said with a confident grin. The air spun so fast it whistled throughout the hallway.

Once he felt it'd been enough, the wind died down and the spell ceased.

"There. See what I can do?" Kyo asked.

Hayner kept his face stoic. "I do see." He motioned around them with his hand. "I see a goblet once on a stand now on the floor. I see your hair a mess, a tapestry tilted, and my own robes needing adjusting." He rolled his shoulders and pulled on his robes so they fit properly again. Motioning behind Kyo, he said, "Not to mention the carpet."

While the carpet beneath his feet remained in place, behind him it sat in a messy, crumpled zigzag across the marble floor. "Well, yeah. It's wind, it does that."

Hayner shook his head. "This shows a lack of control over your own magic and a lot of wasted energy. Even enforcers learn to cast spells without expending excess magic, making the most of their individual magic pools while ensuring they run out of magic at as slow a rate as possible, allowing them to cast more spells before becoming exhausted."

Kyo took in Hayner's words. If enforcers learned this, then no doubt Aurora would see it as basic, even second nature. And here he was, a self-described honorary Aurora being clueless about his own magic.

"I won't waste my time with someone who can't even cast such a spell without ruining the area around him. Come back to me when you figure that out." Hayner dismissively walked past him and didn't bother to look back. "And clean up the mess you've made before you go."

Kyo's heart raced as he watched him leave, eyes narrowed. But then a grin spread across his lips. He stared down at his open palm for a second then clenched it into a fist. "Fine, I'll show you I can do it."

If that's what it took to get more specific guidance on spells and techniques, then so be it. Hayner was transparent in his attempt to teach Kyo by making him want to prove him wrong, but he'd play along if it meant getting stronger.

Chapter 5

It was only for one night. Kyo repeated this in his mind, grimacing as he looked in the mirror. Why would anybody ever be happy to dress up like this?

The pants were too tight, and the jacket closed with two columns of golden buttons that made it difficult to raise his arms above his head. While he wouldn't have chosen blue for himself, he accepted it for its dark hue. The suit had been left for him while he was out of his room.

"Just suffer through it, Kyo. Do it for Rosette," he grumbled to himself.

Upon learning Rosette never had a proper birthfete with friends, Krysta insisted one be thrown for her for her eleventh birthday. Rosette's face had lit up at the idea, and she squealed when Krysta suggested she be princess for the day. While he was happy for her, why did they all have to dress formally?

He adjusted the collar of his jacket, gave himself one last look in the mirror, and shrugged before leaving his room. While navigating the halls of the palace, he kept his arms at his sides, a moderate wind swirling around his left hand. This had become a habit ever since his talk with Hayner about two weeks ago. Whether he ate, showered, or wandered the city, he did his best to maintain a simple spell without letting the air affect anything around him. It disgusted him how weak it had to be to achieve this at first, but through diligent training, he'd managed to noticeably improve. Though using so much magic throughout each day meant he passed out at night as soon as he hit the bed.

Kyo opened the thick wooden door to the great hall, only certain it was the correct place by the noise on the other side. Stretching along the middle of the room sat a single lengthy table with all sorts of food: sweets and baked goods, meat including an entire cooked cockatrice, various fruits and vegetables, and an assortment of bread, which would be his first stop. Everyone wore elaborate suits and dresses, and Rosette's sparkling white gown and tiara made her easy to spot. That and the small crowd around her.

"Hey, munchkin, happy birthday," Kyo said as he pulled her into a hug.

"Watch her hair," someone he didn't know cried.

Rosette giggled and hugged back. "Thank you. You look good in a suit."

"Don't get used to it. As soon as this party's over it's right back to my usual shorts and hoodie. But you sure look pretty. I'd never know you weren't a real princess." He gave her a big smile. "Your hair looks nice too, Your Highness."

It had been done up into a bun with two wide blond strands framing her face. He stuck out his tongue, to which she responded in kind.

"Thanks! They wanted to do something fancier, but I didn't want to sit there forever."

"Understandable. Want to get to the party and start eating all this food, right?" Kyo asked with a grin. Rosette nodded enthusiastically.

Roland reached his hand toward her head but released a slight grunt and retracted it. "No ruffling the hair tonight," he mumbled under his breath. "She does look great though, doesn't she? She's always been a mix of a girly girl and a tomboy, but I've never gotten to see her go this far on the girly side of the spectrum."

Roland's suit was identical to Kyo's, except deep crimson with white trim. On second thought, maybe his own midnight blue suit wasn't so bad after all.

"I might be all dressed up, but I can still beat you up," Rosette said, balling up her fists and throwing a faux punch.

Roland laughed, putting his hands up defensively. "Yeah, you sure can."

"Well, while you two duke it out, I'm going to grab a bite to eat." Kyo made a beeline to the plates of bread on the food table, grabbed the first buttered roll he saw, and took a big bite. He closed his eyes and smiled, enjoying the rich taste and fluffy texture.

"At least grab a plate. You will make a mess otherwise."

Kyo opened his eyes to see Marsh standing to his right, dressed in his usual cleric robes.

"Why do you get to dress normally?" Kyo asked in disbelief with his mouth still half full.

Marsh raised an eyebrow then began loading up his plate with various food. "Please swallow before speaking. And cleric robes are considered formal wear. No one asks a cleric to change into something else." He side-eyed Kyo with a smug grin. "Therefore, I get to be comfortable regardless of the affair."

"Well, aren't you lucky?" Kyo mumbled after a hard swallow then snatched a plate from the table, set it down, and used the same hand to place bread and fruit on his plate, wanting to maintain the spell around his left hand.

"It cannot be too bad. You might even pass for a royal," Marsh said.

"Ha! There is no way the islander would pass for anything of the sort." Krysta appeared at Kyo's left side. Today, her hair had been done in a bun in the back and weaved into a double helix on both sides, nearly identical to Rosette's. Maybe they were going for some sort of sisterly theme. Her dress matched his suit in color with puffy shoulders and lower half reaching her ankles.

Kyo took the bulla fruit off his plate, jiggling the juice-filled balls connected to the core. He motioned to the bulla fruit for emphasis. "Hey, look, you match."

Krysta glared. "It looks to match you more."

"Please, both of you. Not during Rosette's birthfete," Marsh pleaded.

Kyo glanced past Krysta to see the king greeting Rosette with a large smile and bellowing laugh. With no children of his own and Krysta grown up, he bet His Majesty missed having a young child around. "Even the king is having fun, huh?"

"It's rare my uncle gets to take a break and enjoy something like this," Krysta said. "I bet it reminds him of when I was young."

Kyo pulled a fruit ball off the bulla core and popped it into his mouth. After everything that happened to them, it was good to see Rosette smiling. She had said she wasn't afraid, but he couldn't imagine a ten- now eleven-year-old going through dealing with Sybilla and coming out unscathed. A mere child battling shades, undead, and fighting Sybilla as fiercely as any enforcer might, if not more so. The harsh, nomadic nature of her and Roland's lifestyle had certainly toughened her up, but those events had to have left some mark on her mind. They'd certainly affected his, memories of those days playing constantly. And on top of it all, his concern for Alden.

"By the way, has anyone made any progress in finding Alden that you know of?" Kyo asked.

Krysta sighed. "None. The word has been spread across Feracael, but no one has seen any sign of him yet.

It's honestly impressive, given he won't have Blanq's illusions to rely on when hiding like a coward."

"Watch your mouth," Kyo said with gritted teeth. "He is no coward."

"No? Giving Sybilla and Blanq access to an accrue stone, resulting in hundreds of deaths if not more to protect himself. Seems rather cowardly to me."

He fully turned to face her. "And if he hadn't, I and all Mistwell would probably be dead right now. Plus, they already had an accrue stone at that point anyway, so what happened in Calmarock wouldn't have changed."

"Both of you, please. That is enough," Marsh interjected.

But Krysta ignored him. "An accrue stone that Sybilla herself said Alden helped them get. So yes, he would be responsible either way," she shouted, stomping her heeled foot. "Do you honestly believe a man connected with the Aurora wouldn't have had a way to contact them, have them help deal with those two before anyone got hurt?"

Marsh reached his hand out, but Kyo swatted it away.

"Arguably the most powerful Aurora specializing in finding things still had a very hard time tracking those two down even when they were in the same city," Kyo said. "If Alden went against them, what do you think the consequences would have been? Prissy little princess thinks she knows everything but doesn't know us *commoners* can't snap our fingers and summon powerful mages to their side."

"Excuse you." Krysta shoved against Kyo's shoulder. "I know more about how the world works than you ever will. You're just letting your attachment to him keep you from thinking clearly."

Baring his teeth, he shoved her shoulder back. "And you think you're not doing the same with your attachment to Layla?"

"Both of you stop this instant," the king roared.

Krysta ignored her uncle, reaching for Kyo, who caught her hands in his. Their fingers interlocked, pushing against one another. He growled and she grunted, their arms flailing this way and that to get the upper hand on the other.

How dare she talk that way about his only family. She had a vendetta against Alden, wanted to see him imprisoned forever for what Sybilla and Blanq had done. He knew she wasn't entirely incorrect in saying allowing them to get the accrue stones made the devastation worse. But all they needed was an enchanter. If not him, then someone else could have done it. Kyo's grip weakened as he considered Alden contacting the Aurora for help. Had he tried? They couldn't do more than speculate what may have happened if he had. But as far as he knew, Alden had no direct method of contact for them. Not even chancellors could easily contact them when needed, as they rarely stayed in one place. They had to contact other chancellors to see if they were near their town or city. No, he *had* to believe in the man he knew his entire life.

"Wow, look at that cake," Rosette shouted, clapping.

Kyo sure wouldn't mind shoving Krysta's face into a cake.

Krysta's foot slipped out from under her, causing her to fall forward. Her weight sent Kyo stumbling backward, struggling to regain his footing. They both bumped into someone, who cried out as they tumbled together.

A second later, something fell onto them. Something soft, creamy, and sweet.

The room became silent as he adjusted himself to find them covered in what remained of Rosette's birthfete cake, white icing in their hair and on their clothes, large chunks of golden cake and strawberries scattered across the floor.

The scent of crushed strawberries and sweet icing contrasted with the awkwardness that permeated the room. Kyo's lips tightened, and he cringed as the stillness was broken by a few quiet sobs. Rosette rushed out of the room, and Roland hurried after her. All eyes were on them, and all Kyo could do was sigh and stare at the ground. After Krysta adjusted herself and flung some icing out of her hair, their eyes met. The anger was gone, replaced by shame. How low did he have to be to ruin a little girl's birthfete?

He glanced up at Marsh. "Sorry." Marsh extended his hand and Kyo took it, rising to his feet then did the same for the chef he had knocked over. "You too, sorry."

No witty or sarcastic comments came to mind, no words to lighten the mood.

Krysta struggled to rise, her heels slipping on the icing. Kyo grabbed her arm and hoisted her to her feet, letting go when he was sure she'd regained balance. She swiped more cake off her dress.

"Thanks," she said. "We should find her."

Kyo nodded and followed her wordlessly into the hallway. He hoped Rosette had run off to her room. Otherwise, he couldn't begin to guess where to find her. Thankfully, Krysta must have had the same thought, leading them to Rosette's room and slowly opening the door to peek inside. Roland sat on the bed with his arms around Rosette, her face buried in his chest.

"Hey, um…Rosette?" Kyo started.

The young girl tightened her grip around Roland and buried her face deeper. He pretended not to notice Roland's disappointed gaze.

"We're very sorry," Kyo said as Krysta stepped inside and he followed, closing the door behind him. "We totally made a mess of things."

Krysta knelt beside Rosette and placed a hand on her knee. "We'll have a new, better cake made. And we'll clean up the old one and get right back to the party."

Rosette didn't look at them as she shook her head, mumbling into Roland's chest.

"What was that, kiddo?" Roland asked in a gentle voice.

After a few seconds, Rosette inhaled deeply and pulled away, her eyes red and puffy. "You two are always arguing. Every time you see each other. Why can't you get along?"

Krysta looked back at Kyo with dejected eyes. He didn't even feel like flinging icing into her face. After a long few seconds, she turned back to Rosette.

"I'm sorry. You're right. I promise we'll try our best to get along better from now on." She turned back to Kyo with wide eyes, as if encouraging him to say the same. As if he needed her to.

"Yeah, we'll do our best. No more arguing, okay?" He wiped a bit of icing from his shoulder and rubbed it off on Rosette's nose, getting a tiny smile from her. "I didn't know it upset you that much."

Rosette nodded. "I like you both. I don't want to see you argue all the time. We fought Sybilla together. We should be best friends."

"So, you weren't upset about the cake?" Roland asked.

"The cake part was funny," Rosette said with a smile. "So, you two swear not to argue anymore? And get along?" When they both nodded and made their promise, she perked up. "Then give each other a hug and make up."

Kyo tightened his jaw as he looked at Krysta, who had a similar expression—trying not to show disgust at the request. But they sucked it up and wrapped their arms around each other, further spreading the remnants of cake over their clothes. Neither spoke, and he did his best to suppress a groan before they released each other.

"Now kiss!" Rosette exclaimed.

That wasn't an image Kyo needed in his head. His stomach flipped at the thought, more akin to nausea than excitement.

"Rosette," Roland said with a warning tone.

"Okay, okay."

"Should we return to the party then?" Roland asked?

Rosette nodded. At least she was smiling again. "Mm hmm."

"Sorry again," Kyo said. "If nothing else, we both sure like you a lot."

"We sure do. A whole bunch." Krysta glanced down at her messy dress. "I suppose I should clean up before returning to the party."

Roland stood. "Actually, I have a much better idea to fix all of this."

Kyo cocked a brow and shivered at the older man's mischievous grin. He'd never seen that look on him before, and he didn't like it.

They headed back to the party, more and more Kyo wishing he could clean himself up. Some bits of cake and icing were inside his clothes and places he'd rather not mention. When they returned, it seemed no one had left, and all eyes turned to them. Shame overtook him again, his body shivering and heating up at the same time.

Roland pulled Rosette along then spoke softly into the king's ear, who nodded and cleared his throat. "Now that everyone has returned, I think it is only fitting that Her Highness, Princess Rosette, decide a fitting punishment for the two troublemakers."

Kyo stared at Roland from across the room. Who knew he had such a devious streak in him? He almost respected him more for it. As Rosette cupped her chin to think, he stood straight and exhaled deeply. What punishment could an eleven-year-old dish out anyway? Then again, if it was one clean punch, he'd be taken away with broken ribs.

Rosette stood on one of the chairs at the food table and cleared her throat. "For ruining my birthfete, I sentence the both of you to spend the night in the prison."

Kyo suppressed a chuckle. To the dungeons with them, huh? He didn't know how they would play this out, but he'd go along with it to make the young girl happy. Leaning closer to Krysta, he whispered, "Good thing they wouldn't actually do that, or we'd be in trouble. Is it even used anymore?"

Krysta stared back with wide, concerned eyes. "It's not yet. There have been talks of putting the corrupted there as a last resort, but that hasn't been officially decided yet. Which makes placing us there that much easier."

Two members of the royal guard whose names he didn't know approached, and his heart sank.

Thirty minutes later, Kyo sat on the cot in his cell, feet on the ground and leaning forward as he stared at the brick walls through the bars. Hayner remained in sight to keep an eye on them for the time being. He guessed the king wasn't completely comfortable with having his niece down here even for a single night.

"This is your fault," Krysta said from the cell beside him on the other side of the wall.

Kyo sighed, opening the palm of his right hand and channeling wind to rotate above it. "Yeah, I hate you too."

Chapter 6

The roads of Alderdeem were bustling with activity. Families strolled together hand in hand, and shops and restaurants lured people into their businesses with various goods, employees holding signs outside the doors, and mouth-watering aromas. So far in the northeastern corner of the continent, people wore cold weather suits and dresses that likely cost more cryst than everything Kyo owned combined. And here he was in his usual hoodie and the most casual pair of black pants he could find in his room's wardrobe. Not that he cared what others thought of his clothes, but he couldn't shake the feeling of being a cockatrice among zus.

While the palace had its charms and uses, he needed to occasionally escape so he could be himself without feeling like he'd do or say something wrong or weird. Even if no one said anything to him about his appearance or actions, he occasionally felt eyes on him when roaming the palace. No wonder Krysta had to run away. And after having to spend the previous night in a prison cell on the whims of the all-powerful birthfete girl, a sense of freedom brought a smile to his lips, despite her giggle fits when she saw Krysta and him the next morning.

The city circled The Ancient, its roots separating each sector, and so long as he could see the palace sitting against the trunk, he could breathe easily knowing how to return any time.

He let his hand gently drag along the bark of a massive root as he strolled underneath into a popular shopping district for tourists. With little cryst to his name, he intended no more than window shopping. The idea of getting some sort of job in the city made him shudder, so he'd resist the temptation to earn spending money for as long as possible since the palace met all his basic needs.

A pair of children ran past him into a shop. There was a poster on the window advertising a new issue of a popular comic book about thieves with unusual powers sailing the seas, one he'd fallen out of reading several years ago. At some point, he'd have to check what he'd missed. After recent events, he could relate to those characters and their hardships more than ever.

The first shop in the next block had various weapons on display in the window — swords, axes, even a metal whip. Kyo paused and examined them for a second before shifting his gaze to his right. A man with a thick black beard caught his attention. Maybe it was paranoia left over from Sybilla and Blanq, but he swore the man stopped walking when he did and proceeded to gaze around at nothing in particular.

Returning his attention to the window, Kyo calmed his body and mind. Though not visible, strands of magic seeped from him, extending outward. While far from proficient, his father's spell that had helped make him so formidable could be useful here, if he could maintain it long enough. His breathing became heavier, and his body tightened as he struggled not to lose the intricate control needed. Kyo turned, took a few steps to the next shop window, then pretended to be interested in the toys on display. Anyone that unknowingly moved through his strands of energy triggered a slight vibration. According to Garret, Kyo's father could glean so much information from them that he'd been able to tell one person from another and their physical attributes. All Kyo knew was if someone moved or didn't. In this case, the man behind him once again stopped moving when he did.

What could this man want? If he intended to attack, he wouldn't find the opportunity in the crowded roads or shops. He released a heavy breath. He was letting his imagination get the better of him. There was no need to jump to conclusions. The spell ceased, his body immediately able to relax. That spell required a lot more practice. He could still test his theory without it.

Kyo continued down the road, passing multiple shops at a leisurely pace. He'd find one to stop at, enter for a while, and see if the man was still around when he left. A bakery up ahead became his target and a good excuse to get a treat for himself for having to deal with this annoying situation.

But before he reached it, the man grabbed his arm and pulled him into nearby alley.

Kyo stumbled, and before he could right himself, the man chucked something at the ground. A burst of light filled his vision before he could blink. He squinted and raised his hand in front of his eyes. Though many people strolled by, it was as if they hadn't noticed. The light faded, leaving Kyo seeing spots as his vision attempted to correct itself.

As soon as the man turned to face him, Kyo summoned a sword in his right hand and charged, using his shoulder to knock him against the brick wall and held the tip of his blade to his throat. After all he'd dealt with, not a lick of fear touched him. Certainly not because of a random stalker.

"All right, what do you want, fuzzy face?" Kyo demanded.

The man stared wide-eyed with his hands up beside his head. "Easy there. I only want to talk. It looks like you've become more perceptive and cautious after what you've been through."

Kyo's heart pounded as he heard the familiar voice, his breathing shaky. The man's face shifted like a ripple, becoming far more recognizable. Kyo's sword vanished and he took several steps back. "There's no way."

The beard disappeared, and the man's previously black hair stood on end, short and bright scarlet.

"Alden?" Kyo asked.

A chuckle escaped Alden as he rotated his shoulder. "Good to see you, you little dullfish." Alden stepped forward and wrapped his arms around him, squeezing tight. "By the Altruists, I've missed you." He pulled back, hands gripping Kyo's biceps. "Are you eating okay? Getting plenty of sleep?"

Kyo shook himself from his daze. It was really him. "I…yeah, I'm fine. I've been staying in the palace. What are you doing here?" he asked, holding back tears. "And how did you do that with your face?"

"A little trick I picked up during my time with Blanq."

"Please don't say it like that. It makes it sound like you were friends or something."

Alden shook his head. "I did *not* say that. But any skills I can learn from the enemy can be useful. If only I could have learned how to teleport instead." He retracted his arms and paced, pulling his notebook from his pocket and flipping through the pages. "I'm sure you have a lot of questions, but I can't stick around for long. I came to find you for two reasons. The first was to see how you were doing."

His head swam, but Kyo still rushed to embrace Alden tightly, burying his face into his shoulder. "I'm damn happy to see you." Kyo did his best to keep his voice steady but couldn't stop the tears from flowing down his cheeks. "You're an idiot, you know. Deciding things on your own. 'Oh, I'm just going to go around Feracael and destroy the accrue stones while I'm being hunted by every law enforcement organization in the world. No big deal.'"

Alden patted his back gently. "One reason this minor illusion spell is so useful but definitely not foolproof. I know Cedric would see right through it, and he's not the only one."

Kyo pulled back and wiped his tears away with his sleeve. "How did you manage to find me anyway?"

Alden pinched the sleeve of Kyo's hoodie between his index and middle fingers. "Being the protective guardian I am, I may have placed a tracking enchantment on this before I gave it to you."

That explained all the times Alden seemed to know where Kyo was when he was trying to be sneaky. He mentally kicked himself for never considering it before. "Speaking of Cedric, the Aurora come by the palace on occasion. Don't you think they'd understand if I told them what you were doing?"

"They probably would. But while they're highly respected, they have no actual authority even compared to the smallest town's chancellor. An annoying truth Kei and Iris had to deal with a lot. I'll be happy to turn myself in and face whatever my fate will be *after* I do what I can about the accrue stones. If I can't destroy them, maybe I can find a way to make them useless." Alden turned his attention back to his notebook, using a finger to glide down the page as he skimmed it.

Kyo glanced between him and the page. "Is that what that notebook is about? You only got that one a few months ago, right?"

He only then noticed the dark circles under Alden's eyes that hadn't been there before. Research had always been a part of his job, learning new enchantments to offer to clients. But he must be burning the candle at both ends to figure out what he can do about the stones.

Nodding, Alden didn't look away from the pages. "Ever since I was forced to collect that first accrue stone for Sybilla and Blanq, I've been working hard to figure out a way to deal with it. And I'm making progress, thankfully. I'm sure of it. Which brings me to the second reason I came to see you." He closed his notebook, using a finger to save the page. "I need you to steal something for me."

"What?" Did Kyo hear that right? That wasn't something someone casually requested. Especially in his position. Kyo gripped Alden's coat. "We want people to think you're innocent, not make them hate you more by committing crimes."

Alden released a nervous laugh. "I know, I know. Listen." He eased Kyo's hands from his coat. "There is a tome I've been looking for that should help me make further advancements in my research. It's called *Binding: A Master Enchanter's Compendium*. I've searched high and low. At every shop and library I've visited, I've asked about it. But even the Pantheon's Library in Ueno didn't have a copy. The woman who heads the Pantheon's Library, a feisty old bag, said she'd seen it before and suggested it could be in the Alderdeem palace's library."

"I...I don't know." Kyo pace about the alley, gripping his hair as he mulled over Alden's words. If he asked the same but to steal it from a shop, he'd agree, only because of how important the research was. Even the Aurora were at a loss on how to destroy the accrue stones, but they and various chancellors agreed it would be for the best. Lives depended on it. But to steal something from the palace—after they housed him, fed him, even helped train him—churned his stomach. "There has to be another copy somewhere, right? Maybe there's places you haven't looked yet. I might like to sneak around sometimes, but I'm hardly a seasoned thief."

This wouldn't be like slipping a bar of candy in his pocket and walking out of a store. This type of thievery required time and planning from people who knew what they were doing. And if they were caught... Kyo could handle others being disappointed in him, but it would immensely hurt Alden's chances of remaining free and acquitted of the charges against him.

Kyo groaned and stomped his feet in frustration. "I know you're right, but it still feels icky. And the books in that library can't leave the palace anyway."

"I'm running out of options and time. And it's not at all fair to include you in this. I should be taking the risk myself. But I can't wander the halls of the palace disguised as a random person no one has ever seen there before, and my skills in illusion spells are mediocre at best. Not nearly good enough to fool a palace full of lifetime workers and royal guards." Alden motioned his head toward the road and the people wandering close by. "Even this enchantment won't fool everyone forever. The only reason I'm asking you is because I have no other options, and we can't risk a repeat of Aquarin, Oasis, and especially Calmarock." He paused, eyes shifting. "Wait, what do you mean they can't leave the palace?"

"Marsh has been doing his own research, trying to find some hint of the source of the corruption. He told me that every single book and tome in that library is enchanted so it can't leave the palace grounds."

Alden leaned against the brick wall. "If it's an enchantment, I'm confident I could lift it. Though that means I'd have to enter the palace grounds myself to do it. But I'd be stupid to try to enter the palace itself. I didn't think it'd be easy, but it's riskier than I thought. Especially for you. I only approached you because I thought you walking around the palace with a tome wouldn't be suspicious. I'll find another way. You shouldn't be seen with me. That flash created an enchantment so no one would notice us here, but that's likely to be detected soon." He sighed. "I shouldn't have thought to involve you."

Those stones were the reason Kyo's parents were dead and the driving force behind so much death and destruction. Even if Sybilla and Blanq could never use them again, that didn't mean others wouldn't try. Was a betrayal of this magnitude of those who helped him justified for the right reasons?

Even as Kyo thought it, his stomach tightened. The hard part would be on Alden, having to enter the palace grounds undetected. All Kyo had to do was find the book and bring it to him.

Simple, if he ignored the extra weight on his conscience.

"On the west side of the palace," Kyo started, "outside, there's a training ground. Open space, bushes, practice dummies. If you could get there, I could bring the tome to you. Midnight?"

"So, you'll do it? You're sure? I could try to find another way."

Kyo nodded. "For something this important, yeah."

"Thank you. Really, this could be what determines whether those stones hurt anyone again or not." He pulled Kyo into another hug. "No matter what happens, I love you. I promise I do."

Hugging back, Kyo released a heavy breath and allowed himself to take in his godfather's familiar embrace. "I love you too." He let the hug linger before pulling back. "I did say in Oasis to let me help you. I guess this is me getting what I want, huh? But be careful, okay?"

"I will. You too. I'm sorry for pulling you into this." Alden ran his fingers over his face, taking on the disguise he wore earlier. "If everything goes well, I'll see you tonight." He reached into his enchanted travel pouch at his side and pulled out a brown paper bag, handing it to Kyo before turning and entering the street, mixing with the crowd.

Kyo watched him disappear before opening the bag, immediately taking in the aroma of garlic from the rolls inside. He grinned. "You really know how to bribe me."

Chapter 7

Kyo couldn't quite tell if the eyes of those he passed through the halls of the palace lingered on him more than usual or if it was his imagination. It must have been paranoia, his conscience getting the better of him. No one could know he planned to steal a tome from the library. Even thinking about it opened a pit in his stomach. His body shivered and burned simultaneously as he walked the palace halls. Knowing that stealing from the palace would help not only Alden but potentially all of Feracael did little to help his unease. How had Marsh done this? Even if it had been to survive, he must have developed nerves of steel.

He entered the library and once again stared in awe at multiple floors of books and shelves. First things first, finding the tome. If it was here, the card catalog would say so. And if not, then he wouldn't have to steal anything, and he'd have peace of mind. He did his best to offer a smile to the librarian behind the desk without appearing nervous, though the older man didn't smile back.

The cabinets containing the card catalogs were categorized by genre and alphabetical order. Tomes had their own section, separated from other books, which was standard for any library or book shop.

"What was it called again?" he asked himself in a whisper. The title came to him a few seconds later, *Binding: A Master Enchanter's Compendium*. He flipped through the cards, reading the titles. "B. B I."

His heart stopped when he found it. Damn it, it was here after all.

Rather than take the card for easy reference, he committed the location to memory then set off to find the tome's location. It took a solid ten minutes of wandering the lower floor and reading the section names and numbers before realizing what he needed was on the second floor. Up the set of spiral stairs, eighth row of shelves to his right, he started scanning the titles on the spines of the tomes.

Maybe it wasn't here. Someone could have checked it out, or it may have been lost. Or maybe… Damn it, there it was. An unusually thick tome with the exact title Alden gave him stared back from the shelf. Yet he didn't reach for it. He could hear his heart pounding in his ears.

It's for the good of Feracael.

Not everyone believed in Alden, particularly a certain princess. As much as Kyo argued against her, he occasionally found his mind battling between her words about what Alden could have done differently and reminding himself there were too many unknown factors, especially regarding how Sybilla would act.

As his eyes bored into the tome's spine, his mind drifted to Sybilla and Blanq, the horrible things they'd done, the people they'd killed. Could Alden really have prevented all of that by contacting the Aurora? Or would that have caused them to act sooner, leaving Mistwell in the same state as Calmarock, or worse? Too many what-ifs, too much speculation. Like previous times he found doubt seeping in, he thought back to his childhood: the birthfetes, the babysitting, the games they played…and how Alden was there after Kyo's parents died. In hindsight, he thought back to those days and weeks after the tragedy and recognized how upset and broken Alden had been. Even when he thought Kyo wasn't watching. He couldn't have been faking that. Their deaths hit Alden hard.

And that knowledge Krysta didn't have was all he needed. He believed in Alden.

Those stones were the reason Kyo's parents and Alden's best friends had been killed. His desire to destroy them had to be genuine.

Kyo's shaky hand reached for the tome, fingers gripping it tight. With a heavy breath, he pulled it from the shelf. He leaned against the bookshelf behind him and sighed. Unfortunately, this was the easy part. Somehow, he had to get this tome out of the library and somewhere he could give it to Alden later without a single person knowing he had it.

The best thing to do for now was gather other books so he could hide this one among them. He remained on the second floor to remain out of sight of the librarian. Not bothering to read what category the books nearby belonged to, he took five off the shelves, sandwiching the tome in the middle. He carried them to a table and chair next to a window and set them down, dropping into a cushioned chair with a heavy sigh.

Checking the tome out wasn't an option, and he couldn't hide such a thick tome under his clothes.

"Think Kyo, how can you get this thing out of here?" he said barely above a whisper.

"Get what out of where?" a voice asked.

Kyo stiffened, turning his head to see Roland standing next to him. Shit. What was he doing here?

"I…information. Figured I'd help Marsh a little with his research, though I'm kind of shooting at random. I have no idea where to actually start." The words flowed from his lips like second nature, a result of the many times he had to lie to Mistwell's enforcers to stay out of trouble.

Roland picked up the book from the top of the pile. "I'll say. *Marriage, Love, and How to Raise the Perfect Family.* I doubt you'll find any information on the corruption in there."

What was a book like that even doing in this library? He should have paid more attention to what he grabbed. "Well, even I want to think a bit about the future when this is over. Something wrong with that?"

Roland laughed. "No, just unexpected from you. I can't recall you ever showing an interest in love. Though I guess you were too busy trying not to be killed, huh?" He lightly tapped the top of Kyo's head with the book then set it back atop the pile.

"Yeah, well, what are you doing in here anyway? Are you a big reader?"

"More than you'd think. But I'm here looking for you, kid."

Kyo's brow raised. "Me? What for? And I'm surprised you'd even look here."

"Someone saw you come in here thankfully. Made the search a bit easier. And I'm here to extend an invitation. I've been doing quite a bit of thinking since our fight with Sybilla. Rosette wants to get stronger, and I do too so I can better protect her. I've already been working with a royal guardsman to help with both magic and weapon use, but it doesn't feel like enough." Roland opened his jacket, pulling out his flask and taking a swig from it. "Then an idea hit me. Well, a few actually. I think we could all benefit from learning from each other. Expand our horizons a bit on what type of spells we cast, become more well-rounded to handle various situations. Hopefully, there will be no need, but we can't assume that."

Somehow, Kyo managed to pull his attention away from his attempted heist. "So...what? You mean give each other lessons? That's actually not a bad idea."

Roland grinned. "Of course it's not. Give me some credit. Being older means I have wisdom. I still need to run the idea by Krysta to see if she's interested, but Marsh already accepted. Once I find out who's on board, we'll be able to start."

Kyo nodded. "Yeah, sure. That sounds good. But if you decided *not* to tell Krysta, that'd be fine too."

Narrowing his eyes, Roland leaned closer. "You promised Rosette you two would get along. I'd better see some progress with that, got it? You won't get off so easy if you make her cry again."

Gulping, Kyo forced a smile, not wanting to challenge the firm tone in the older man's voice. "Of course, don't you worry. We'll be closer than the heads on a hydra."

"You'd better be." Roland stood up straight. "I'm going to find Krysta. Enjoy your…recreational reading." He glanced at the pile of books before heading off.

Kyo slumped in his chair and closed his eyes. Of all times. He thought he was going to pass out. Forcing himself from the chair, he stepped to the nearby window, turning the handle and pushing it open. The fresh, cool air washed over him, and he hung the upper half of his body outside. Below were the training grounds he'd used plenty of times since arriving in Alderdeem. A stretch of lush bushes lined the outside of the palace wall, and an idea struck him. He turned around to find nobody. No voices, no footsteps, no hint that anybody was nearby.

He grabbed the tome from the middle of the pile, double checked it was the correct one, then held it close to his chest as he leaned out the window again. He released it, casting air from his hands to gently carry the tome down away from any windows below and tucked it carefully behind the bushes.

Seconds passed, his body remained motionless, expecting someone to appear behind him and question his actions. When no one did, he dared look behind him to find himself alone. He waddled back to the chair and sat, letting the tension leave his body. Part two of his grand mission had been a success. All he had to do was meet with Alden, give him the tome, and let him handle the rest while ensuring neither of them were seen. What he wouldn't give for Marsh's shadow spell. If only they had started learning from each other earlier, this may have been easier.

* * *

Kyo zipped his hoodie as the cold night air left him wishing he grabbed a heavier jacket. Minutes from midnight, he sat on the grass in front of the bushes, waiting, and hoped Alden didn't get caught sneaking onto the palace grounds. He'd never known him to be stealthy, but so far, he hadn't been caught while traveling across Terrorigo.

Sadly, Kyo could hardly make out more than a few stars through The Ancient's canopy. This would have been an amazing place to stargaze from. His fingers rubbed against each other as the minutes crawled by. The sooner this ended, the sooner he could relax. Maybe his anxiety would be replaced with pride that he was able to provide Alden some help. And hopefully some good would come from this.

"Psst."

Kyo startled as he looked to his left to find Alden crouching next to him, swearing he hadn't been there a second ago.

"Geez, are you trying to give me a heart attack?" Kyo asked, hand on his chest and trying to calm his pounding heart.

"Sorry. Were you able to find it?" Alden asked.

Kyo nodded, turning around and reaching into the bushes, pulling out the tome. "I thought I was going to shit myself trying to sneak this out. Though it turned out not to be too hard. Probably because it's still technically on palace grounds." After a moment's hesitation, he wrapped his arms around his godfather,

65

who returned the gesture, holding on tightly. "I wish you could just stay or we could go back to Mistwell and live normally again. This whole thing sucks."

The embrace lasted a few seconds longer before Alden pulled away. Kyo set the tome on the grass.

"I know," Alden said. "Me too. And I'm not going to lie, getting caught and put on trial is more a matter of when, not if. But if I can destroy the stones, I can live with whatever happens. You're getting older and stronger. I don't have to worry about you as much these days, provided you don't get involved in something this crazy again."

"I don't plan on doing anything crazy any time soon, no need to worry about that."

"You'd better not. Keep yourself safe." Alden pulled two small lockboxes out of his pouch, one filled with golden dust and the other with translucent white crystals, different from the type cryst was made of. "Keep your eyes and ears open while I remove the enchantment."

Kyo glanced around, searching and listening for any hint that someone might be coming, but he heard nothing except the shifting of crystals and the chirping of crickets. On occasion, he'd be drawn to Alden's work, sprinkling the dust onto the tome, setting the crystal on top, then casting a spell from his hands. He leaned over the tome to try and hide the glow it created. A violet shimmer spread across the tome then seemed to shatter.

Alden sat upright again. "Easier than I expected. The enchantment was basic, probably due to how many books they had to apply it to." He returned his items, including the tome, into his pouch. "Thank you. I know this was difficult for you to do."

"So that tome will help you destroy the accrue stones?" Kyo asked.

"No, I'm still working on that too, but I'm not entirely confident I'll be able to. What's in this tome may help me with my contingency plan in case destroying them isn't an option."

Kyo stood, and Alden followed, both taking soft, slow steps and keeping their eyes open for guards. With his godfather behind him, Krysta's accusations came back to mind.

"I have to ask," Kyo started. "Once you knew what Sybilla and Blanq were trying to do, could you have contacted the Aurora?"

"Maybe. They aren't the easiest bunch to get in touch with. I couldn't have done it without involving the chancellor. But even if I wanted to, they kept a close eye on me. If I had tried, it would have been a disaster. For you and Mistwell." Alden gripped Kyo's shoulder, sadness in his eyes.

"That's what I thought. I hope they understand that when—"

"Who's out here?" a feminine voice called out.

Kyo's eyes widened, a light growing brighter from around the corner. He turned back to Alden, but he was nowhere to be found.

"Oh, it's you."

Two royal guards approached him, both familiar, at least in passing. The woman held her palm up, a light illuminating her pretty face, emphasizing her naturally bronzed skin, eyeliner with wings, and black lipstick. She ran her fingers through her black-and-blonde hair as she stared intensely at Kyo. Next to her stood a man with hair that seemed a mix of his own and Marsh's: blond, a bit messy, but also long enough to tie in the back. While the woman gave off a fierce aura, the man's facial features appeared softer, kinder, giving a more curious than authoritative look.

"Hey…uh, sorry, I forgot your names," Kyo said. "Or never knew them to begin with. I can't remember which."

The man smiled. "I'm Jaune. And this is Kira."

"And you're one of Her Highnesses friends," Kira said in an accusing tone.

While Kyo would debate the word *friend*, this wasn't the time to argue anything. "Yeah. Sorry, is it too late for me to be out here?"

Kira glanced from him to the training dummies then back to him. "Not necessarily, no. So long as you don't disturb anyone's sleep. But we didn't expect you to be out here at this time. Were you talking to someone?"

Kyo tensed, trying to keep his breathing steady. "Just myself. Working on a new spell and talking out loud helps."

"Yeah, I get that. I do that too sometimes," Jaune said. Unlike his partner, he didn't seem to have any suspicions at all.

Kira took a moment to look around then stared at Kyo again. "Well, don't make too much noise while you're out here. And maybe wear heavier clothes, yeah?"

"I'll probably go back inside soon anyway," Kyo said. "Thanks though."

The two turned to head back the way they came.

"See? Nothing to worry about," Jaune assured her.

"Shame, yeah? Would have been fun to bust someone's head in," Kira replied, thrusting her fist into her other hand.

Kyo groaned silently and pinched the bridge of his nose. That was it. The deed was done. All he could do at this point was hope it'd be months or years before they discovered the tome was missing. And for the short term, he'd head back to his room and get some well-deserved sleep. A part of him remained upset at Jaune and Kira for making Alden leave without a proper goodbye. But being able to hug Alden and laugh with him again brought a smile to Kyo's lips.

Chapter 8

Guilt had set into Kyo since his act of theft a week ago, but felt confident his actions were for the best. So he didn't feel uncomfortable strolling through the halls of the palace alongside his friends on their way to the training ground outside. A unanimous decision had been reached to take Roland's suggestion of learning from one another to benefit their ability to both fight and survive. When Kyo had arrived in Alderdeem, he'd hoped to learn concepts and spells from some of the royal guard. And while that had turned out to be the case, he hadn't expected to also learn from his friends. While he had never taught anyone how to use a spell, he knew who he wanted to learn from first. For all he knew, none of them were interested in wind spells, so he might be off the hook.

"We should have free rein of the training ground for as long as we need, so no need to rush," Krysta said. For the purposes of training, she returned to wearing her casual clothes, and while Kyo wanted to make a snide remark about it, he'd keep his promise. At least while Rosette was within earshot.

"Good. I know I have a lot to learn. I can't let the pipsqueak stay stronger than her old man," Roland said, nudging Rosette with a grin.

"Nuh uh. I'm always going to be stronger than you because you're old." Rosette stuck her tongue out at Roland.

"Your Highness!" The group stopped and turned to see Hayner rushing in their direction. "Might I ask where you're going?"

Krysta raised a brow. "We're going to the training grounds." Her words were drawn out, as if suspicious of the question.

"Then come along with me. You can use the indoor training room beneath the palace." Hayner waved his hand for them to follow but after a few steps stopped and turned to look their way. No one had moved.

"But it's such a nice day out," Rosette complained.

Marsh nodded. "Not to mention being outdoors leaves less room for accidental damage to any structures."

"I assure you the indoor training grounds will be the best place for you. Come along. Now." Hayner's voice grew stern, and he stared until he knew they were following.

Kyo and the others glanced at Krysta, but all she could do was shrug. They trailed behind Hayner silently, discomfort permeating the air.

Without warning, Krysta paused. "What's going on? I expect you wouldn't hide anything from me."

Hayner halted and turned to face them. His eyes met Krysta's before his shoulders slumped. "Keep walking, and I'll tell you." He rounded the corner and slowed his pace to allow them to catch up. "You recall the other day it was reported that a new outbreak of the corruption has been discovered. Not only in Alderdeem but all across Terrorigo. Like before, it seems those afflicted became so around the same time, according to communications with chancellors. As we'd planned after you dealt with Sybilla and Blanq, we worked together to give those afflicted transport to Spellnix Hold, where Blanq would heal them. And to her credit, she's kept her word."

They arrived at a pair of tall metal doors, revealing a staircase descending beneath the palace.

"Well," Hayner went on, "as we feared, there were those who hadn't made themselves known, likely due to fear. And those people have begun turning into shades. In short, there are shades currently loose in the city, more than we had originally anticipated."

Everyone looked at each other with wide eyes.

Kyo turned to face away from the stairs. "If that's the case, we should go help."

Hayner grabbed his wrist and pulled him down the staircase. "And that is precisely why I would have preferred to take you to the underground training area without explaining the situation. His Majesty and I knew you would want to get involved."

"It is only natural for us to want to help, is it not?" Marsh asked. "We have dealt with shades before."

"Yes, you have. And how did that turn out? As I recall, you couldn't do any harm to them. Estella and Garret had to come to your rescue. And what little you've done to improve your capabilities since you've been here will not change that." Hayner opened another set of metal doors, revealing a massive space nearly the size of the training grounds outside and a ceiling that reached multiple stories. It had much the same setup, including the dummies minus the foliage. "You would be nothing more than additional people that would need protection."

Kyo furrowed his brow, clenching his fists. "Come on. We were able to take down Sybilla together. We should be able to do the same with a shade if we put our all behind it."

"Don't argue," Roland interjected. His eyes narrowed at Kyo then turned to the rest. "Hayner is right. Our fight against Sybilla nearly killed us, and we only squeezed out a win because we were able to use the accrue stone. There's no reason for us to go that far to kill a shade when the enforcers and royal guard are more capable and have greater numbers. We'd only get in the way."

Krysta sighed and lowered her head. "It's true. We're too weak to be of any real help without being a burden. That makes what we're doing here today all the more important. One day, we'll be able to help in these situations, but it's not today."

Kyo grunted, the muscles in his arms tightening in frustration. When they'd come out victorious against Sybilla and Blanq, he'd felt content on letting others handle things from then on. But with danger reappearing outside their door and people's lives at risk, the thought of staying out of it made him sick to his stomach. But he knew they were right, and that admission sparked anger toward himself for his weakness. Anger he'd be more than glad to let out against one of the training dummies. A month ago, he'd fought undead, shades, and Sybilla and barely came out alive. Today, he'd have to stay hunkered down like a helpless child while others fought and possibly died.

"We made absolutely certain any within the palace who had become corrupted were sent to Spellnix Hold, so there shouldn't be any shades appearing here. Even so, stay down here until we give the all-clear." Hayner turned to leave.

But Kyo grasped his arm. "Wait."

When Hayner turned around, Kyo held out his hand, palm up. Air circulated above his palm, condensing and forming into the wind drill he'd used against Sybilla. His eyes remained locked on Hayner's as the spell grew more intense, magical energy traveling unseen down his arm to feed the spell. Yet his hoodie and Hayner's robes barely budged. Though slight, a few strands of hair brushed against his forehead but nothing more before the spell ceased. While not absolute perfection, pride filled him, knowing he'd made a world of difference in his magic control.

"You've come far in such a short time. Color me impressed." Hayner smiled. "You're still not going to go out there to fight shades, but I'll make it a point to teach you a few more direct things that should help you." He patted Kyo's shoulder then turned and closed the doors behind him.

Krysta extended her hand and shouted, a fireball launching and hitting the head of a nearby practice dummy. Like the ones outside, a barrier appeared upon impact, an array of colors spreading from the point of contact before fading. "They'd better eliminate every last shade. And treat the bodies properly afterwards."

"I am sure we can trust them to do what they must," Marsh said. "We should focus on what we came here to do. Perhaps we could split into groups, depending on who wishes to learn what. Does anyone have anything specific in mind to start?"

The other four closed in on Marsh then glanced at each other.

"I guess we all want to learn from him, huh?" Rosette grabbed Marsh's hand, rocking on her heels. "You're popular."

A light blush crossed Marsh's cheeks. "You all wish for me to teach you?"

Roland extended his right arm, his polearm appearing in his hand. "I can definitely see some benefits to making my own barriers."

"Yeah, I was thinking the same thing," Kyo said. "That was first on my list. I sure wouldn't mind being able to heal myself too, but barriers first." He sat and crossed his legs. "Since we all want to learn the same thing, may as well start with that, right?"

The others sat, forming a circle.

Marsh released a shaky breath and sat. "Well, I have never taught anyone how to use a spell before. Remember, I have only been a cleric for a few years. Maybe you all would be better off…" His words trailed off as he glanced between them, all staring back and ready to learn. His face hardened with determination. "I will do my best. Do not become frustrated if you do not grasp it in this session. Learning new spells takes time and becoming truly proficient in them more so."

Kyo knew that well. He'd managed to practically master his father's wind drill spell when it really counted, but it had taken months to truly grasp it. And it would have taken longer if he hadn't been put in dangerous situations that required it to survive. This new spell he'd been practicing would no doubt take longer, being from a school of magic he'd never attempted before. He couldn't wait to get the hang of it though, already having several uses in mind.

"We're ready when you are," Krysta said with a gentle smile.

Marsh nodded. "Very well. We will of course work on creating a barrier from your hands, as that is the easiest part of the body to expel magic from."

While true, Kyo intended to eventually cast them from beneath his feet. But he'd pay attention and learn the basics first then figure out how to do them his way later. Understanding how the others fought, he suspected at least some of them had similar ideas.

"Perhaps Krysta may have the best understanding," Marsh went on. "Much like with ice spells, it relies on solidifying your magical energy. So, we must start there before we can consider creating a full-sized barrier. That, I believe, will be the most difficult part. Once you understand how to accomplish this, the rest should come more easily." He raised his hand with his palm facing outward, strands of sapphire and violet magical energy seeping from it. Within the span of a second, the energy lost its hue, solidifying into a messy shape like a flat translucent blob. "Condense the energy then spread it. That is the first key to solidifying it."

Condense and spread. Kyo inhaled then allowed his magic to trail to his hand. Like Marsh, he could see the raw magical energy escape due to how slowly and carefully he released it, instead of transforming it into wind instantly. That habit proved hard to break. He had always used his magic to create free-flowing air, the exact opposite of Marsh's instructions.

As Kyo continued his efforts, a groan of frustration came from his friends on occasion. Marsh circled the group, occasionally giving tips or encouraging words. For someone who had never taught spells before, it seemed to come naturally to him.

At one point, Kyo swore he heard that faint, all too familiar screech of a shade. He thought it was paranoia, the concern about what was happening outside in the back of his mind, until he noticed the others all had their eyes on the door.

"You don't think there's one in the palace, do you?" Kyo asked.

"I sure hope not. It's hard to tell. Those screeches do tend to penetrate far," Krysta said in a slow, soft voice.

Roland slapped the solid ground several times. "Let's focus on what we came here to do. I'm sure they have it under control out there."

"What if they don't?" Rosette asked.

After a few seconds of silence, Roland returned his gaze to the door. "We'll judge as the situation unfolds. But for now, that screech sounded far away. So back to training."

Over the next several hours, they made varying degrees of progress. Krysta was the first to successfully solidify her magic to be more like a tiny barrier, not even half the size of her palm. Rosette succeeded next, followed by Roland. While Kyo grew closer, he still struggled, staring intensely at his hand. During this time, they had heard the screech of a shade twice more, but the last time was about two hours ago. He hoped that meant the situation was under control.

"Why don't we take a break?" Marsh suggested.

Kyo groaned and laid on his back, embarrassed everyone achieved the basic concept before him. The son of two Aurora in last place.

"Having trouble over there, islander?" Krysta asked with a snide giggle.

Kyo grumbled and pushed himself up with his elbows ready to insult her back, but one glance at Rosette and he relented. He could wait until the kid wasn't around. "I'll get it. In the meantime, I hope they update us soon about what's going on. I'm all for training, but it's different when we're forced to stay in here. I wonder if anyone thought about bringing us food."

"If not, we can at least slip into the kitchen quickly. I doubt Hayner locked the door behind him." Roland stood and stretched his legs. The others followed suit, bending their backs and occasionally getting a crack from various body parts.

"Thanks, Marsh. Once I do get the hang of this, it's going to be helpful," Kyo said. The others thanked him as well, bringing a blush to Marsh's cheeks.

"I am glad to help. After this, I will request I be taught something as well, of course. I already know what I have in mind." Marsh glanced at Kyo for a second and smiled.

If they could successfully learn from one another and be creative in the application of their new spells, they would become a force to be reckoned with. Though there was no telling if they'd ever have the need to fight side by side again. While Roland and Rosette would soon have a house in Alderdeem, Kyo and Marsh would eventually return to their own homes. At present, Kyo's main concern remained Alden and his eventual fate. The way things stood, there was a good chance Alden would be punished for his involvement with the accrue stones. But if he did in fact manage to destroy them or render them useless, perhaps those wishing to sentence him would change their minds. The theory reaffirmed to Kyo that he did the right thing stealing that tome from the library. Once Alden finished his work, they'd see how things played out. Kyo didn't intend to return home any time soon. Aside from having no desire to live in an empty home, remaining in Alderdeem gave him the best chance of survival. Should he become corrupted, he'd have easy access to transport to Spellnix Hold. And he would milk the royal guard's willingness to train him as much as possible.

Chapter 9

Between time spent in the palace practicing new spells since Kyo had arrived four months ago and the occasional corruption outbreak, excursions to the city were rare. It was time for him to relax, let both his magic and body rest, and do something enjoyable. When he compared how far he'd come since arriving in Alderdeem, the difference brought a satisfied smirk to his lips. Sure, he wasn't equal to an Aurora or even a royal guard, but if he kept up with his current pace, he'd reach that point somewhere down the line.

The sun shone brightly through The Ancient's canopy outside, the air flowing through open windows warm enough for Kyo to keep his hoodie wrapped around his waist. He descended the stairs to the main level of the palace. With the city waiting, new things were on the horizon: new bakeries, new spell tomes, all things he still couldn't afford so he'd have to settle for more window shopping. Training had taken such a priority he'd forgotten about finding a job. Good thing the palace provided everything he needed. But when he did have enough cryst to spend, he'd at least know what to spend it on.

Kyo turned into the palace's entryway heading for the main doors, eyes focused on the massive dragon skull on display with other rare and expensive items and relics. He hardly took more than a step before a hand pulled at his arm, causing him to stumble backward.

"Come with me," Marsh ordered, keeping a firm grip on Kyo's wrist. "Hurry."

"Wha? Oh, uh…okay." Kyo regained his footing and struggled to keep up with Marsh's quick pace. "What are you—"

"The Aurora are still here?"

"I think so, but I haven't seen them since yesterday. Did something happen?" They turned a corner, and Kyo suspected they were headed straight for the throne room.

"I believe I have found something significant." Marsh's eyes remained forward, determined.

For the first time, Kyo noticed a small book Marsh held in his left hand, a finger keeping a page saved. "You actually found something?" For the past four months the Aurora had come and gone, absent far longer than present. If Marsh found important information on the corruption, no wonder he was so insistent.

When they arrived at the massive throne room doors that reached to the ceiling, they found Jaune and Kira standing guard. "Are the Aurora meeting with His Majesty?" Marsh asked. "I need to speak with them immediately."

"They are, but you'll have to wait until they're finished," Kira insisted without a bit of hesitation, her fierce eyes locked on the cleric.

"I cannot risk missing them," Marsh said, staring back with a challenging tone in his voice. "I have incredibly important information regarding the corruption that they need to see."

"Don't get uppity with me, cleric," Kira warned.

Jaune stepped between the two, stretching his hands outward to prevent a fight. "Hold on. Remember our orders. Anything regarding the corruption is to be treated as top priority. Give me a moment." He opened one of the doors enough to step through but not enough to invite others in.

Regardless, Marsh stormed past Kira and slipped through.

"Hey!" Kira followed, and Kyo did the same with a sigh. Maybe his own lack of care for authority was starting to rub off on Marsh. Though even he might not be this bold.

"I'm sorry, Your Majesty," Jaune started.

The king sat upon his throne, Hayner standing stiffly to his right. Before them, the three familiar Aurora turned. Krysta, dressed in another fancy gown that matched the hue of her hair, stomped toward them, leaving her uncle's side.

"Kyo," she said, "what are you doing? We're having an important meeting."

"Hey, it wasn't me this time." Kyo raised his hands defensively and looked to Marsh for an explanation.

"Please forgive the interruption, Your Majesty. I need to show the Aurora something immediately." Marsh held the book out, its pages yellowed, the charcoal leather cover and spine frayed. It looked as though the pages might fall right out. "I may have found something on the source of the corruption."

Everyone went silent, looking at each other in confusion and skepticism. Kyo stared with wide eyes. Finding relevant information and finding the source were two different things entirely. There was no way he could have found something in a book so old, right?

Estella stepped to him, and Marsh handed her the book, open to the page he'd saved.

"Please read from this page," Marsh instructed.

PROVENANCE

She examined the book's front and back cover
and flipped through a few pages while saving the
important one. "A journal."

Estella turned to the king, who gave a nod of
approval. Clearing her throat, she read aloud.

*I don't know how it happened or even
what it is that has happened. I have taken
refuge within the caverns the Crossroads
officials have dug beneath the town while in
search of additional water sources. Even down
here, I can hear the screeches. They seem to
penetrate everything. There is no escaping them.*

*One moment, all was well. The town's
center was bustling with traders and eager
spenders. The next, darkness took hold. Women,
children. None were safe. They became savage
beasts of void, slaughtering indiscriminately. I
don't know who else survived or if I am the only
one. Nor for how long.*

*I will bide my time, see if I can find a
means of escape.*

The throne room became silent as the dead. Even
Kyo didn't need someone to explain the similarities
between what Estella had read and what had been going
on across Feracael these past few months.

"So, that story about Crossroads disappearing
overnight is true?" Kyo asked. "And it was because of
the corruption?"

"Just as the stories have said, this entry is dated
over two hundred years ago. Where did you find this?"
Estella asked.

"Tucked away toward the back of the royal
library. After my initial research failed to give any
results, I toyed with the idea of this not being the first

time the corruption had been seen, so I started focusing on journals." Marsh took the book from Estella and flipped through a few pages. "The remainder of the entries are of his attempts to survive, his eventual corruption…and that is all."

Garret approached Marsh and gave him a firm pat on the back, causing him to stumble forward. "That does sound like a significant lead. More than anything we've found so far, ya. That is some damn nice work." He smiled at Marsh then gazed at Cedric. "Worth investigating?"

Cedric had his hand over his mouth for a moment before nodding. "Absolutely. It sounds too similar to ignore. However, I suspect those in charge back then wanted to hide this as much as possible, hence most only see its disappearance as a story. And those who do believe it debate on Crossroads' exact location."

"I can help with that," King Richard said. "I do recall seeing mention of Crossroads while scouring my family's old records years ago, though it will take some time to find. With any luck, that information should include coordinates of where the town once sat." The king rose. "Cedric, our current meeting is hereby postponed. I'd like you to investigate this without delay. Hayner, please come with us to the archives."

"Yes, Your Majesty," Hayner said, bowing his head.

"Estella, Garret, I can't say if this will take hours or days, but tell our airship crew to be ready to leave at a moment's notice. And Marsh." Cedric offered a wry smile. "Brilliant work." He left the throne room, swiftly following the king and Hayner.

Marsh's smile could have put a giddy Rosette's to shame but quickly faded as he stepped in front of Estella and Garret to keep them from leaving. "Take me with you."

"Absolutely not. There's no telling what we might find or how dangerous it could be," Estella moved past Marsh with Garret by her side.

"I can take care of myself," Marsh assured, following them toward the doors. "And if things prove to be dangerous, I will wait aboard the airship. But as you have said, there is no telling what we may find. And that could include a way to cure the corruption that does not rely on shipping people to Spellnix Hold."

Garret intercepted Marsh to keep him from moving forward. "You have done an incredible job here, ya. An extremely important one. So, leave this part to us. If we learn of anything you should know, we will tell you when we return." He ruffled Marsh's hair before leaving the throne room with Estella.

Marsh sighed, his shoulders slumping. "I knew the chances were low, but I still hoped."

Kyo frowned and placed a hand on the cleric's back. "Hey, don't be too upset about it. They might be right. What if they come across old geezer shades that shake their canes at you? The horror."

Marsh tried and failed to hide a snicker.

"And it's not like I'd suggest we tag along without them knowing. Between you and me, we might be able to avoid even Cedric's notice." Kyo said with a mischievous grin. The idea of seeing the source of the corruption firsthand, helping the Aurora to investigate, perhaps even finding a way to stop it could make his parents even more proud than defeating Sybilla. And if he could achieve two successes in a row alongside the Aurora, they wouldn't be able to do anything but accept them into the group. Once Kyo was a bit older anyway. "Not that I'm actually suggesting it of course."

"You will do no such thing!" Krysta cried out, stomping toward them. Without another word, she grabbed their hands and pulled them through the throne room doors.

"Did we hear something we shouldn't have?" Jaune asked in a shaky voice.

"Better hope not," Kyo teased while being pulled past him and Kira.

Krysta pulled them down the hall and around the corner before releasing them. "If you two think you are tagging along and leaving me behind to play princess, think again," she said in a harsh but hushed tone.

Kyo's eyes widened. "If your uncle notices you missing, you are going to be in so much trouble. Please come along with us." He tried not to laugh at the idea.

"You think I care? I left for a solid half year. What we could learn might be imperative to keeping Alderdeem and its people safe and corruption-free. And what if something happens to the Aurora and we never learn about the source?" She shook her head. "The more eyes we have there, the better."

"Krysta, Kyo, please," Marsh said, frowning and with pleading eyes. "I am volunteering because I am fully prepared for the risks. Being so close to the corruption's source, we do not know what effect that could have on us. We could instantly turn into shades without warning. I am sure the Aurora are aware of such a risk as well. Without knowing what we could come across, there is no reason for you to take unnecessary risks as well."

"And yet you insist." Kyo slapped Marsh on the back of the head. "You think I'm letting you do something like that alone while I just sit here and hope for the best? If you go, I go."

"For once, I agree with him." Krysta folded her arms across her chest. "We won't let you put yourself in danger alone. If nothing else, we'll be there to back you up if you need it." With a gentle smile, she booped Marsh's nose, leaving a dusting of frost over it. "Besides, I have a suspicion we won't have to worry about instantly turning to shades. It's a loose theory, but given outbreaks of the corruption aren't worse in one specific area versus another, it stands to reason we don't need to worry about being too close. Now, if the source turns out to be something we can physically touch, we may want to avoid doing that."

Marsh crinkled his nose and brushed the frost off. "I would feel absolutely terrible if anything happened to either of you."

"Feeling's mutual, bedhead." Kyo lightly punched Marsh's arm. "Which is why, like when dealing with Sybilla and Blanq, we need to have each other's backs."

"Yeah, I want to go too!" Rosette cried out, bursting from a nearby corner.

Roland followed, grabbing Rosette's wrist and pulling her back. "Nope. Not happening. I will go. *You* will stay here."

"What?" Rosette stomped her foot. "You said you'd trust me to fight more."

"I did say that, and I do. But this is different." Roland ignored the death glare from Rosette. "It might not be something you can throw a punch or kick at or even have an Altruist help with. There are too many unknowns here. But I'll need to chaperone you kids if you insist on going so the Aurora can focus on their investigation."

"You're not going to try to talk us out of it?" Kyo asked.

"I doubt I could. And why bother trying when I can go to the Aurora right now and tell them you're planning to follow without them knowing? That would put an end to your little trip nice and quick. But…" Roland clenched his lips and tapped his fingers against his thigh. "As amazing as the Aurora are, the fact is if we left events in Oasis completely up to them, we would have had an entire city of shades. It was only because of our involvement that didn't happen. That's why I'm not so against us tagging along, whether they want us to or not. So long as we are careful."

Kyo didn't know if that should make him feel proud or concerned. He'd always seen the Aurora as this unstoppable force who could do anything. Oasis changed that perception and brought thoughts of what his parents may have gone through and the time in Oasis years ago when that young boy died during their battle with the massive scorpion. No longer were they the invincible heroes but exceptionally powerful mages who put everything on the line for others. Still highly respectable, but they were still human, and humans made mistakes and needed help on occasion. That didn't hamper his feelings toward his parents though or the pride he felt when thinking of them and all they'd done.

Marsh nodded. "You do have a good point. And I suppose there is a chance we will not find anything. But there is no doubt they will not allow us to tag along. We will have to keep our ears open to find out when they plan to leave then sneak aboard their airship."

"If we do that, we'll need to give absolutely no indication we are there until we arrive at our destination. They will turn the airship right around with me on board. Not to mention not wanting to give Cedric a reason to use his perception spells," Krysta said, rolling her eyes.

"Then it's settled. Rosette will be staying here. The rest of us will find a way aboard the airship once we know when they're leaving. Right, Rosette?" Roland asked, giving the girl a firm look, and she grumbled in response.

"And if they decide to leave at night, I know the perfect way for us to sneak on board," Kyo said with a grin. Mischievous acts and doing things he shouldn't always sent a tingle through his body. Months ago, they helped bring an end to Blanq and Sybilla's chaos and destruction. This time, they'd help put an end to the corruption altogether, allowing the entire world to breathe a sigh of relief. After that, all that remained was for Alden to do his part, and this whole nightmare could be put to an end.

Thinking of Alden brought his attention to the hoodie around his waist, his fingers caressing the fabric. So long as it stayed with him, Alden would be able to track him. Krysta would blow her top if she knew, but he had no intention of leaving it behind. Besides trusting Alden, Kyo's focus remained on the accrue stones. He tightened the sleeves around his waist, ready to leave at a moment's notice.

Chapter 10

Hours passed since Krysta had gone to help the king and the Aurora in the archives, and Kyo grew restless. For a while, he killed time with Roland and Marsh by talking and playing card games. When that couldn't keep his impatience in check, he ended up lying on the bed in his room, staring at the ceiling, and groaning. He glanced out the window, hardly any sunlight seeping through The Ancient's canopy. If it ended up taking them days to find what they needed, he'd die from a mixture of boredom and eager anticipation. He released a frustrated grunt, kicking his feet.

"Relax, kid," Roland said, seated in a cushioned chair in the corner, feet up on an ottoman. "His Majesty can't put off all his other duties indefinitely. They'll either find it soon or call it for the day and pick it up tomorrow. Either way, I'm sure we'll know soon."

"How is progress going on the house for you and Rosette?" Marsh asked from the stool in front of the vanity table that Kyo insisted he had no use for, despite teasing from the other two.

Roland grinned. "His Majesty says it should be ready for us within the next month. He insisted on a new construction, which I'm not going to complain about. Although…" His eyes dropped, the grin following suit. "I'll be glad to be out of here. Everyone here has been nice and polite, but a certain few can't completely hide the way they look at Rosette. I don't think it's disdain, given how we worked with Krysta, but at least mistrust." Sighing, he placed his hands behind his head. "I'm sure it'll be no different once we have our new home though."

"Such feelings for summoners run deep. However, I would like to think if they understand how she helped their princess, then get to know her personally, your neighbors will come to have an appreciation for her." Marsh offered a reassuring smile. "Give it time."

"Four months hasn't been long enough?" Roland asked.

Kyo jumped when the door swung open.

Krysta clapped her hands once. "They're leaving soon. We all know where to meet?"

"Finally! I'm ready right now." Kyo slid off the bed and made for the door.

"Good for you, but there is no way I'm going without changing into some comfortable clothes. I'll meet you all shortly." Krysta turned to Roland. "Is Rosette somewhere secure?"

Roland rose from the chair and stretched his arms above his head. "Yeah, she's in our room. I'm going to let her know, then I'll meet the rest of you."

"With no more preparations needed from me, Kyo and I can head straight there. We will see you soon." Marsh followed Krysta out of the room and waited.

"Let's get going. Time to figure out what's going on with this damn corruption." Kyo patted Marsh on the back then led the way. He did his best to act casually, not wanting to give any guards or staff they passed reason to suspect anything. Marsh did his part by forcing casual conversation to passersby during their walk to one of the palace towers, allowing them to reach one of the highest points.

From the window of the northeast stone tower, they could see the airship dock in the distance. So long as Cedric had no need to use his perception spells before taking off, they should be able to sneak aboard without issue. Even so, his heart pounded from both nerves and excitement. Another mission alongside the Aurora, the chance to discover the truth about the corruption, and finally putting some new spells to good use. He could hardly stay still. He smiled wide when Roland and Krysta arrived, the latter wearing the same long-sleeved striped shirt and denim shorts she wore before returning to the palace.

"Okay, everyone ready?" Krysta asked. "Be sure to keep quiet."

"Also stick close together," Roland said. "Marsh has to maintain two spells at once. Don't put more of a strain on him. You're sure you'll be okay?"

Marsh nodded. "Absolutely."

Kyo unlatched the window and pushed it open. "Then let's get to it."

He hopped onto the window ledge, pulled the zipper of his hoodie up a bit more to protect him from the chilly breeze, then took his first step into the open air. His boot pressed upon a solid square barrier only a bit longer and wider than his foot. Each subsequent step created a new barrier to use as a walking platform. The others followed, using the same spell to keep themselves high in the air without issue.

A long exhale escaped from Marsh as he extended his hands, darkness seeping from him and enshrouding the group, blending into the night. Not a sound escaped from them as they walked along the sky, peering through small gaps in the shadow to ensure they traveled in the right direction and descended at a reasonable pace.

Roland's lips were tight and his eyes wide. Out of the four of them, he had no way of saving himself should he falter with his barriers and would have to rely on the others. It almost made Kyo chuckle. The poor man. Of course, he'd grab Roland if it came to it and could surely save him well before reaching the ground.

Something hit the back of Kyo's head. He turned to Krysta, who had more tiny snowballs in one hand, the other motioning to come back, as he'd put too much distance between himself and them. Mouthing an apology, he made his way back to the group and worked to keep his steps in line with theirs. He waited for Roland to move ahead of him in case something went wrong with his spellcasting.

Marsh put his arms out to signal a stop. A gap opened in the shadow, and after a moment of peering through, he altered his direction for the others to follow. He took large steps downward, increasing the rate of descent as they neared the Aurora's airship. Much like their robes, it didn't stand out much. No special markings or emblems. While a bit longer and wider than the average airship, it still looked like a wooden sea ship with magic-tech engines on the back and bottom, no different than many others. Always trying to blend into the crowd and keep attention off of them. At least until it came time for a fight.

Once again, Marsh paused and peered through a gap in the darkness, this time for much longer. Unable to feed his curiosity as well as contain his impatience, Kyo considered shaking Marsh to ask what the holdup was. Before he had the chance, Marsh waved them on. "Be quick."

They descended until their feet hit solid ground in front of the airship, with an audible sigh of relief from Roland. Marsh guided them around the hull until they came to the entryway into the lower level. He held his hand out to signal for them to stop. Kyo gazed over Marsh's shoulder and strained his ears yet picked up no sign of anyone nearby. The urge to push his friend forward almost took over, but then a man holding a clipboard exited the airship. Right, former thief. Kyo had nearly forgotten and reminded himself to put more faith in Marsh when it came to sneaking around.

They entered the lower level of the airship, nearby voices and footsteps of the crew reaching their ears. Slow and steady, they weaved past doorways to other sections and peered into other rooms until they found one for storage filled with crates and barrels of who knew what and boxes of assorted mechanical parts.

Krysta gently closed the door behind them.

"So long as we can stay hidden, we'll be fine," she said barely above a whisper.

Roland picked up a crate and as gently as possible moved it against the wall, repeating this with several more until there was a gap they could slip through. "It won't be a comfy ride, kids. But if we don't want to get caught, we'd best stay hidden back here until we arrive at our destination."

"And this is where the secret to dealing with long travel comes in. The more you sleep, the easier it'll be," Kyo said, heading for the back wall and finding a spot to sit down with his legs outstretched. Once the others did the same, Roland moved some of the crates and barrels to cover them while giving them some room to stretch out.

"I am anxious to discover what we will find at the site. Remember, we must be as careful as possible." Marsh ran his hands over his knees, breathing deeply.

"So am I." Roland propped one knee up and rested his forehead against it. "Truth is, I spend every day worrying the next time I look at Rosette, she'll be corrupted. If we can at least keep things from getting worse, it's worth getting directly involved."

Kyo decided to follow his earlier advice and sleep through as much of the trip as possible. He closed his eyes for a few minutes before the hum of the engines and the shaking of the airship signaled their departure. Perfect. So long as they kept quiet, they should have no trouble staying hidden until it was too late for the Aurora to turn back. The white noise of the engines helped lull him to sleep.

When Kyo opened his eyes, he did so to a hand reaching over and covering his mouth. He glanced at Roland then strained his ears to listen.

The clink of the doorknob turning had everyone's attention. The door opened, and footsteps echoed against the walls. Kyo tensed, his jaw clenching while hoping whoever was on the other side of the supplies had no reason to search where they sat. Everyone eyed each other nervously. Whoever it was rummaged through a barrel or crate by the sound of it, then silence. Did he miss the footsteps of them leaving? Was the door still open? It'd be best to assume so, and that meant remaining in complete silence.

More rummaging through barrels and crates. Of course it was inevitable for someone to come to the supply room on a trip bringing them halfway across the continent.

"All this stuff is boring," a voice said from the other side of the supply crates. A young, feminine, and familiar voice that made Roland's eyes go wide in a mixture of surprise and anger. He lunged forward, clearing a path until all four of them could see Rosette standing there, eyes wide, her hand covering her mouth for a second before lowering it, revealing a wide, toothy smile.

"Wow, funny seeing you here. In the same room too." The smile vanished when Roland grabbed her wrist, pulled her into the gap in the back of the room, and covered them again.

"What do you think you're doing here? I was explicitly clear that you were not getting involved in this." No amount of whispering could hide the frustration in Roland's voice.

Rosette pulled her wrist away. "What if you need my help? You might need an Altruist to help you and then what?"

"We'll figure it out. I told you to stay put until we get back," Roland said harshly.

Tears welled in Rosette's eyes, though they remained focused and narrow. "And what if you don't come back?" she barked back in a hushed voice. "What if you leave me behind and something happens to you? You're always going on about protecting me because I'm a kid. But I want to protect you too. You're my dad!" She pushed against Roland's chest. "We've done everything together, and I don't want you to go alone." The anger gave way to a deep frown before she wrapped her arms around Roland, who fought between continuing to show anger and giving in to understanding and sympathy with a frown of his own. "I thought about what if a shade gets you, or you become corrupted, and I never see you again. And I cried." She buried her face in his stomach. "I don't care that you think I'm too young. We're a team, and we need to look out for each other."

Roland shushed her as her voice threatened to get louder. "Okay, okay. Just keep your voice down."

Sighing, he rubbed her back and remained silent.

Kyo and the others could do nothing but let them deal with this as a family issue. He took his place against the wall again. Though he wouldn't say it out loud, having Rosette here brought him some comfort. Despite her age, she had more magic than any of them, and the ability to summon avatars of deities made her the most well equipped to get them out of a tight spot.

The others took their seats, Rosette sitting in Roland's lap as they spoke in hushed tones—apologies, some firm words. Kyo tried to tune them out. He understood both sides but had no reason to pick one. Let them figure it out.

For the remainder of the trip, Kyo could do nothing more than sit in boredom or continue sleeping.

He closed his eyes but let his mind wander. What would they find when they arrived? The stories stated Crossroads was once a bustling hub, popular with traders from all over, then one day vanished. Not only the population but the buildings, the roads, everything. So, what were they going to investigate besides a massive empty plot of land? And the more pressing concern—was it due to the corruption everything vanished? If so, could the same happen with these new outbreaks? He shuddered at the idea they'd only seen the beginning of what the corruption could do.

Chapter 11

A sensation of weightlessness and Kyo's ears popping signified they were landing. They had managed to avoid detection during the trip by remaining hunkered behind the storage supplies. Though he wasn't sure how long the trip had lasted, it seemed long enough to get a full night's rest despite the uncomfortable accommodation. He stretched his arms above his head and groaned, ready to be free and not stuck shoulder to shoulder with the others.

Roland held out his arm to keep Kyo in place. "We should still wait a bit. Give them time to settle before we make ourselves known. Hopefully once they start their investigation, they won't want to interrupt it to bring us back."

Kyo sighed and slumped against the wall.

"Where do you think we are?" Rosette asked.

"Well, I know where we are geographically, but I know nothing of the area and what we might find." Krysta leaned forward, reaching for her toes in a deep stretch. "If you were to look on a map, we're around the center of Terrorigo, which makes sense, given what a popular trading hub Crossroads was. Beyond that, we'll have to wait and see."

Marsh bent backward to stretch his back. "I suppose we will not need a plan to leave the airship undetected. Perhaps fifteen minutes before we leave? Not that we can accurately tell time from inside here, but we can estimate."

They agreed, spending that time stretching, making whispered small talk, and hastily moving their legs and fingers in eager anticipation. When enough time had passed, Roland moved the storage containers out of the way, allowing them to be free of their self-made prison.

"Finally, let's get out of here." Kyo led the way, opening the door and immediately seeing several of the airship crew, all dressed in royal blue pants and long-sleeved shirts and white engineer's hats, who turned to look at them with cocked brows and hanging jaws. "Hey, smooth trip, thanks. Don't mind us. We'll see ourselves out."

The crew remained silent until Krysta left the storage room. An older man with a trimmed gray beard and muscular arms spoke up. "Your Highness. What are you doing here? Your uncle…uh…he won't be happy, nah?"

"That's for me to worry about, not you," Krysta replied in a slightly harsh tone. A second later, her face softened. "I'll make sure none of you are held responsible for this. If the Aurora didn't know we were here, how should you?"

"Tutelvus help us," the man muttered. He dragged his hand down his face and released a heavy sigh, the other crew members murmuring among themselves.

Kyo gave a small smile and wave as he walked past them and to the gangplank leading outside to a bright sunny day.

Krysta inhaled deeply. "Ah, fresh air. It was way too stuffy in there. I wouldn't doubt if the islander was to blame for that."

"If I blasted you with wind from anything other than my magic, you'd know," Kyo said, narrowing his eyes.

Marsh nudged Kyo and pointed north. In the distance among the expansive grassy field stood the Aurora, staring at the ground for a moment before hopping into it, vanishing from sight.

"Where did they go?" Rosette took off toward where the Aurora had stood a second ago.

"Rosette, wait!" Roland ran after her with the others in tow.

Kyo stepped around Roland to find Rosette crouched, staring down a deep hole dug within the ground, easily wide enough for a grown adult to jump into with plenty of space around them. "Where do they think they're going?" He kicked a small rock from upturned earth into the hole and leaned down, listening for the impact. Seconds passed and, after a full minute, gave up. "Wow. That's deep."

"I wonder what they think they will find down there," Marsh asked, peering into the darkness of the hole.

"There's only one way to find out, isn't there?" Krysta suggested, a snarky grin on her lip. "We didn't stow away to sit idle. Kyo, why don't you see what's down there and we'll follow."

Kyo shrugged. "Okay."

It couldn't be any worse than leaping from the tower in Oasis. Without hesitation, he jumped into the hole, barely hearing Krysta's call to wait. A barrier appeared under his feet to act as a platform to stand upon. It vanished, allowing him to drop a fair distance before another appeared. He repeated this cycle, as it used up less magical energy than constantly slowing his descent with wind.

Unable to see his hand in front of his face, Kyo reached into the pouch at his side, feeling around until he pulled out a translucent orb. Pushing a minute amount of magic within it, the orb illuminated the area with a faint turquoise hue, allowing him to see the rock and dirt around him. From above, he could hear the faint sounds of his friends following him, but he decided not to wait. He didn't need his head accidentally crushed by their feet or a barrier.

After several minutes of descending, the rock and dirt gave way to a massive open space he couldn't see the end of, illuminated by natural glowing crystal stalagmites and stalactites of various colors. His jaw dropped at the beautiful scene, wanting to stare at the hues like he often did the stars. Though tempting, he tore his eyes away to continue hopping barriers to head downward. As the ground drew closer, he realized there was far more than dirt below him. Buildings, roads, an entire town nestled deep underground.

"What the…" Kyo hadn't expected they'd make a discovery like this. It had to be Crossroads.

Kyo couldn't stop the wide smile spreading over his lips. A chance to explore a place no one else had in over two hundred years. Though the smile faded when he remembered the town had vanished with its people. Would he find the roads littered with bodies like Calmarock? A shiver ran through him at the thought. By now they'd be nothing but bone. While not quite the same, images of the victims of Calmarock flooded into his mind. He clenched his eyes and pushed the thoughts away as he continued downward until his feet touched solid ground. He stared up from where he'd come, making out faint hints of the others coming his way.

When they joined him, they kept their eyes on their surroundings, eyes sparkling in awe.

"This place is beautiful," Rosette said, her words coming out slowly.

"That it is." Roland took a few steps to a radiant yellow crystal slightly bigger than his hand. He pulled but it wouldn't budge. "Rosette, give me a hand." The girl nodded and gave the crystal a swift kick, breaking it from its base within the ground. "Good job, kiddo. I wonder how much this will go for."

Kyo searched the area for other clusters of crystals. "They might have the right idea."

"Please focus." Marsh stepped out in front. "We are here to investigate what is plaguing the world. We should find the Aurora and join them right away." He led the others down a cracked road, little more than a barely noticeable path after several centuries.

The homes they passed weren't too different from Mistwell, albeit smaller in width and one story tall. Kyo could tell the light-colored wood used to make them was weaker, flimsier than what was currently used, and that was ignoring the awful disrepair of every structure they passed. The wood was frayed and rotted. Some homes had large holes in their walls; others were covered in deep gashes. Going inside to explore may cause them to collapse if they weren't careful.

"This is highly reminiscent of Calmarock after the shade attack. It's getting harder to deny a connection." Krysta diverted to a nearby building, gently running her fingers along claw marks in the wall. "These poor people." Her gaze fell, her body unmoving.

"This way. I see them," Marsh called, pointing down another road.

Sure enough, down the road were three figures in plain robes. Kyo and the others ran toward them, but as they drew closer, the three turned, each readying a glowing spell in their hands.

"Whoa, easy there," Kyo said, his hands raised defensively. "It's just us, your best friends who you'd never get angry at."

The three Aurora stared in wide-eyed disbelief.

Estella pinched the bridge of her nose. "Please tell me I'm hallucinating." She opened her eyes then released a deep sigh. "And the princess too. The king will have our heads if he finds out."

"Not if we never go back to Alderdeem, nah," Garret said with a chuckle.

"No one will have our heads." Cedric stomped forward, eyes narrowed. "What are you doing here?"

"We're here to help," Rosette responded with a big smile. "You needed our help with Sybilla and Blanq, so we figured you would need our help with this too."

Cedric's face softened, but he couldn't stop a long, low groan from escaping his throat. Kyo thanked the Altruists for having a cute kid with them to help ease the blow.

"I'll wager you snuck aboard our airship. Stowing away is a crime. I have a mind to—" Cedric's gaze rose, then he rushed past the five, holding his arms out to keep them behind him. "Stay back!"

Kyo and the others turned to see a shade appearing from a nearby home. In appearance, it was the same as those they'd dealt with before, the smokey void aura with the glowing golden eyes. Had this shade been down here all this time? Did they not age?

"If there is one shade remaining down here, then there must be others," Marsh said, slowly turning in a circle. "I see several already."

Cedric readied a spell in his hand, engulfed in the black-and-purple glow of his gravity spells. But he paused, keeping his eyes on the nearby shade, which shuffled in front of them as if they weren't there. Slowly, Cedric crept forward until he was within an arm's reach. He cautiously reached out and pushed against the shade's arm. It paused, looked directly at him, then continued on its way.

"It's docile?" Krysta asked, following it with her eyes.

"Well now, isn't that an interesting development, ya?" Garret approached the shade, grabbing its hips so it'd face him then cupping its face, examining it closely. The shade made no move against him, acting more like Blanq's mindless undead than the vicious creatures they'd run into previously. "There is still so much we don't know about these shades. Clearly being trapped down here for over two hundred years has affected them in some interesting ways, ya."

"It also tells us they do not need sunlight to survive. We cannot rule out water entirely until we have further explored the area, but I find it unlikely they would have found enough food to last them for so long." Marsh broke from the group, approaching another wandering shade but stopping halfway, examining it from a distance.

Estella stepped past him to the shade. She forced its mouth open and peered inside. "Even after all this time, the corruption appears to be as strong as ever. I would have to put a lot of power behind my magic to kill it or to reveal who lies beneath."

"So, would what lies beneath be a skeleton at this point?" Kyo asked.

The comment made Estella pull away and shudder. "There is one way to find out, but that's not something I want to test currently. They may be docile now, but committing a violent act against them could change that. Still…" She stared as the shade wandered away, bumping into the exterior of a home, changing direction, then continuing. "It's possible the corruption turns its victim into a self-sustaining organism. That would be incredible."

Cedric cleared his throat loudly. "Back to the immediate issue at hand. Her Highness and her party. You have no reason to be here. Nor will we take responsibility should anything happen. We will not spend our time babysitting."

"Do you really think we need babysitting? We might not be as powerful as you, but you know we're fully capable of handling ourselves." Kyo crossed his arms over his chest. "Oh, and gentle reminder. If it weren't for us, you and all of Oasis would have become shades months ago. So, consider letting us tag along as your official thank you."

"That aside," Roland said, pushing Kyo away to stand in his place, ignoring his protest, "it'd be a good idea to have two groups during an investigation, especially one as uncertain as this. We have no idea what we're going to find. If anything were to happen to you, no one would know if you discovered anything. What would that lead to? Another group coming to find you only to suffer the same fate?" He held up a finger, the other hand reaching into his inner pocket, pulling out his flask and taking a swig. "The main investigation can be left up to you three, but consider us backup if you need it."

"You know what? Let them," Estella said, stomping back to the group. "And once we get back, they can take full blame for what they've done. In the meantime, you listen to what we say and obey without question." She turned to Cedric. "We're not about to leave and delay the investigation by a full day or two, are we?"

After a deep breath, Cedric stormed off, everyone else following but keeping their distance.

"Sounds like we've come to a consensus, ya. Maybe I'll get to see another Altruist," Garret said, ruffling Rosette's hair as he strolled past her. "When the Aurora were formed, it was agreed we wouldn't be given nor accept any actual authority to command anyone outside of our group, so as to lower the risk of abusing power. But that means we can't even order a bunch of kids to go home, nah." Laughing, he looked among the five mages. "Ridiculous when you think about it."

"It's time to focus. Keep your eyes open for anything unusual." Estella grabbed Garret's arm and pulled him toward Cedric.

"Because there's nothing unusual yet, right? Why don't we spend the night? Try the local cuisine, do a little shopping in this perfectly normal town," Kyo said.

Krysta clicked her tongue and rolled her eyes. "You know what she means. There has to at least be a hint of what's causing the corruption down here."

Kyo wished he could search from above, but he didn't dare stand on the roofs of these crumbling buildings. As for the barriers, he wanted to conserve as much magic as possible in case the shades decided to turn hostile. Not knowing what they sought, he moved away from the group, peering into old homes and businesses, watching for unusual sights, listening for odd sounds. Roland did the same on the other side of the road. Krysta and Rosette kept their eyes on the ground beneath them while Marsh searched above.

Eventually they found themselves in the town's main square. A stone statue of a woman lay on its side next to the circular fountain it once stood upon. Wagons and stands populated the perimeter, some still intact with various merchandise such as clothes covered in layers of dust and dirt, accessories well out of fashion, and jewelry with gems worth who knew how much. Others were toppled on their sides with the goods sprawled across the road.

Kyo sidestepped large holes and cracks that split the road in various places. The buildings around them were in worse shape than any they had seen so far, with one having its entire side wall missing. He could imagine the scene: people turning into shades, others running, screaming. A re-creation of what he saw in Aquarin Port multiplied many times over. Shaking his head, he pushed the thoughts from his mind and focused on their goal. "Maybe a trader brought something with them that caused the corruption to spread."

"If you're going to search the wagons, be careful what you touch," Roland said,

The group split but remained within the main square. More shades walked among them but paid them no mind, though Kyo still kept a wary eye on them. He crouched behind a wagon, examining the goods it held before moving on to another, sure to open the small cabinets in the back, he assumed where the vendors kept their money or other valuables.

"What's going on?" Krysta cried out.

Kyo rose to find her engulfed in an all too familiar white light. The same surrounded Cedric, Estella, and seconds later, all of them.

"I don't like—" Krysta was interrupted when she vanished into thin air.

Rosette ran for Roland but disappeared before she could reach him. Kyo looked to where the Aurora were a moment ago, but they were nowhere to be seen. His heart pounded in his ears, muscles flexing, unable to do anything but wait. The wait was brief as he felt his body shudder and stretch. Then…darkness.

Chapter 12

The cries of Kyo's comrades echoed in his ears before they were drowned out by deafening silence. Nothing to hear except his own heart pounding in his ears, and he couldn't see his own hand in front of his face. He stood completely still as he attempted to register what had happened. Even his breathing came out in deep, silent gasps. While his mind hadn't yet registered what had occurred, his body knew it had gone through something intense. From head to toe, his muscles trembled. He listened for words, the shuffling of feet, anything to signify the others were nearby, but heard nothing.

"Okay," Kyo whispered to himself through a deep exhale. "First things first." He bent his neck left and right, rolled his shoulders, waved his elbows like cockatrice wings, then wiggled his fingers. Nothing missing up top. He continued to test various parts of his body until reaching his toes, curling them in his boots. No pain and nothing felt out of place.

With a body check out of the way, he slid his hand into his pouch to grab his light orb. A touch of magic had it illuminating the area around him. His breathing halted as he stared at a shade who did the same with its golden eyes, so close it could easily reach out and touch him. Yet it did nothing. Not even a hint of curiosity or any sign it had a working mind. Looking ahead without truly seeing.

With a shaky hand, Kyo grazed the shadowy aura. Unlike Ruby's, it didn't lash out or react in any way. He sighed with relief and stepped around it without taking his eyes off the creature. While it gave him a scare, the presence of a docile shade suggested one thing: He may not be in Crossroad's central square anymore, but he must still be somewhere in the area.

He shuffled like the shambling shades in town as his mind reeled with what had happened. To be transported to a new place without warning, how could such a thing take place? Were they close to The Flow? It was one possibility. Natural magic could have interesting and sometimes unexpected effects on the environment, but he'd never heard of something like this before. His eyes narrowed, remembering the white light that had engulfed them.

He *had* seen such a thing occur. As much as he didn't want to admit it, he couldn't deny the eerie similarity between that event and the way Sybilla and Blanq teleported.

Kyo groaned and rubbed his eyes. "Forget it. I can think about that crap later."

For the first time, he took in his surroundings. Smooth rocky walls stood tall, leaving enough space for a caravan to roll through. The flat nature of the walls and consistent width suggested they were dug by humans. Likely by magic, since there were none of the typical wooden structures in place to support the walls or ceiling to prevent a cave-in. The journal said something about finding an alternate water source. But if the source of the corruption really was related to Crossroads, what did they find instead?

With no clue where he was, he had no choice but to pick a direction and hope for the best. He strolled through the cavern, keeping his eyes open for more shades and ears open for his friends. If they had all teleported like him, they should at least be physically unharmed. He hoped no one had ended up in an area with no way out. Of all of them, he worried most for Rosette. While she could handle herself, she was still a kid and might freak out if she ended up alone. An image of her crying, shouting desperately, came to mind. She might try to punch her way through a wall only for it to collapse on her. The pace of his steps increased as he strained his ears for any sound related to what his imagination conjured up.

With intent, he slowed, taking a deep breath. She was strong, and with Cedric's perception spells, she wouldn't be alone for long. She'd be okay. Kyo had to focus on himself first if he wanted to help anyone else.

The path occasionally weaved and turned, bringing him to find another shade that ignored him. A diverging path to his right stretched about half the width of the tunnel he'd walked so far. Though, after a minute of investigating, it led to a dead end. Another had a similar width but stretched much farther. Was all of this really necessary just to find more water? It was like they'd dug a labyrinth.

Another shade crossed his path, and Kyo stepped aside to let it pass. "Oh, excuse me, good sir."

Like the others, it shambled by without noticing him.

Kyo came across a wider tunnel to his left. About a minute later, he froze, straining his ears. He swore he heard a voice far in the distance. It was so faint he couldn't tell if his imagination was getting the better of him. Attempting to follow the distant voice led him to pause at another path to his right. He listened closely, then took a few steps into the alternate path. The same sound seemed to come from both and neither louder than the other. What he wouldn't give for Cedric's magic or even a saber to sniff the others out.

After a brief internal debate, he took the side path, hoping to find either one of the others or a way back to the town. If they found it, they could get back to the surface. He could always use his wind to dig a hole straight up, but he didn't want to think about how long that would take and how many rests he'd need to recoup his magic in the process.

He reached the far side of the tunnel greeted by a wide underground lake faintly illuminated by more of the glowing crystals. "Whoa. I guess they found a water source after all."

On the other side of the lake and to his right was an elevated rocky platform and the entrance to another tunnel. "So why keep digging?" Kyo walked along the water's surface using barriers as steppingstones. Due to the dim white light of the crystals, he couldn't see far beneath the surface, but the fact he could at all hinted the water must be relatively clean.

While debating if he should take a sip, water burst upward on his right side. A massive fish with jagged gray scales and rows of sharp pointy teeth lunged toward him, threatening to consume him entirely. Kyo thrust his hands toward it, emitting a blast of air that stopped the fish's advance and launched himself backward, skidding across the water before sinking. Barely able to see and chilled to the bone, he frantically swam to the surface, gasping for air. He searched his surroundings while treading water but found no sign of the feral. The water shifted around his feet as the creature emerged from under him, its teeth closing around him.

"Oh no you don't." He stopped it with a barrier from each of his hands. "If anyone here is going to be dinner, it's you." Kyo grunted, straining to maintain the barriers and keep the teeth from impaling him. Wind burst from his feet, launching him into the air high enough to touch the white crystal stalactites. Another barrier appeared under his feet as a platform, giving him a chance to rest while catching his breath. "Ha. Stupid fish. Can't get me up here, can you?"

His clothes clung to his body, dripping and sagging. "This is great." He brushed hair from his face and stood upright, walking in the air toward the cave entrance he'd attempted to reach before. Streams of multicolored energy caught his eye from beneath the water, congregating to one spot. "Oh shit."

As the natural magic collected, the water below swirled into a whirlpool then burst into the air as a waterspout, engulfing him.

The water twister tossed his body like a toy. He had no idea which direction was up. He couldn't breathe and could barely see. Through squinted eyes, he saw glimpses of the feral riding the swirling water before it slammed into him. Kyo's eyes bulged, pain radiating from his chest as he clenched his lips to keep whatever air he could in his lungs. He tumbled, unable to gain a sense of direction before the fish rammed him again, this time knocking the air out of him. If he didn't stop this and get air quickly, he'd drown and become this thing's dinner.

He would not let his life be ended by a damned fish. The feral charged again, swimming upward as if the water wasn't spinning at a rapid pace. Kyo extended his hands and blasted air from them. At first, it made him rotate faster, but altering his angle allowed him to escape the waterspout, taking a deep gasp of air before his back hit the rocky wall hard.

Panting desperately to fill his lungs, the world spinning around him, he fell toward the lake. He managed to focus enough to create a barrier beneath him, catching him before he hit the water. Coughing, lying with his body still, he wanted to close his eyes and make the spinning stop but doing so meant becoming easy prey.

The waterspout slowed then vanished. Silence followed. His vision focused enough to identify the tunnel he wanted to reach, but that wouldn't be enough. No, this stupid fish had to pay for what it did, preferably before it gathered more natural magic. So long as it could do that, it wouldn't magically exhaust itself.

Then again, maybe letting it gather more was what he needed. He couldn't see beneath the surface with the water so turbulent in the aftermath of the feral's last spell.

"Come on, try it again." As if responding to his dare, more streams of multicolored energy converged beneath the water's surface. "Got you."

Kyo opened his palm, forming a wind drill in his right hand and summoning a sword in his left. The barrier vanished, wind from his feet launching him into the lake. Once he broke through the water, he pushed his spell against the fish's back, the rotation of his spell causing another whirlpool. However, the wind at his feet kept him and the feral from being caught in it like before. The hard, jagged scales cracked and broke off like shattered glass, exposing the softer flesh beneath. Not wanting the spell to launch the fish away, he put a stop to it and stabbed his sword into the creature's vulnerable flesh.

It shook and flailed, but Kyo held on to the hilt with both hands, using them to transfer some of his magic into the blade. Once enough had been gathered, wind burst forward like an extension of the steel, and he pushed downward, slicing the feral in two. He watched for a few seconds as the two halves floated away from one another. Satisfied with his victory, he swam to the surface.

"Ha…that's what…you get," Kyo said through heavy pants. He elevated himself out of the water with more barrier steppingstones and reached solid ground. At least if the others came this way they wouldn't have to deal with that thing.

Lying on the cold bumpy ground and soaked to the bone, he closed his eyes and let his body rest. Hayner would be receiving a thank you when he got back to Alderdeem. If not for his magic control lessons, Kyo would have expended a lot more magic in that fight.

How did that thing come to be here in the first place? There must have been a tunnel under the water that led outside to the ocean or maybe a river. It'd be worth investigating if they needed a last resort to escape the tunnels.

Kyo shimmied his hoodie off then sat up and removed his shirt, shivering when exposed to the open air. He wrang as much water out of both as possible. Next, he removed his boots. He half expected a tiny fish to emerge along with the pools of water he dumped out. If only Krysta were with him, she could make a fire to warm him up, though she could feel free to leave after that.

These tunnels had more dangers than expected, and the shades could turn hostile at any time. So, he decided not to waste magic on something trivial like drying his clothes. He put the damp shirt and boots back on, tied the hoodie around his waist, and stood to continue his exploration.

For several minutes, he walked in silence, unable to hear the voice from earlier. Maybe he'd gone the wrong way after all. He clicked his tongue, annoyed that he had a chance to find someone and missed it.

Kyo swore he saw a colored dot float past his vision and squinted. Maybe the time without air had affected him more than he thought. But then he saw another. He pulled his magic from his orb to dim the light and could still see it—a tiny purple dot glowing like a light bug. "And what are you exactly?"

Farther down the tunnel, the glowing dots became more prevalent, floating in a beautiful display. He still had to watch his steps as they weren't bright enough to light up the floor and walls. But if he were to turn his light off completely, it'd be like walking among the stars, and he was tempted to do so. The tunnel curved to the right, and Kyo had to catch himself on the wall to keep from falling into a gargantuan, circular pit with no bottom to be seen.

Chapter 13

An underground town and docile shades were surprising enough, but with the discovery of this massive pit, this place had no end to its mysteries. Kyo crouched at the edge and peered down, though didn't expect to see anything beyond the violet lights dancing around. Two homes from above could fit side by side and be dropped into the hole with room to spare. Though the light he held to guide his way didn't reach the far side, from what he could see the walls were smooth and curled, as if they'd been melted.

He took a few steps back, scanning the ground until he found a rock, tossed it into the pit, then leaned down to listen. After about a minute, he resigned to the fact he wouldn't hear an impact. It felt like déjà vu from testing the hole on the surface before jumping in. "Why are you so deep?"

His gaze drifted upward, finding the hole stretching toward the surface, but he saw no sign of it while outside. It stood to reason something so large would have been covered up for safety's sake. Tightening his lips, he sat and crossed his arms. A hole above, below, and a tunnel dug in the middle.

"Okay, so, they were digging these tunnels and came across this pit?" he asked himself. If his life depended on it, he couldn't think of a reason they'd need to create such a massive gap in two directions. He blinked as one of the glowing violet dots passed through his vision. "And what are these things?"

More important questions entered his mind. How much of this had been known by the king and others—the town, the shades, all of it? The story of Crossroads was known by many across Feracael, but any details were speculation at best. Yet with the king's help, the Aurora were able to find it with little issue. If two hundred years had passed without a proper investigation, details must have been kept quiet on purpose. And that had come back to bite them in the ass in the form of the corruption. Could it have been prevented if this place hadn't been ignored?

Kyo groaned and stood. He had two things to worry about: find the source of the corruption and get back to the others. Let the Aurora figure out the more complicated details.

If he could find the lake again, he could guide the others back here. Once more, he leaned forward and peered into the pit. He squinted, straining his ears as a faint rumbling came from below. It grew louder, and before he had a chance to react, the cavern shook as an invisible force burst from the pit and sent him flying backward. He skidded across the ground, stopping before hitting the curved wall of the tunnel. Panting, his heart pounded as he shifted to his hands and knees.

He stumbled to his feet and shook out his limbs. Nothing missing, no pain. A strange event to add to the many mysteries of this place. He retrieved his light orb and returned to the pit. It appeared the same as before.

Then a violet mass stretched from the pit and struck him with such swiftness he couldn't determine the size, shape, anything other than its color.

The cavern blurred, refocused, then with a scream, he shot upward to the tunnel's ceiling, through it, dirt and rock surrounding him on all sides. No impact, no air rushing over him from the sudden launch, but he phased through the earth like a spirit. He emerged from the surface, the sky growing closer, darker, and within seconds, he stopped.

"W-what the…what?" Kyo gasped, certain his heart should be pounding, yet he couldn't feel it, as if his sense of touch had completely vanished. His mind swam with myriad questions drowned out by internal screaming and a primal fear not even Sybilla had brought out of him. Darkness surrounded him, but far more concerning was what he found below.

Feracael. His world, the land and oceans, the entire sphere seen from above.

"Go back," he muttered, clenching his eyes shut. "Go back, wake up, I don't care what just be back in that stupid cave." His voice choked, barely escaping his throat.

After a shaky breath, he opened his eyes again. As soon as he did, he zipped through the darkness of space, planets and stars flying by at unthinkable speed. No, he wasn't going anywhere. More like the cosmos sped by him.

"Make it stop. Make it stop!"

This didn't make sense. It wasn't possible. He shut his eyes again, but even that no longer helped. Open, closed, it didn't matter — he still saw all of existence fly by, far more than the constellations and named stars he had learned about.

Again, it stopped. Still, darkness surrounded him, at least he thought so. Lightheaded would be putting his state mildly, as if someone shook him, distorting his vision, thoughts, all his remaining senses blurred.

A form materialized into existence before him. Even within the darkness of the cosmos, it stood out, a deeper, darker void than he ever thought possible. The form shifted like liquid, stretching tall, wide, taking on a vague humanoid shape as if trying to mimic him. Most concerning, it appeared as though the form had been ignited, like dancing flame from a candle. As the form filled his vision, he couldn't help compare it to a shade. A pair of golden eyes opened, what looked like webbing surrounding the iris and stretching to the edges. Then another. More appeared, a column of five, and an extra single eye on each side of the center row. And they all stared at him. Kyo could do nothing but stare back, frozen from fear or some other means, likely a combination of both.

The creature…being—whatever it was—emitted a sound akin to a mix of sloshing of the mouth and clicks and vibrations of the throat. Was this thing trying to talk? Kyo couldn't speak and didn't want to. He wanted to be back with the others, on solid ground, safe. The same sounds repeated, but alongside them he heard a whisper, a deep breathy voice uttering one word in his language.

"Mordibrae."

The word echoed in Kyo's mind, pounding away, digging into him as if to bury itself so it'd never be forgotten. It overtook all other thoughts, growing louder and louder. Then it ceased. At the snap of a finger, he could think, he could move his incorporeal body. He finally found the will and means to speak, but before he could, the universe again shifted around him. Worlds and stars shot past him for a few seconds before he descended to a planet's surface.

Kyo found himself in what he assumed to be the middle of a town or city, but everything appeared hazy and vague, as if someone had painted a picture then smeared their hand over the fresh paint. But he could still make out the shapes of tall buildings, people wandering about, and flora. Even if it were another world, it was familiar enough to bring a minute sense of calm, enough to wonder if this was real or an illusion. Could he truly be shooting through the cosmos, to other worlds? Were there really other beings with cities they knew nothing about? One walked by close enough to touch. When Kyo reached his hand out, it phased through as if he weren't there, and the humanoid kept walking without noticing.

This was too much, and worse, he didn't know if he should tell anyone. No one would believe him. He hardly did, not knowing if he'd gone insane or if he saw the truth. Amidst the haze, a light appeared in the distance. A sense of peace and calm came with it, something he welcomed at that moment. In an instant, it washed over the area like a wave, and its wake left every 'person' illuminated. As if of one mind, they all turned, marched together, stiffly, like wooden puppets.

Another wave approached, this time one of an unmistakable darkness. Unlike the previous wave, this one engulfed half of the beings marching in unison. It enshrouded them in shadow, and they returned to how they were before. Some went their separate ways, while others conversed in small groups as if nothing had happened.

"What is going on? Let me go back home!" Kyo cried.

If he could feel the sensation of breathing, he would've been close to hyperventilating. What if he never returned or lay dead in the cave? He fell to his hands and knees, his gaze glued to a single rock on the ground.

"Send me back," he whispered.

But frantic movement pulled his attention to his surroundings.

The beings of light and darkness faced each other, and a fight broke out. Focused punches, savage slashing, the two sides clashed fiercely. The number of people on both sides grew by the second. His body rose into the air against his will, as if an invisible hand lifted him to give him a better view. The city was one of many pockets of these fights across the planet's surface. What he witnessed couldn't be mistaken for anything but all-out war.

Kyo shot through the air once again, leaving the world behind. This time, every planet he came across had a veil of light or darkness. More and more zipped by, faster than he could perceive until it all became a blur. He screamed as hard and loud as he could then gasped as he once again stood within the cavern, the giant pit lying inactive before him. With eyes wide and heart pounding in his ears, his body quaked.

After a few seconds of taking in his surroundings, he scrambled away from the hole, falling backward. His hands covered his face as he closed his eyes and rolled onto his side, lying still. What was that? What had he stumbled upon? He took mild comfort in the hard ground beneath him, glad he could feel something again. More than anything, he wanted to be out of this place. He didn't care where, so long as he was under the sun, somewhere safe. Alderdeem, Mistwell, anywhere. He had to get out. But his body wouldn't move.

The things he'd witnessed continuously flashed in his mind. He tried to focus on anything else, anything that would calm him enough to think properly. Something relaxing, peaceful, though at the moment he did not want to consider his usual go-to of stargazing.

Kyo focused on thoughts of his time in Alderdeem. One particularly peaceful and happy memory came to mind. He and the others sat around a table, eating delicious food, smiling, laughing. They made jokes and reveled in the moment of peace that came shortly after the events in Oasis. At the time, they were happy to be alive. Rosette bragged about how she punched and kicked Sybilla, Roland congratulating her but also offering his usual words of concern. Marsh expressed disbelief in what he'd been dragged into and never imagined being part of something so violent and significant. Krysta spoke about how they were pivotal in allowing many to see justice served. He'd never forget the relief and pride that had filled him at the time.

Lying still on the hard floor of the tunnel, Kyo had no idea how many minutes passed. Over time, the wild visions were pushed away from the front of his mind as he focused hard on the more peaceful memory. Hard enough he almost drifted off to sleep. He moved his hands from his face and opened his eyes to stare at the ceiling illuminated by his light orb.

"I need to get out of here," he mumbled, forcing himself to stand and gently slapped his face. "And sleep for a week."

The path he'd taken had led to a dead end, so he'd double back, hopefully avoiding hostile fish, and find another way. He clicked his tongue, annoyed he'd gone the wrong way when previously trying to follow the faint voices. With any luck, Cedric would have found at least some of the others, assuming none of them were teleported halfway across the world instead of below Crossroads.

Kyo wandered through the tunnel until he reached the lake. After a moment of observation, he hadn't noticed any activity within the water, so he walked across and reached the intended path without issue. Eventually, he found himself back where he'd made the wrong turn and continued the way he should have gone.

The voices were long gone, but he hoped to hear them again soon. As he wandered, he came across more docile shades, all the same in appearance as the others. At first, he froze, their form too reminiscent of that being, that Mordibrae. After a few deep breaths, he continued. When the darkness took over the people in that other world, was that representing the same shades Feracael was dealing with?

The next one he saw, he took its hand and gazed into its golden eyes. "I'm sorry."

It didn't respond, didn't acknowledge his presence. He let go, and it continued to wander aimlessly. As frightening as they could be, underneath the darkness, there were people whose lives had been stolen from them. It felt wrong to say nothing.

More dark tunnels, none of them housing the glowing crystals that would have made his journey easier. Thank goodness he thought to pack this light orb when he'd left Mistwell. Something caught his eye, something that made him smile wide—a figure in a white robe seated and slumped against the wall.

"Marsh! Finally, I found someone. I guess staying put would have been a good idea for me too. But glad I found you." Kyo stepped toward him, but Marsh waved his arm.

"Go away," Marsh said in an unusually monotone voice.

"What do you mean 'go away'? We need to find the others so we can get out of here. There's some weird shit down here." Kyo grabbed his hand, but Marsh quickly retracted it.

"You must leave. Find the others and go. Do not worry about me." Marsh shifted his body to the right, as if hiding under the cloak.

Kyo narrowed his eyes. "Are you dumb? Come on already."

He roughly yanked on Marsh's shoulder, and time seemed to stop as Kyo stared down into the cleric's face. Well, half his face. The other half, as well as the right side of his body, was enshrouded in a shadowy aura.

Chapter 14

How could this have happened? When Ruby became corrupted, she complained of not feeling well half a day beforehand. Marsh had given no indication anything had bothered him. Was he hiding it from them? Or maybe something else. Estella had told them location didn't seem to have any effect on being corrupted, but if they truly were right on top of the source, that may not be true after all.

Kyo reached out, but Marsh batted it away again, refusing to look at him. A part of him wanted to grab Marsh, shake him, force him to his feet, but memories of how Ruby's corruption reacted to hostile actions made him think better of it.

"I knew the risks," Marsh said barely above a whisper. "I knew tagging along came with the distinct possibility of falling victim to the corruption." He stared at his open hand enshrouded in the shadowy aura, shifting like a flame. "Even so." A tremble accompanied his voice as he turned to look up at Kyo, tears streaming down his face. "I'm afraid."

The sight broke Kyo's heart. Even without looking, he would have known Marsh was frightened.

His speech pattern only changed during moments of extreme emotion. For a second, his face became Ruby's — desperate to be saved. Another victim of the corruption, another friend he'd fail. His chest quivered as he inhaled, eyes starting to water.

No.

He wouldn't fail again. Marsh would make it. Kyo would make damn sure of it. His body tensed, forcing those heavy emotions down. This time would be different. They had a solution waiting for them.

"Hey, don't you worry about a thing." Kyo pressed his back against the wall and slumped next to Marsh, placing his hand on his uncorrupted shoulder and gently shaking it. "We have everything we need to get you all fixed up, right? They've been doing it for months. We'll find the Aurora, get back on the airship, and take you right to Spellnix Hold to get Blanq to cure you, no problem. You'll be back to your normal self by tomorrow."

Marsh stared at the ground. "That depends on us finding the others, as well as a way out of here." He curled his legs and wrapped his arms around them. "We can't leave anyone behind to deal with my condition."

"We'll find them, even if we have to shout our lungs out through these tunnels. And the second part is easy. Worst comes to worst, we head straight up, right? I'm sure the Aurora can dig through the rock and dirt like they did to get down here in the first place." Kyo roughly patted Marsh's back once but refrained from doing so again after the dark aura twitched in response. Instead, he gently rested his hand against him. "You'll be okay. We'll make sure of it."

"Some cleric I turned out to be. Unable to help even myself or listen to reason. The Aurora are more than capable of handling this on their own. I was simply stubborn, desperate to be of some use." Marsh picked up a pebble and mindlessly tossed it against the opposite wall.

"You've been extremely useful though. We wouldn't have made it this far without you. You saved Donavi from Sybilla's poison, healed our injuries plenty of times—"

"It. Is. Not. Enough!" Marsh shouted, his words echoing down the tunnel, the corruption flaring in response. "It's never enough." He ran his fingers through his hair, gripping it tight. "Even before becoming a cleric, I have seen so much pain, suffering, and death."

Kyo froze, stunned by Marsh's shift in emotion. The surprising change made his heart jump. It reminded him of a saying he'd heard: Do not test the fury of a gentle man. Maybe it came down to the effect of something unexpected, but even without the corruption, he'd rather not test that saying.

"Marsh. You can't fix everything by yourself. Don't even try it. Even the Aurora can't save everyone." A lesson Kyo had learned that day on the Oasis beach when he was young and reaffirmed during the battles against Blanq and Sybilla years later.

"Why not?" Marsh asked, turning to stare at Kyo with wide, intense eyes. "Why can't I save everyone? Why can't I figure it out?" His jaw clenched, and he slammed his fists into the wall behind him. "I'm not stupid enough to believe I can travel the world, cure every sickness and ailment before every individual succumbs to them. However, if I can figure out this corruption, maybe find an alternate cure that does not rely on Blanq, maybe learn to drain their magic like Sybilla had, then I can save everyone from that at least." Silence followed, their eyes not moving from one another's. Not even the shambling of a docile shade nearby broke their focus. After a long moment, Marsh rested his forehead against Kyo's shoulder. "I am sorry."

"Hey, you have no reason to be. You're fine, I promise." Kyo wrapped an arm fully around Marsh, receiving no pushback from the corruption.

"Before I became a cleric, I was far from the only orphan in Riftdale. It was a poor town nestled in the southern corner of the continent, south of the Alderdeem region. Although it was built by the sea, using it as a port for merchants and travelers never caught on. All the town could do to generate cryst was fish, and only one type in that region was worth anything. So Riftdale became known as a dirty, poverty-stricken place no one wanted to visit. I was one of many children who had to make their own way."

Kyo focused on Marsh's words but still made it a point to keep an ear open in case any of the others happened to come close to them.

"What happened to your parents?" It never felt right to ask this out of the blue, but he'd always been curious.

Marsh sat up again, wiping his tears with his sleeve. "They passed from illness. Not uncommon. Though in a way I am one of the lucky ones. Imagine being a young child or teenager, knowing your parents left Riftdale, abandoned you to better their own lives elsewhere. I knew a few in that situation"

"I'm sorry. I know that's rough, to put it lightly. Especially if you didn't have anyone else." At least he had Alden to rely on. But Marsh had to make his own way from a young age. Most of his life he'd been nestled in the corner of Kattelink Island. But now that he'd left, met new people, he found his situation wasn't so unusual.

"It is okay." Marsh inhaled deeply. "I remember their faces but not much else. I do not have the memories of them you have of your own parents. But it did lead to a rough life. Nights, sometimes days, going hungry before I worked up the courage to start stealing food, finding a safe place to sleep. Naturally, those of us in the same situation came together, got to know one another. The older ones would teach us the best techniques to steal, the best paths to flee, that sort of thing. Thankfully even during the cold months, temperature was of little concern, given our geographic location."

What else could Kyo do in response but tighten his grip around Marsh. Becoming corrupted broke the poor guy down. For the moment, he'd sit quietly and listen.

"Of course, forming a group," Marsh went on, "even making friends came with an emotional toll. Every so often, someone would fall sick and be gone days later. More than one fell to 'appropriate punishment' if they were caught stealing by the wrong person. These were the risks of trying to survive."

"That is just wrong." Kyo clenched his fist. "What is wrong with people? Something needs to change there." He couldn't imagine physical harm or death being a valid punishment for stealing. Such a thing would never fly in Mistwell. While he'd never been a thief, he couldn't imagine the types of punishments Riftdale had in store for a mischievous kid like himself.

"I agree. And one day I hope to bring that change to Riftdale, somehow. It will take more than a skilled cleric, however. That is merely one piece of the puzzle. The true solution would be an economic boom, bringing the people out of poverty. That is not something I have figured out yet. One thing at a time. But someday. Or so I hoped until..." Marsh glanced at his corrupted half.

Kyo retracted his arm and nudged Marsh. "You'll still reach that goal. We'll get you cured once we find the others."

"Assuming they are down here with us. There is no telling if they were transported elsewhere or not. Speaking of, did you notice the similarity? The light that engulfed us?"

"Between what happened to us and how Sybilla and Blanq do it? Yeah, I noticed. But I'm not going to pretend I understand the connection. That's just one of several mysteries down here."

Marsh raised his brow. "Did you find something?"

Kyo exhaled. "Hoo boy, did I. Though at this point I'm wondering if it was even real or if I imagined the entire thing." After briefly recounting his battle with the fish, he described the pit he found, the violet lights in the area, and what happened afterwards. He found it easy to describe it in detail, every second of it burned into his mind. As he explained his experience, he felt a weight lifting from him, finding relief in telling someone.

"Mordibrae," Marsh mused. "Not a word I am familiar with. I cannot say I can make sense of what you experienced, but it certainly comes off as disturbing. Though one thing I feel certain of — there must be a connection between what you saw and the source of the corruption. The Aurora have to be made aware of this."

"So, you don't think I'm crazy, or it was just some hallucination?" Kyo asked.

"No, I do not. While I do not fully understand, there are a few key factors that stand out and cannot be ignored. Especially such a thing happening here, in an underground town filled with shades."

"Well, I'm glad you believe me, because I hardly believe myself. Can you stand?" Kyo asked, rising and extending his hand to Marsh.

Marsh took the offered hand and stood. He carefully stretched his limbs, bent his back, and tilted his neck. "What choice do I have? The corruption stifles my movements somewhat, but not so much I cannot walk."

Kyo grinned. "Good. If you refused to move for much longer, I would have flung you over my shoulder and carried you. Glad I don't have to do that now. Like I said, we'll find the others, get out of here and head straight to Spellnix Hold." Assuming Blanq would be willing to do so. Sybilla, absolutely not. But Blanq…she was hard to figure out. He hadn't heard of her refusing to cure anyone yet, but that might change when it came to Marsh.

"I hope you are right. I will be relying on you heavily, Kyo. I have been unable to use any spells since becoming corrupted. I may be able to exert enough magic to power that light of yours but no more. So should something happen, I will be powerless to help."

"This time, I'll be the one to protect you. Don't you worry your bedhead about it." Kyo walked alongside Marsh, keeping a slower pace than usual. He suspected Marsh wouldn't be as defenseless as he thought. The corruption had a habit of protecting its host, like when Ruby's lashed out and destroyed three blobs at once. So long as it didn't lash out at Kyo, they'd be okay.

For a while they moved in silence, listening for any hint of the others, bypassing a shade here and there, choosing together which diverting path to take. But eventually, they decided so long as the shades were docile, there was no harm in calling out for the others.

"Hey! Anyone there?" Kyo shouted. His voice echoed off the walls. There were too many tunnels for his liking, and he wished he could go back two hundred years and slap whoever decided to dig them like this with no plan in mind.

"Kyo, how much time would you say passed between when that energy surge knocked you off your feet and when you found me?" Marsh asked.

"I would say probably around thirty minutes or so? Hard to tell exactly down here, but that's what it felt like."

"That seems to be the timeline from when I became corrupted and when you found me. I believe there is a direct cause and effect between the two. Though why you escaped unscathed, I cannot say."

"I'm guessing the same reason why people anywhere become corrupted but others in that area don't. We've already seen that no location around Feracael has a higher rate of corruption than anywhere else, right? It seems so random. I guess that's true even this close to the source of it all."

"I suppose I am simply unlucky. However, it is only now sinking in that you may have truly found the source of the corruption." Marsh turned to stare down in the direction they came from. "We have not traveled far. I think it would be a good idea to mark our path so the Aurora will easily be able to find it again. Should they find their way back down here, that is."

He had a good point. Maybe they could even use this as an excuse to avoid getting a lecture about the consequences of his actions, which he was sure would come once they reunited with the Aurora. Wasting time backtracking didn't sit well with him while Marsh had to get to Blanq as quickly as possible, but in this case, it had to be done.

"Okay. Let's go." Kyo summoned a sword and used the dull end to mark arrows along the tunnel walls, making sure they were big enough to be easily found. He did so all the way back to the lake but felt no need to go farther after drawing an arrow on the ground, pointing to the platform on the other side. "From there, it's a straight shot to the pit I found."

"That should be good enough. Now, let us keep our eyes and ears open for the others. If they are anywhere nearby, I am certain their voices will echo throughout the tunnels."

They headed back to the wide thoroughfare and once more decided together which way to go. He would not let Marsh fall to the same fate as Ruby. No matter what it took, he would get his friend out of here and make sure Blanq cured him.

Chapter 15

Every minute they remained down there was a minute they were not on their way to Spellnix Hold. Kyo stomped through the tunnels, frequently pulling ahead of Marsh then forcing himself to slow his pace so he could catch up. His condition brought an enormous sense of urgency, and the constant dead ends they ran into didn't help. While Marsh remained mostly silent, Kyo shouted for their friends and restricted a frustrated grunt whenever he received no response.

"There are way too many tunnels down here. I'm about to lose it." Kyo slammed the side of his fist against the rocky wall. Problems he couldn't resolve by attacking them frustrated him more than anything. Swinging a sword or blasting something with wind were preferable over patience and critical thinking.

"The more I traverse these tunnels, the more I suspect they weren't merely seeking new sources of water as the journal suggested," Marsh said.

Kyo glanced behind him, shining a light in his direction. His movements were stiff and forced, as if he were actively fighting against an invisible pull on his limbs. "You're probably right. Even back then they should have had a better way of finding water than blindly digging into the ground, right?" He inhaled, then cupped his hand around his lips. "Hey!" he shouted, extending the word for several seconds.

His voice echoed off the walls before fading into silence. No response came.

"These tunnels are pissing me off. This way, that way, looping around, oh and just for fun, let's stop most of them before they connect to anything." He gritted his teeth, but once his eyes rested on Marsh, he took a breath to calm himself. If he freaked out, Marsh might as well. He didn't want to worry the poor guy even more. "I almost expect to find a minotaur in this damn place."

"Let us be grateful those do not exist. This would be an appropriate place for one to be found." Marsh gave the slightest of smirks before it faded as quickly as it appeared. "I do wonder if they experienced hints of the corruption before tragedy struck and were seeking the source like we are now."

Marsh's eyes remained fixed on the ground. Kyo couldn't imagine what must be going through his head.

"I guess that would make sense." Another minute passed before he called out again. "Anyone there?" Kyo shouted. They'd bypassed enough shades not to expect their horrifying screeches as a response. In fact, he didn't expect a response at all, so when a distant hello echoed back, his eyes widened. "Did you hear that?"

Marsh quickly nodded, a smile forming on his lips.

"Where are you?" Kyo shouted.

After several seconds, the voice responded, "Stay put."

A female voice, not young and not annoying. It must be Estella. Having an Aurora by their side would relieve a lot of their built up stress. Kyo and the voice played a game of vocal tag, each time hearing it draw closer.

"I see a blue light, is that you?" the voice called.

Kyo raised the light orb above his head and waved it back and forth. "Yeah, Marsh is with me too."

Contrary to his own, a red glow drew closer and closer, and footsteps rushed their way, far too many to belong to one or two people. The faces of his friends came into view, and Kyo released a deep sigh in relief, smiling wide.

"Kyo," Rosette cried, rushing to wrap her arms around him.

He chuckled and patted her head. "Hey. So, you all found each other, huh?"

He glanced between them. The three Aurora were accounted for, but someone appeared to be missing.

"Everyone but Roland," Rosette said in a sad tone.

Krysta crouched down beside her. "Don't worry. We'll find him. He can take care of himself. And once he's back, we'll get out of here."

"About that. The sooner the better. We have a…situation." Kyo took several steps to stand beside Marsh, illuminating him to show the others the shadowy aura encompassing half his body.

"Oh no!" Krysta rushed toward him but stopped short of reaching out to touch him. "I-It's okay, right? We should have at *least* a day." She turned to the Aurora. "We'll get him to Spellnix Hold and have Blanq cure him, won't we?"

"Quite the unfortunate turn of events, ya," Garret said, arms folded over his chest.

Cedric approached Marsh, reaching out to touch his corrupted arm. The shadowy aura twitched and stretched, but Cedric batted it away. "But not an unexpected one. This is exactly why you shouldn't have come, why you should listen to those more experienced." He took a deep breath to calm his rising voice. "But Her Highness is correct. Right now, you don't need a lecture. You need to be cured. As soon as we find Roland, we'll leave."

"Have you found a way out?" Kyo asked.

"Not yet, but if doing so becomes too troublesome, we'll force our way up," Estella said.

"That's good to hear. I'm sure you can do so a lot easier than me. Just don't cause a cave-in or something," Kyo said, glancing at the ceiling.

"You can give us more credit than that. Of course we wouldn't be so careless." Estella approached Marsh, gently pushing Cedric to the side and taking the cleric's hand in hers. "Don't worry. We'll make getting you to Spellnix Hold our priority. We've seen more than enough to know this is where we want to focus our investigation. An extra day or two won't hurt."

Marsh smiled, a tear running down his cheek. "Thank you. And I am sorry. I should have listened. Should not have been so hasty."

"He'll be okay, right?" Rosette asked, her bottom lip trembling.

"Blanq has cooperated in curing anyone we've brought to her so far. He should be fine by the end of the day," Cedric said, motioning with his hand for the others to follow. "Let's get a move on."

As they followed Cedric, Rosette and Krysta periodically called out for Roland. Kyo kept his eyes and ears open but his mouth shut, not wanting his voice to drown out a possible response. He tried to keep his body from shaking in anticipation of nearly being rid of this place.

"Kyo, perhaps now would be a good time to tell them what you found," Marsh said.

"Oh, right." Kyo tugged on the arms of the Aurora to get their attention before recounting what he found. The massive hole, the lights, and the vision.

"That is certainly something. Are you sure you didn't just hit your head?" Estella asked.

Kyo rolled his eyes. "Yes, I'm sure. I even left marks along the walls to find my way back there. I don't know what it was, but whatever's down there needs to be looked at a lot more closely."

"I'd have to agree, ya. Finding that hole should be the focal point of our investigation once we come back." Garret sighed and shook his head. "Once again, these yolks are showing us up. Are we washed up?" He turned and grabbed Estella by the shoulders. "Do we even have a purpose anymore?" he asked in exaggerated fashion, eyes wide and lips turned down.

Estella grunted, pushing Garret away. "Stop being overdramatic."

"Roland," Rosette called again.

This time, a faint voice called back.

She gasped and hopped in place. "Roland, we're here!"

The group continued forward through the tunnel, Roland's voice growing louder. The second he came into view, he and Rosette dashed toward one another. Roland picked her up in his arms, spun her around. and held her close.

"You're okay! Thank goodness." Roland placed kiss after kiss on her cheeks, bringing giggles from her as she tried to push him away.

"Glad to have you back. Now everyone is accounted for," Krysta said.

Roland set Rosette down and looked among the group. "Good. So, are we continuing to look around or…" His eyes fell upon Marsh, frowning. "Oh man. Hey, you're going to be okay, kid." He turned to the Aurora. "Right?"

"We're leaving immediately to bring him to Spellnix Hold. Best not to waste time," Estella said.

Roland motioned behind him. "Good. I don't know if it leads out of here, since I don't have a clue where we are. But I did find a tunnel that led up, so that's a start."

Cedric nodded. "Up is good. Lead the way."

Kyo made it a point to stay next to Marsh. "See? We'll be out of here in no time. And we have an airship to take us right to where we need to go." Although he spoke the truth, he couldn't get rid of the sinking feeling in his stomach.

Marsh nodded. "Yes. I am sure I will be fine. Though there is no helping the anxiety that comes with being corrupted and knowing what could happen." He stared down at his corrupted right half. "An infection of the magic. But why only our magic? As far as I have heard, there have been no reports of ferals being corrupted, correct?"

"No, we've heard nothing of the sort, nah. That's another part of the mystery. Among the three types of magic—human, feral, and natural—only human magic seems to be susceptible to the corruption. On the one hand, that's good for us, yah. Well, not ideal, but imagine trying to deal with corrupted ferals or how it might affect land, rivers, and the sort." Garret rubbed the back of his neck. "On the other hand, it's a real head scratcher, yah."

Cedric kept his eyes forward. "Slightly less so if you take Kyo's vision at face value. Something I do not want to do, but it would be foolish to dismiss anything outright. Perhaps we will experience something similar when we return and find that hole."

The path slanted upwards and curved. Given the distance between Crossroads and the surface, it amounted to little more than a step in comparison, but Kyo would take any progress in getting them back under open sky. "Cedric, any chance you can dig a hole straight up so we can hurry this along?"

"I'd prefer leaving that as a last resort. Digging up is not the same as digging down. There is no telling what we might accidentally disturb by being careless. Imagine heading upward through a hole I've dug, only to cause a cave-in on those below me. We still do not know how deep we are. It's not something I want to rush into." He turned toward Kyo and Marsh. "Don't worry. We won't forget our time is limited. If our search takes too long, we'll take the risk."

The path leveled off, continuing straight with another breaking off toward the right. Roland paused then, without consulting the group, headed toward the alternate path. After a few steps, they found themselves in a massive room with no glowing crystals to illuminate it.

"Should we go back? We can't see anything in here," Rosette said.

Krysta turned both palms face up, each holding a flame. "I'll give us some light."

Cedric gasped. "Your Highness, don't!"

It was too late. Nearly a dozen flames flew into the air, emitting enough light to see the entirety of the massive room. The ceiling stretched about half as high as the area that housed Crossroads, the walls meeting on the far end forming a curved ceiling, like a jagged dome.

Kyo turned to the gargantuan form nestled against the wall next to the entrance they walked through. He and the others froze, breath and all. The deep void, the flickering aura, there was no mistaking it. A shade, comparable in size to Blanq's bone giants she'd formed during the battle in Oasis. How could one be so large? It certainly wasn't once a giant person.

"We should go back," Roland said barely above a whisper.

The shade's golden eyes opened, shifted, then settled upon them. It rose, pushing against the wall behind it, stepping forward and blocking the exit. Its exhale was audible, echoing within the cavern. Slowly, its head reared back, its jaw opened, and it released a terrifying, high-pitched screech.

Chapter 16

The piercing screech shook the walls, rock and dirt breaking away and falling to the ground. Kyo hunched over and covered his ears in hopes of suppressing the vibrations permeating his entire body. His gaze darted to the exit leading back toward the tunnel, but his legs refused to move, and apparently neither would the shade's foot that blocked the way. Estella and Roland were in his field of view reacting in much the same way. Even the Aurora couldn't handle such a shriek.

In the blink of an eye, silence fell over them. Kyo panted and trembled as he stared up at the hulking shade, the darkness of the room partially cloaking its massive claw swiping toward him. A few wobbly steps weren't enough to get him out of its path.

The shade's claw stopped mid-swing, the faint purple glow of a spell emitting behind it.

"Move!" Cedric cried out, maintaining a gravity spell to keep its limb from moving any farther.

Kyo found strength in his legs again and dashed toward Estella and Roland, keeping the massive claw in sight as it fought against Cedric's spell. His heart jumped when he heard the man grunt. Cedric Felmont, the powerhouse of the Aurora, was struggling to hold this thing back.

"If you have anything that emits light, bring it out, ya!" Garret shouted.

Kyo pulled out the light orb from his pouch, infused it with a hint of magical energy, and set it on the ground near the wall. While far from bright enough to light up the entire room, any little bit would help. Those who had one brought out a similar light to help brighten the massive space. Estella brought out her own and rolled it across the ground between the shade's feet. Krysta created several more fireballs and launched them into the air, spreading them out and leaving them hovering.

A few dark corners remained but nothing that would hamper their ability to fight. Despite its gargantuan size, it still maintained the same humanoid shape every other shade possessed. Could there really be a human body in there somewhere? They didn't need more mysteries around the corruption than they already had.

Cedric released his spell, taking deep breaths as the shade turned its attention to him. It raised its foot then brought it down to crush Cedric, but golden ropes wrapped around his torso and yanked him out of the way.

"Are you all right?" Estella asked.

"I'll manage. Whatever caused this thing to increase in size seems to have greatly boosted its resistance to magic compared to an average shade." Cedric stood upright and rotated his shoulders. "Make for the exit!"

Marsh stood closest to the way out. As soon as he made a run for it, the shade turned to him and swept its foot across the ground. He managed to stop in time to avoid being hit, but it crashed into the wall, sending chunks falling to block their way out.

Garret built electricity around both hands then fired lightning bolts at the shade's face. It cried out and shook its head before setting its sights on the elder Aurora.

Kyo glanced at Roland. "An attack like that took out two shades before, in…" A pang of sadness struck him as Ruby's face flashed in his mind, but he shook it off. "How are we supposed to deal with this?"

Roland extended his right hand outward and summoned his polearm. "The only way we can, kid. We have eight mages here. There's no reason we can't take this thing out."

Kyo considered summoning his swords, but remembering how little effect they had on normal shades, what was the point? "Why is this one so hostile when the others aren't?"

"Save your questions for later. Focus." Raw magical energy engulfed the spear-end of Roland's polearm as he crouched and launched himself toward the shade's shin.

The shade raised both hands, balled them into fists, and brought them down. Krysta and Rosette leaped out of the way, the impact leaving an imprint and deep cracks behind. Rosette ran forward and threw a punch at the shade's wrist then a spin kick. The resonating sound of the impact was enough proof of how much power she had behind her attacks, though they only seemed to annoy the shade.

Estella fired glowing purple arrows from a magically created bow, pelting the shade on the side of the head. It swiped at them as if they were insects. Krysta extended her hands, coating the ground beneath the creature's feet in a sheet of ice. The next time it budged, its feet slipped out from under it, landing with a heavy thud that shook the room, knocking several of them off their feet.

Magical arrows, lightning bolts, fireballs. Everyone used their spells to attack the giant shade in one form or another, yet they did little to harm it. Marsh remained to the side, his scowl showing his frustration in being unable to help as he rose to his feet again.

While Kyo doubted his attacks could add much to the assault, he wouldn't stand by and do nothing. He formed a wind drill in his right hand and jumped into the air, creating a barrier to land upon as a platform. It rotated with him crouched on it, and he launched himself down, thrusting his spell against the creature's neck. The muscles in his arm tensed as he grunted, pushing with all his strength, increasing the amount of magic behind the spell. The dark aura fought against him. A shadow overtook him, and he glanced up as the shade's massive claw smacked him away, sending him flying into the far wall.

The impact sent a harsh shock throughout his body, his mouth opening in a silent cry. He fell hard, coughing, unable to move. Each breath sent a sharp pain through his back and chest. Carefully, he stretched his back muscles and took lighter breaths, shifting to a sitting position.

"Kyo! Can you stand?" Marsh asked, crouching beside him.

"Maybe in a minute." Kyo rotated his shoulders, taking in the battle before him. No matter what they did, it didn't seem to be enough. The shade's cries and body language hinted at the spells causing some miniscule level of harm, but at this rate, they'd all run out of magic before they defeated it. With Marsh's help, he stood and took a deep breath. "What now?"

"I do not know. I would suggest making a run for it, but now that this monster is active, I fear what would happen if it chased us to the surface."

The shade scraped a claw across the ground toward Krysta and Garret, but Estella cast a wide barrier between them. Unlike her usual spells, the barrier caused the creature's hand to bounce backward, reflecting the attack, though the barrier shattered under the strength of the impact.

"Yeah, we need to deal with this thing now. But how?" Air and swords were what Kyo had to work with. Raw power wouldn't help in this situation. He could never hope to put out as much magic as a single Aurora, let alone three.

The shade released another screech, causing everyone to stop in place and cover their ears.

"This damn thing," Kyo said through his clenched jaw. He glared at the monster, building magic within his hands. "Let's see how you like it." Whirling air shot from each hand, but instead of attacking the creature, he flung the spells toward its head. He focused on keeping them in place next to its ears, spinning at high speeds.

The screeching ceased, the shade stumbling as it attempted to swat away the spell to no avail. It shook its head and stomped its feet in aggravation. The air whistled throughout the room as Kyo extended his hands and maintained the relatively simple and magic-effective spell.

"That was a genius move, ya. Keep it up for the time being," Garret said as he and the others approached Kyo and Marsh.

The shade stumbled back against the wall, its fist slamming against it, causing more debris to fall.

Estella erected a barrier to shield them from the raining rocks. "Let's not take too much time in plotting our next move. We can't leave until this thing is dealt with."

"Okay, but how? We're not outputting enough power to do serious damage," Krysta said, staring at the shade. "I really hope there aren't more like this."

"When the effects of Cedric's spells are limited, you know we have a problem, ya." Garret's eyes met Cedric's. "Though we do have one option left."

Cedric stared back for a few seconds then sighed. "Indeed so. Since we haven't received any hostility from shades up until this point, it should be okay." He made sure everyone was paying attention. "It's risky, but our best bet is to vent our magic."

"Risky is an understatement," Marsh said. "If it fails, you will be left completely defenseless."

Rosette raised her hand. "Um, I don't actually know how to do that."

Roland shrugged when Cedric looked at him with a raised brow. "I planned on teaching her when she was a bit older

The shade stomped its feet and slammed its body against the wall. Everyone huddled under Estella's barrier to keep themselves shielded while she kept her eyes firmly on the shade.

"That may be for the best. Marsh obviously cannot do anything with his magic currently. Kyo, we want you to keep doing what you're doing, so you won't be venting. Neither will Rosette, which is fine. If it fails, we'll be relying on her strength to break through the rubble blocking the exit. As for everyone else, are you ready?" Cedric asked.

Roland released a heavy breath. "I'm not going to like how it feels afterward. But fine, let's get it done." He took his flask from his inner pocket and took a swig from it.

"Okay, get to it. While I *can* do this all day, I'd rather not." Though effective, Kyo would like to be rid of the giant shade as soon as possible and not risk something else getting in the way of their escape.

Estella ceased casting her barrier and turned to face the shade alongside her partners, Roland, and Krysta. They extended their hands outward, facing the agitated shade.

"Krysta, crouch a bit more and keep your feet firmly planted," Roland said. Krysta glanced down at her feet and adjusted her stance accordingly.

Cedric was the first to release his magic, consistent waves of azure and violet energy striking the shade, causing it to screech loudly. Garret followed, then Estella. The cry the shade released couldn't be mistaken for anything else but pain. Krysta and Roland joined a few seconds later. The shade shook its head, its hands attempting to bat away the magic assaulting it.

Despite the impressive display of power before him, Kyo did his best to focus on the shade's head, keeping his spells as close to the creature's ears as possible during its wild thrashing. Though never one for prayer, he hoped with all he had this would be enough. Once a mage began venting their magic, it couldn't be stopped until they had practically none left to give.

He'd only seen someone vent once in his life, and the memories came flooding back. His parents had taught him how when he was nine years old, his mother the one to demonstrate. The display of magic and its sparkling colors had been hypnotizing, but he'd rushed to her when she collapsed. His friends were certain to do the same once they finished. They'd have nothing left to fight with, and their bodies would be vulnerable without magical protection.

This had to work.

"Come on, you can do it," Rosette whispered while sticking close to Kyo's side.

Through the vicious magical onslaught, the shade managed to take a heavy step toward them, attempting to use its hands to block the coordinated attack. Whenever it did, they'd adjust their aim, trying to keep it focused on a single point on its chest. It took another step forward.

Kyo increased the intensity of his spell, the air swirling faster, the whistling fighting for dominance over the shade's cries.

Krysta's flow of magic stopped, and she fell to her knees, panting, wobbling from side to side. A few seconds later, Roland followed, keeping himself propped up on trembling arms. Two mages down, and the shade still stood. While its head shook harshly to get away from the whistling air, it still took occasional steps toward them.

The Aurora stood firm, their robes flapping from the force of their magic. Any other creature in this world, even a dragon from Morterra, would have fallen long before now. If even one giant shade like this made it to the surface and the Aurora weren't around to stop it, Kyo had no doubt it'd be a far greater threat than any Relinquished had ever been.

Estella fell to one knee, her waves of magic shrinking. Soon after, Garret and Cedric could no longer stand, and together, their waves of magic vanished. Estella fell on her side, catching her breath, and all anyone else could do was stare up at the monster towering over them.

The shade took another step forward then fell to its side, its body dragging along the cavern wall until it crashed into the ground. The shadowy aura rose from its body like smoke from a flame, vanishing soon after.

Little by little, it disappeared until a normal human body remained. A teenage boy.

Everyone released a collective sigh, allowing themselves to slump and fall in various ways. Kyo let his hands fall to his sides. Rosette jumped up and down, cheering and punching the air, and Marsh could do nothing more than smile.

"Thank the Altruists. I was truly worried it would not be enough," Marsh said.

"I think we can postpone…any further investigation," Garret suggested, rolling onto his back, chest heaving, "until later…ya?

"As soon as we're back on our feet, I'm ready to leave this damn place behind." Roland forced himself to sit up, only to be knocked back down from Rosette pushing her weight on him while giving him a tight hug.

"That's incredible," Estella said, her eyes staring at the body of the boy. "I can only assume he is from two hundred years ago when the people of Crossroads were first corrupted, but he looks like he could have been walking around yesterday. His skin, clothes, everything is perfectly preserved."

Kyo glanced at where the exit sat covered by the massive rubble, straining his ears. As the others spoke among themselves, he waved his hand at them.

"Shut up for a second." He remained still, swearing he heard a screech in the distance. Maybe the giant's cry still hadn't left his brain. He was ready to dismiss it until he heard another and another, several at the same time, with more joining the frightening chorus by the second. "So, somehow I don't think the other shades are happy about what we just did."

"They were all docile. Why now?" Estella asked in a shaky voice.

"Perhaps they're linked in some way," Cedric said, forcing himself to stand on shaky legs. "But those are questions for later. This is bad. We need to get out of here, now."

Kyo's heart pounded, a chill running through his body. All the shades he'd seen up to this point, including those that remained hidden, there had to be at least a hundred at minimum. Now they were pissed and coming for them.

Chapter 17

The symphony of screeching continued to assault Kyo's ears, penetrating the dense rocky walls of the cavern. There had to be another way out, but they couldn't waste time blindly searching. One wrong move and they'd find themselves face to face with tens or hundreds of shades while stuck at a dead end.

Kyo hurried to retrieve his light orb. "Okay, let's get out of here quick. We need to—"

He paused and took in the others' condition. Run? Could they even do that much? They stood on wobbly legs or sat while hunched over, panting, trembling. Venting their magic took a huge toll on their bodies. If Cedric hadn't vented, he could burrow a hole straight up and to the surface like he'd stated earlier as a last resort. Clearly that was no longer an option.

"What are we supposed to do?" Kyo asked, burying his face in his hands.

"Kyo, Rosette, how are you on magic?" Marsh asked.

Rosette bounced on her heels. "I'm okay. I have a bunch left."

"I'm hardly topped off, but I'm fine," Kyo said. He focused on the magic flowing within him, flexing it like a muscle. Knowing how much he had left was like a sixth sense working together with a slight warmth flowing through his body, unnoticeable unless he focused on it. Despite his earlier fight with the fish, he still had over three-fourths remaining.

Marsh raised a hand into the air. "Everyone, please gather around me. If we are to make it out of here, I suggest Kyo and Rosette transfer a bit of magic to each of you to ease the fatigue enough to run."

The others rose and wobbled over to Marsh, following his guidance to form a straight line.

"Good idea, ya. We don't need to fight, only make it back to where we came in and ascend." Garret said.

Kyo stood behind Cedric and Estella, while Rosette took a position behind Garret and Roland, each placing a hand on their backs and transferring some of their magical energy into the others. Their hands glowed the same azure and violet as a human's raw magic. Audible sighs escaped from the recipients. Once their exhaustion eased, Kyo did the same for Krysta.

"Thank you. We should at least make it back to the entrance like this." Estella couldn't hide the worry in her eyes. "Though getting us back to the surface will be up to you two. You're the only ones who can cast spells currently."

"Not only that but they're the only two able to defend us while we make our way there." Roland crouched in front of Rosette, placing his hands on her shoulders. "I'm sorry, kiddo. A lot is going to ride on you."

Rosette nodded and tightened her fist. "I'll knock those nasty shades away. I could summon an Altruist. I have one in mind, but it wouldn't be able to carry all of us."

"Save it for now, but if things get dicey, do what you think is best." Roland kissed her forehead gently.

A loud screech forced their attention to the boulder blocking the exit of the cavern room. At least one had arrived, with more undoubtedly on the way.

Those who had separated from their light orbs rushed to retrieve them.

"We'd better get going. Rosette, you can break that boulder, right?" Krysta asked.

Rosette nodded and turned toward their intended exit.

"Once you break through, I'll take care of the shade on the other side, then we run for it," Kyo said, building wind above his palm. Though he spoke with confidence, his heart pounded like it wanted to break free of his chest. At least he didn't have to kill the shade. He hadn't successfully done so yet. All he needed to do was knock it away enough for the others to run without the risk of an immediate attack. "Roland, you said you found a tunnel leading up, right? You'll have to guide us."

"You got it," Roland said.

Marsh stepped next to Kyo. "I suggest Rosette take the front and you take the rear, with the rest of us in the middle. If something happens to Rosette, we will all see it so we can help. Though you may be the only one capable of anything."

Kyo nodded, forming his favored drill spell above his palm. He took slow, deep breaths, eyes fixed on the exit. Rosette crouched then dashed at the fallen debris and jumped into the air. With a single kick, cracks spread throughout the solid rock, and it crumbled. The second they were free, the shade leaped for Rosette, but Kyo got to it first, thrusting the wind drill against its side, pushing against the shadowy aura. The wind compressed then exploded, sending the shade launching hard against the wall with enough force to kill most typical creatures. Shame shades were not ordinary.

"Everyone, move!" Cedric ordered.

Rosette took the lead with Roland behind her, holding out his own light orb. Next were Krysta and Marsh surrounded by the Aurora and Kyo taking up the rear. They turned right out of the room, ran down the tunnel, and seconds later heard a screech from behind.

Garret kept a hand on the uncorrupted side of Marsh's back to keep pushing him onward. While the others had received a magic boost, nothing could be done to mitigate the corruption's slowing effect on Marsh's body.

They turned a corner, and Rosette shrieked in surprise as she nearly ran into a shade, her body reacting by punching it in the stomach and knocking it on its back. Kyo mentally noted never to startle her. As they passed it, he jumped to barely avoid it grabbing his ankle. He glanced over his shoulder as the shade scrambled to its feet, joined by the first, both giving chase.

The group followed Roland's directions, making turns when instructed. "Rosette, make sure you don't hit with the intent to injure," he instructed. "It's not going to help much. Punch and kick with the intent to put distance between them and us. Push them away."

"Okay," Rosette cried out.

Rosette protected the group well as they passed shades one by one. One recovered quickly and dashed at the group from behind, but Kyo was able to trip it with a powerful burst of air that took its legs out from under it.

"Turn right. This leads up," Roland ordered.

They followed his direction, running up the incline of the tunnel. It eventually leveled off, and after a few more seconds, they found themselves back in the massive cavern housing Crossroads. The light orbs were turned off, the illumination from the glowing crystals more than enough.

"Oh, thank whatever Altruist needs to be thanked," Kyo mumbled.

Shrieks echoed throughout the town and beyond. The sight of shades from all directions coming for them made Kyo's blood run cold. Some ran on all fours like beasts. Others dashed like humans, forming groups of five or more as they drew closer. Running and putting distance between them was all they could do. If that failed…he didn't want to think about the shade's digging their claws into them for a painful death.

"Does anyone remember where we came in?" Krysta asked through heavy pants.

"Only vaguely," Cedric said. "We'll run through the town, use buildings and any other structures to slow their pursuit."

Estella's pace slowed before she grunted and picked it up again. "Not ideal but it's better than open space on all sides."

Shades drew closer, hunting like ravenous predators. As they ran down what was once a residential street, a shade leaped at the group from a rooftop.

"I got it," Kyo called, building air around his hand then thrusting it forward to send the shade crashing against the exterior of a neighboring home. While his wind drill would be more effective, he had to conserve what magic he could. Unfortunately knocking a shade back required much more magic to be put into his spells compared to any other creature.

"Come on. You can do it, ya. Keep moving," Garret said, weakly pushing Marsh from behind.

Marsh's limbs moved as if he had weights strapped to them. "Apologies. It is difficult to run like this."

More shades emerged from between homes and through side streets. The previously docile, lethargic creatures had become determined hunters. Rosette thrust her fist into a shade, sending it tumbling into a home. Kyo slowed his pace to allow a shade from behind to reach him then ducked a swipe of its claw and placed his hands against it for a point-blank burst of air to launch it across the road.

"There," Cedric said, pointing down a side road.

The group turned, and Kyo's heart lifted. The town square. Which way did they enter this area last time? Wasn't there a vendor wagon on his right?

Before Kyo realized it, shades attempted to flank them from both sides. Three to their left, four to the right.

There were too many. Some would slip through, and they only had two defenders.

Time seemed to slow as his mind reeled. A spell from all four limbs would send him flying away from the group. Still, he had to try something.

With enough magic, a wider reaching spell should still work. Kyo gathered his magic into his hands. The shades closed the distance between them. He couldn't gather the magic he wanted quickly enough, but he had to act.

With a determined cry, he thrust his hands forward and cast his spell, wind launching two shades away from the group. His eyes widened as the remaining two reached for their prey, one aiming for Krysta, the other, Marsh. On the other side of the group, Rosette had managed to land blows on two, but the third passed her, aiming for Roland.

No. Kyo couldn't react fast enough to do anything, only watch as his friends' horrified faces stared at impending death.

The shadowy aura stretched from Marsh's body like thick tendrils, wrapping itself around the shades' heads and torsos, stopping them in their tracks before slamming them into the ground then hurling them away. The corruption protected its host, much like it had done for Ruby.

"I did not mean to—" Marsh stammered.

"Don't worry about it. Right now, it's a benefit, so let it happen." Krysta said.

Garret hesitated before pushing Marsh along. "I hate to say it, but if more shades break through, put yourself in the path of them, ya. Your corruption is sure to act when you are in danger."

"I…" Marsh released a heavy breath. "Yes, I will."

The group continued to run as fast as they could, keeping themselves close together for the added protection of Marsh's corruption. More shades leaped at them only to be knocked away. One managed to break through, ripping its claws across Estella's arm. She cried out in pain as Kyo blasted it away.

"Are you okay?" Cedric asked.

"Just keep going," Estella ordered, ignoring the blood flowing down her arm like streams and dripping off her hand.

Upon reaching the outskirts of the underground town, the area looked familiar to Kyo but not enough for him to know exactly where they had entered from. And when they found it, he and Rosette would have to lift them all out at once. They were close. Soon they'd be free from the threat of harm, and their ears could rest from the nonstop screeching that permeated their skulls.

Kyo glanced behind them, and a chill struck him to his core. Every shade they had fought off, as well as others that hadn't reached them yet, chased them as one massive group, like an all-consuming void seeking to swallow them whole. There must have been nearly one hundred shades who sought to tear them limb from limb. Once they reached the way out, they'd have almost no prep time.

"How close are we?" Krysta asked.

"We can't be far. Keep your eyes open," Cedric said, constantly glancing upward.

"There's a lot coming from the front," Rosette shouted.

Nine shades dashed toward them but were raised into the air by shadowy tendrils bursting from the ground. The creatures flailed and screeched while the group passed them. A second later, they began tearing through the shadows to continue their chase.

"How'd you do that, Marsh?" Kyo asked.

"That was not me," Marsh replied, examining his body and hands as if looking for something new.

"Of course it wasn't. Now keep running!" ordered a harsh, feminine voice. More shadowy tendrils rose from the ground, this time aiming to trip the shades behind them. Some fell forward, the ones behind them doing the same, while others leaped over their fallen brethren.

A fierce-looking woman emerged from the shadows to join them, one Kyo recognized as one of the royal guard who had nearly caught him that night with Alden.

"Kira! What on Feracael—" Krysta started.

"Later!" Kira said. "Look ahead."

Only seconds away, Jaune stood opposite Hayner with a glowing barrier between them. Kyo didn't know why or how they got here, but they were saved.

"Hurry, we're doing this rapid fire," Jaune shouted.

As the group approached, they hopped on a barrier in groups of two and launched toward the hole in the ceiling, barely a second after one another. When Kyo hopped on, his face scrunched as the air assaulted his face and his heart pounded. He zipped through the hole previously made by Cedric, the rock and dirt flying past him. Light from the surface grew brighter by the second until he found himself out of the hole and hurling into the air. He used his wind spells to keep his descent to the ground slow and gently landed on the lush, green grass. By the time his senses settled, everyone had made it to the surface.

"We made it," Kyo said, so relieved he couldn't stop himself from laughing.

After taking a few moments to gather themselves, everyone allowed their bodies to relax. Rosette crawled into Roland's lap, and he showered her in praise. Jaune knelt beside Estella, casting a healing spell on her arm.

"Thank you. You've gotten us out of a nasty situation," Cedric said, extending his hand to Hayner, who shook it firmly then pulled him to his feet.

"I'll say," Hayner said. "I did not like seeing so many shades in one place. But is that confirmation you've found the source of the corruption?"

Cedric glanced back at Kyo for a moment. "Perhaps. We'll give our full report to His Majesty after some rest. Most of us had to vent our magic."

Krysta hugged Kira tightly. "How did you find us? And what are you doing here?"

Kira returned the hug before pushing Krysta back, glaring at her. "What do you think? When His Majesty realized you were gone, he was furious and ordered us to retrieve you immediately. I don't envy your return, Your Highness."

Krysta frowned. "That's fine. After what we've been through, I almost look forward to a simple lecture."

Hayner gazed past Cedric to Marsh. "I see Estella is not the only one having trouble."

"Yeah, and time is a factor. I know you need to get Krysta back, but we need to get Marsh to Spellnix Hold so Blanq can cure him." Kyo approached Marsh and smiled. "See, just a simple airship trip and you'll be good to go."

The members of the royal guard glanced between each other. Jaune sighed and stood. "That brings up another reason why we're here. We already have to make another stop before returning to Alderdeem." He approached Marsh, placing a hand on his uncorrupted shoulder. "I'm so sorry."

"What's wrong?" Krysta asked.

Jaune's gaze fell, and he took a deep breath. "Sybilla and Blanq have escaped Spellnix Hold."

Chapter 18

Jaune's words struck Kyo like a brick to the head. This couldn't be happening. After all the damage and death those two had caused, he'd thought they were locked up for good, unable to hurt anyone again. While they no longer had an accrue stone, they were powerful enough to repeat the tragedy of Calmarock if they chose. He turned to Marsh, whose eyes were wide and face pale. An unmistakable look of terror with no hope. What could they do for him?

"What do you *mean* they escaped?" Kyo asked, his voice raising with each word. "You're telling me they managed to get away from a prison on a floating island. Above the ocean. Where the nearest landmass is home of the world's most powerful ferals? How does that happen?" By the end, he was screaming, hands balled into fists and heart pounding.

All eyes were on Jaune, but Hayner raised his hand for attention. "I'll explain. We received a report shortly before we left Alderdeem. As unbelievable as it sounds, a pair of dragons flew from the coast of Morterra to Spellnix Hold. A battle ensued, and there were unfortunately many casualties, guards and prisoners alike. So dire was the situation that the guards removed the nixium shackles from prisoners so they could assist in fending off the dragons. I imagine in such a panic, the guard that decided to do so for Sybilla and Blanq and forgot, or never knew, they could teleport to another location."

"Dragons?" Estella asked. "Unprecedented but not impossible. They only live in Morterra, but what could have attracted them to the prison?"

Kyo glanced around. Krysta's wide wild eyes made her look as though she'd kill something there and then. Rosette leaned closer to Roland. Marsh… His movements were slow, dragging his hand across his face as his chest heaved. Blanq and Sybilla were his only chance at removing the corruption. There were no other methods they knew of.

In an instant, hope was lost.

"This is not the sort of news I wanted to hear. Those two could be anywhere," Cedric said, his attention falling to Marsh. "What terrible timing. We'll need to contact every chancellor we can in hopes of getting a clue as to their whereabouts."

"That process has already begun," Hayner said.

Cedric marched toward the airship as quickly as his legs would allow without another word.

Kyo stepped beside Marsh. "Hey, we'll figure something out. I'm sure they can be found. All of Feracael will be on the lookout for them." He turned his head, shifting his gaze between the royal guard and the Aurora for reassurance. "Right?"

The uncertain looks on their faces didn't instill trust.

Krysta approached Marsh and gently took his uncorrupted hand into hers. "It'll be okay. We'll find a way to cure you."

Marsh kept his eyes down, not acknowledging her words.

"You can't become a shade!" Rosette insisted.

Roland said nothing, removing the flask from his coat and taking a long swig.

"I brought this on myself. I knew the risks of coming along. And so I will accept my fate," Marsh said, nearly losing the last few words in a poorly held back sob.

"My ass you will," Kyo turned to Estella and Garret. "You'll be looking for them, won't you?

"Well, of course. But this time, we have an entire world to search through, ya. Those two are powerful enough to hide out in Morterra if they choose, at least for a little while. We have no idea where to begin," Garret confessed.

Estella shook her head. "And even if we found them today, it'll be days before our magic recovers enough to engage them in battle after venting."

"You, maybe," Kira said, cracking her knuckles. "We might not be as powerful as you Aurora, but we royal guard of Alderdeem would sure give them a run for their cryst. You can be the eyes, and when you find them, we can be the muscle."

"When it comes to Marsh, unfortunate though it may be, there is nothing we can do. He has a few days at most." Hayner's eyes weren't without sorrow as he spoke. "Looking at the bigger picture, an exceptionally close eye should be kept on Alderdeem. It's entirely possible those two will want to retrieve the accrue stones we took from them upon their capture."

"You can't give up on Marsh," Rosette shouted.

Hayner sighed. "If you have an idea on how to save him, we're all ears."

Rosette grunted in frustration and stomped her foot too hard, struggling to pull it out of the soft dirt.

The magic-tech engines of the Aurora's airship hummed, growing louder by the second.

Cedric returned to the group. "We'll begin the hunt immediately, starting with getting more details from those at Spellnix Hold. Garret, Estella, we're leaving now. Marsh…good luck. And to all of you, thank you for the assistance."

Garret ruffled Marsh's hair, and Estella carefully embraced the cleric before following Cedric to the airship.

"Well, I guess there's no point in sticking around here, right?" Jaune said, motioning everyone toward their airship parked west of them. "Let's get going. We can think more on the way."

"You mentioned a stop before returning to Alderdeem. Where do you plan on going?" Roland asked.

"Northwest, to a site not far from Ueno," Kira said.

Kyo's eyes widened. "Ueno? That's where my dad is originally from."

"We're not going on a sightseeing tour. About a day and a half walk east of Ueno is an unusual place. Think of it like a bog combined with rocky cliffs, caves, and the like. It's also home to some nasty ferals." Kira smirked. "And according to His Majesty, deep in there lies another accrue stone, which we're going to add to our growing collection."

"Don't say it like that," Jaune begged. "It makes it sound like you're up to no good."

Kira waved him off. "Nothing wrong with a little dash of chaos here and there."

"If all that's protecting that accrue stone is a bit of murky water and some ferals, I'm surprised Sybilla and Blanq didn't go after that one first," Krysta said. "It sounds like it would have been much easier than the one in Mistwell."

"There is one more detail about this place that makes it extremely dangerous," Hayner warned, walking backward to face the others as he spoke. "This location is also the largest natural repository of nixium ore in Terrorigo. Even in its natural state, it retains its magic suppressing properties. And with so much of it around, no one who ventures in there can expect to cast a spell or even have their magic provide the usual natural defense for their body that's taken for granted. In short, it'll be as if we have no magic at all."

Kyo shuddered at the thought. Unable to cast a spell and one strike from a feral could mean death. The image of a feral piercing his stomach flashed in his mind. "So how do you plan on getting it then?"

"The same way people mine the nixium ore. With solid weapons and protective armor. We'll show you after we take off," Jaune said with a proud smile.

The group boarded the airship, the initial hum of the magic-tech engines causing it to vibrate. The crew wore similar garb to the royal guard, but white and sky blue, with an extra emblem depicting an airship on the right breast. As the crew worked to get airborne, Hayner led the group into a room on the lower deck, various melee weapons and leather armor pieces set neatly in separate piles.

Rosette dashed past everyone else and picked up a cedar-colored leather chest piece with thick shoulder pads and heavy stitching, examining it with curious eyes. "Wow. Are these better than our magic defenses?"

Jaune shook his head. "No, under normal circumstances, there's no point in wearing them. For anyone who trains their magic for the purpose of fighting, their natural defense provides better protection without the extra weight and burden. But it does come in handy for situations like this." He took the chest piece from Rosette and slipped it on, posing with his fists on his hips.

"Allow me to go with you," Marsh said.

Kyo stared at him in disbelief. "Did you already forget what happened the last time you said that?"

"No, I did not. But as we have seen down in Crossroads, the corruption can be a benefit before I turn."

"I don't know about that." Kyo's lips tightened and twisted. "They put nixium cuffs on Ruby in Aquarin Port. It managed to suppress the corruption enough that the enforcers could handle her. So, it might not be too useful in there."

"Then allow me to mention another perspective." Marsh turned to Krysta. "I would assume you intend to leave Krysta here while you retrieve the accrue stone. Should the unthinkable happen, do you truly wish to leave me here with her and put her life in danger? I may have days until I turn—or only hours."

Kira grunted and rolled her eyes. "His corruption isn't something we intended. We can't leave him alone with Her Highness."

"You're right. We can't." Hayner drummed his fingers on his thigh. "Nor can we trust his friends to do what needs to be done, should he turn. Logically, the best course of action would be to leave him here, far from the nearest town."

"We will *not* be doing that," Krysta growled angrily, gritting her teeth.

Hayner held up his hand. "I said logically, but I'm not a cold-hearted monster. Marsh will come with us. But know we will not risk everything to protect you when it comes down to it, given your current condition."

Marsh nodded. "I expected as much."

"Marsh, are you serious?" Kyo asked, but he knew the answer before the words left his mouth. "Well then, count me in. I'm going as Marsh's bodyguard to make sure nothing happens to him. I've got my own weapons to use."

Hayner pinched the bridge of his nose. "Do you all crave life-or-death situations?"

"I'm not letting Marsh go in there unprotected." Kyo glanced at Marsh but didn't smile. Something felt off about Marsh's request this time, but he couldn't put his finger on it. "Besides, it's also about getting that accrue stone so Sybilla and Blanq don't. At this point, we're practically veterans when it comes to this sort of thing."

"The kid's right," Roland said, summoning his polearm. "My suggestion is to let the three of us join you. Rosette and Krysta can stay aboard the airship with the crew until we come back. So long as they have their magic, those two are plenty capable." He clenched his fist and smiled at Rosette. "You going to be the princess's bodyguard until we come back, kiddo?"

Rosette thrust a fist in the air. "Yeah, I'll beat up anything that comes near her! But will you be okay? You just vented your magic."

He nodded. "I should be by the time we get there. It'll take a few days to fully recover my magic, but physically, I'll be okay after some hours of rest. It doesn't take as much of a toll as when Sybilla and Blanq force the magic out of someone." He turned to Hayner. "What do you think?"

"Fine," Hayner said, glancing at the three in turn. "Marsh may be a detriment in his current state, but I know you two aren't. But don't forget you're used to using your weapons alongside your magic. You have until we arrive to rid yourself of that mindset." His gaze fixed on Krysta. "I trust you'll have no intention of following us, being your usual sneaky self?"

Krysta shook her head. "Not into a place like that. But please be careful. All of you." She stepped forward, taking Kira and Jaune's hands in hers and standing before Hayner. "Don't make me return home without any of you."

"We don't intend to, Your Highness. Honestly, we would have liked to have a few more royal guards with us, but we needed to leave as many to defend Alderdeem as we could with those two free." Jaune hit his chest with his fist. "But we can handle it, I think. If nothing else, one glare from Kira should send any ferals running off."

"What do you mean by that?" Kira asked harshly, narrowing her eyes.

"See? There it is." He grinned.

Kira slid her arm under a piece of leather armor, that same arm appearing from a shadow on Jaune's back cast by a light on the wall. Her hand wrapped around his throat. "I can still use my magic until we get there, you know."

"Okay, okay. Sorry!" Jaune begged through her chokehold.

"Both of you, enough," Hayner said. "We have an important mission ahead of us. Be sure to get some rest before we arrive. There's no telling what we might run into."

The airship trembled as it lifted from the ground. The crew could be heard relaying orders and setting their destination.

Kyo kept his eyes on Marsh. Venturing to a place he couldn't rely on magic wasn't something he'd typically do by choice, but he had to stay by Marsh's side. Despite his words earlier, he couldn't think of a way they'd be able to cure him. Even if Sybilla and Blanq were found, how would they convince them to do so without being blackmailed? Time was as much an enemy as those two or any feral. He'd stick by his friend's side and ensure his end didn't come until the very last second.

Chapter 19

Kyo tugged at the strap on his side to secure and buckle his cuirass while Roland helped by doing the same with the straps on the shoulders. The added weight would take a bit of getting used to, but it wasn't as heavy as Kyo expected. At least it was sleeveless, providing a wide range of motion, though it left his arms vulnerable. One bite or slash from a feral could do significant damage. Having no idea what sorts of creatures dwelled in the bog had his imagination running wild, picturing everything from massive lizards with razor-sharp teeth to giant skitters. The latter coupled with not having his magic to protect him made his body run cold with nerves. If he saw something like that, he'd likely curl up in a corner.

"There. You're good to go, kid. Not too bad, right?" Roland asked.

Kyo turned to face him, his usual trench coat discarded in place of a similar cuirass over a dark blue T-shirt. The design had a strong appeal, multiple rows of overlapping leather scales connected to a leather backing. Shame they weren't made of dragon scales, if such armor even existed, but if it protected them, he had no complaints.

"Yeah, it's fine," Kyo confirmed, firmly beating the chest piece with his fist several times. "At least I hope it is. I have no idea what we might run into while we're in there."

"I have a bit of insight on that," Hayner said as he walked into the room holding a large bronze disk. "Kyo, this is for you. Without your magic to support you, dual wielding swords becomes impractical."

Eying the disk, Kyo took it and flipped it over, revealing straps on the other end. "Oh, a shield?"

Hayner nodded. "Given how you are used to moving around swiftly, I figured a smaller, lighter one would suit you best. Though that means your aim will have to be better, but I trust you will have no issues with that."

Kyo glanced down at his cuirass then at the table where leather greaves, bracers, and a helmet sat waiting for him. "Hoo boy, this is a lot. Thanks though."

"Meet us outside once you're ready. Marsh already has his armor and is waiting for you," Hayner said as he left.

Roland stared at Kyo with a serious look. "Speaking of which, keep an eye on Marsh while we're in there."

"Mm, I know. He's been acting off lately. Which makes sense, but there's something else I can't figure out." Kyo sighed, tapping his middle finger against his thigh for a few seconds. Maybe he was overthinking, but he couldn't shake the feeling the corruption wasn't the only thing to watch out for with Marsh.

Once they completed attaching their armor, they left the airship to join the others. Rosette and Krysta remained off to the side while Marsh, Kira, and Jaune stood side by side in front of Hayner.

"Everyone, be sure to follow my lead," Hayner ordered. "I've been given instructions on where to find the accrue stone. Our goal is to get in, retrieve it, get out, and return to Alderdeem. Remember to keep the mindset of not relying on magic. Also remember the ferals can't use magic either, so that's one less concern."

Kira grinned, reaching forward and pointing her morning star mace toward their destination. "Which means they only have what protection their bodies provide. So, we'll smash and cut our way through any that stand in our way."

"Or preferably not come across any at all," Jaune replied in a meek voice, gripping the handle of a wood-cutting axe. "It'd be nice if things went smoothly. Hey, maybe the ferals here are docile." He looked around for any signs someone agreed.

Hayner pulled his claymore from the dirt. "I'm sure not every single feral will attack us on sight, but assume any feral is hostile. I shouldn't have to tell you that."

"Right," Jaune said with a sigh.

Rosette ran to Roland and hugged him tightly. "Be careful. Don't get hurt while you're in there, okay?" She gazed up at him with wide eyes and a frown.

"Heh, don't worry, I'll be fine kiddo," Roland said, ruffling her hair. "You just focus on keeping yourself, Krysta, and the crew safe, okay? And stay aboard the airship while we're gone. The princess has had some time to recover her magic but not a lot. So, you're the powerhouse here."

Rosette nodded and punched her right fist into her open palm. "I'll keep everyone safe."

"I really hate being so helpless. Do you at least need me to light a torch for you or something?" Krysta asked.

"The day has just started, so we'll have plenty of sunlight. Remain on the airship with the crew until we get back. And do *not* think about coming after us, Your Highness." Hayner glared at Krysta.

"We've been over this. As if I'd go wandering into a place like that without my magic," Krysta grumbled, folding her arms over her chest.

Kyo gazed beyond Hayner to where the grass stretched tall in the distance. Based on Kira's description, it wasn't going to be a fun time trekking through overgrown flora and pools of murky water. At least they wouldn't be going in completely blind. Assuming the accrue stone hadn't been moved by something, maybe it'd be a quick trip.

"All right, everyone, let's get moving." Hayner turned and led the others, Rosette and Krysta saying their goodbyes.

"Good, the sooner we get this done the sooner I can take off this helmet. I look incredibly stupid," Kira said, her lips twisted.

Jaune chuckled. "It's not too bad. You should wear it next time you come over to my place."

Kyo's eyes widened. "To your place? Is there something about you two I didn't know?"

Kira narrowed her eyes and lightly stamped the knob of her mace against Kyo's helmet. "Don't get any dumb ideas. For whatever reason, his little brother and sister love me. Can't imagine why."

"You say that, but you get along with them so well. And they'd get a kick out of seeing you in that leather getup." Jaune reached for the helmet, but Kira slapped his hand away. "At least bring that."

Face flushed, Kira pointed her mace at him. "There is no way in Feracael I am wearing this when I don't need to."

While the two of them went back and forth, Kyo stepped beside Marsh. "Hey, you doing okay? Remember to stay close. We're not sure if the corruption will protect you with all the nixium around."

"I am aware. Interesting, is it not? In its refined form, there must be physical contact for it to have any effect, but in its natural form, its effect radiates some distance. I wonder why that is," Marsh mused, eyes glued to the sky.

"I'm sure people smarter than us know why it's that way. Let's just be careful. Hopefully, there won't be much to worry about." Kyo felt a tap on his shoulder and turned. Roland showed him his polearm, a reminder to summon his sword into his right hand before they entered the area of the nixium's effect. He gripped the hilt, resting the dull end of the blade against his shoulder.

As they ventured into the bog, they stuck to as much solid ground as they could. Deep pools of water, narrow paths of solid dirt, interlaced with the occasional mineral vein or additional rocky, serpent-like path they could walk along. In the distance, Kyo spied several larger rock formations. A strong earthy scent filled his nostrils, not entirely unpleasant, similar to the smell in the air when it started raining during the warmer months. His steps took a bit more effort, as if a weight pressed down upon him, so subtle it could be ignored in time. This feeling must be a sign the environment was suppressing his magic. An uncomfortable sensation but not so much he'd verbally complain. The farther they ventured, the taller the grass became and the more frequent the tall rocky formations towered over them. On occasion, they did see an intimidating, lizard-like feral that could likely bite them in half, but those seemed more interested in resting in the pools of water.

Kyo's lips twisted in annoyance. As much as he tried to stay clear of the water, his boots had already been soaked through. "This is gross. I don't like hearing my feet squelch whenever I take a step. This would be so much easier if we could make barriers to walk on."

"That would definitely be nice," Jaune said, his entire lower half wet from previously falling into a pool. "The perfect place for my spells and I can't use them."

"That brings up the question — what magic do you use?" Kyo asked. "I don't think I've ever seen you cast a spell."

"Well, it's not like we've had much interaction before now. But my forte is barriers." A proud smile spread across Jaune's lips. "I use various types depending on the situation."

Roland raised a brow. "Only barriers?"

"He has attempted to teach me a thing or two during our time in Alderdeem," Marsh said. "Though there is so much more to learn."

"Well, I guess it has its uses," Kyo replied in an unenthused tone.

"Don't let the description fool you." Hayner glanced over his shoulder. "He may only use barriers, but he is exceptional at what he does, capable of using them both defensively and offensively. When it comes to barriers, his skill is superior to Estella's." He paused for a few seconds, scanning their surroundings before making a right turn and motioning to follow him along a narrow dirt path between a short rocky cliff and a pool of water. "Be sure to remain vigilant."

The group followed. Kyo gave their surroundings a once-over. "If that's true, why not join the Aurora?"

Kira suppressed a cackle. "Because he'd be way too afraid to deal with the things they do regularly."

"Hey, that's not it," Jaune said unconvincingly, the grip on his axe tight and close to his chest. "Well, not entirely. The main reason is money. Being a royal guard pays well, so I'm able to send money back to my family in Riftdale. They rely on me. I can't see them as often as I'd like, but it's worth it to make sure they're doing okay."

"If they are in Riftdale, then the situation is understandable. I grew up there for a time. Nothing is more common there than poverty." Marsh shook his head. "It is good your family has you, Jaune."

"Hayner, I have a question," Roland called out. "Why are we not seeing nixium be mined currently? The cuffs have been shown to suppress the corruption. Shouldn't making as many as possible be a priority?"

"Unfortunately, this is only true for the first stage. Once someone becomes a shade, the effects are insufficient." Hayner pointed out, his lips tightening. "The loss of several enforcers taught us that hard lesson quickly."

Kyo's head snapped to the left just in time to see something coming for him. He raised his shield in front of his face, the impact sending him onto his back with a heavy grunt. Several thick, intertwisted vines retracted before Kira could bring her mace down on them. On the other side of a pool stood three bipedal creatures composed entirely of shifting vines.

"You little shits," Kyo hissed, returning to his feet.

The ferals outstretched their arms, the vines shooting across the pool to strike before retracting. The group dodged, swinging their weapons to beat back the appendages while Hayner and Roland rounded the pool to flank them.

Marsh shifted between Kyo and Kira to stand in front of them, a vine thrusting at his shoulder to the side of where his armor protected him, knocking him to the ground. He cried out, gripping the impact point.

"You okay?" Kyo asked, taking a split second to look down at his friend before returning his attention to the attackers. Only the feral in the middle attempted to strike them from across the pool with the other two otherwise engaged.

"It hurt, but I think I am okay. While it seems I cannot rely on the corruption to attack like last time, it still protects my body while suppressed. At least somewhat," Marsh said, rising and returning to stand behind the group.

"Well, don't count on it too much," Kyo warned.

Roland pierced one of the ferals with his polearm, raised it into the air, and flung it into the pool. Hayner swiftly cut the head off another before both mages struck the third, killing it instantly.

Kyo released a sigh of relief. His heart pounded, the moment he blocked the first attack flashing in his mind. He had no magic protection. If he hadn't noticed when he did, that strike could have killed him before he knew what happened. "I don't like this place."

"Maybe it's time to end the casual conversation and keep our attention on our surroundings, huh?" Roland asked with a fresh scratch trickling blood along his cheek.

"Agreed. Let's keep moving. We've been lucky to make it this far before being attacked. But we aren't far from our destination." Hayner once again motioned for them to follow as he started forward.

"How do we know where we're going without a map or something?" Kyo asked.

Hayner pointed to a tall rock formation. "Landmarks. Rocks, pools, and the like shaped in certain ways."

The group continued, remaining focused on the environment. No longer lax, Kyo gripped the hilt of his sword firmly. The occasional aggressive feral approached them, most easily dispatched with little more than a few scratches or a bruise as a result. Two crocodiles were able to be chased off without a fight. Despite the lesson learned previously, Marsh continued to put himself to the front of any battles, taking hit after hit to various parts of his body. Thankfully, he expressed no concern of injury, only throbbing pain.

"That's it. If we get in another fight, you're staying behind us, end of discussion," Kyo snapped, eyes narrowing at Marsh. "You're a cleric. You should know how to protect yourself. What's wrong with you?"

Marsh stared at him with apathetic eyes. "It is fine. They have not been able to seriously harm me." He sounded almost disappointed, which angered Kyo further.

"I don't care." Kyo gripped Marsh's collar. "You don't leave my side until we're out of this place, got it?" When Marsh didn't reply, Kyo forced him along by his arm.

"I know what you're doing, Marsh," Roland said. "And I understand your mindset." Marsh turned to look at him. "But remember, your careless actions might end someone else's life instead of your own. Ask yourself if you're okay with that."

Kyo stared at Marsh, a chill running through him. In a soft tone, he asked, "Are you actually trying to get yourself killed?"

Marsh remained silent, but his gaze drifted to the ground.

"We're here," Hayner said. They stood before a towering, curved rock formation with a jagged circular hole near the top. "At least this landmark was obvious. The stone should be here somewhere. Start looking but stay close."

Kyo kept Marsh with him, scanning the ground for the stone as if it were any lost household item. To his credit, Marsh also searched carefully.

"Almost done with this place," Kyo muttered. And he hoped that, once they left the bog behind, that would eliminate Marsh's attempts to end himself. Typical Marsh. Even with death looming, he wanted to go out being useful, taking a hit meant for someone else. Marsh may have given up, but Kyo wouldn't let anything happen to him until there were no options left.

Enough time passed so that the sun's position change in the sky became noticeable. After two attacks by ferals, Roland stopped his search to stand watch. Jaune started using his axe to dig up dirt in case the stone had been buried, and Kira sat in front of a pile of rocks, moving them one by one. At one point, Kyo swore he saw her pocket one.

"Didn't the king tell you exactly where the stone might be?" Kyo asked.

"He did," Hayner responded. "And it is no longer in that spot. It was expected a feral may have done something with it."

"So, it might be on the other side of the bog for all we know?" Jaune asked.

Hayner nodded. "Entirely possible. But if that is the case, it is likely safer than if we brought it back to Alderdeem. I can't imagine anyone finding it if a feral ran off with it, maybe buried it in one of the thousands of pools."

Kira shouted and shot to her feet. Everyone's attention snapped to her. She held a grainy, transparent orb in her hand. "Is this it?"

Everyone gathered around. Though no magic swirled within it, there was no mistake.

Kyo stared at the orb. The image of Sybilla holding the orb came to mind. "Yeah, I'm pretty sure that's it."

"There is a way to be certain," Marsh suggested. "Your magic is severely suppressed to the point of being useless in battle but not completely. Though you cannot cast a spell, if any of you can squeeze a bit of magic into the orb, that would confirm it."

Kira nodded and took a deep breath. Her grip on the orb tightened, and her breathing came out in heavy gasps.

"Come on," she muttered, her arms trembling.

Then, where her palm held the orb, a small, thin strand of azure-and-violet energy slipped inside.

"That confirms it. Well done, Kira," Hayner said with a smile, patting her shoulder. "We're free to leave."

"Thank goodness," Kyo sighed. His gaze drifted up to the top of the rock formation. Did it move, or were his eyes playing tricks on him? He narrowed his eyes, and at first, nothing happened. As he was about to give up, it shifted.

Not the rock but something resting atop it. It skittered through the hole fully into view — a massive black centipede that could easily swallow them whole. And its beady eyes were fixed on them.

Chapter 20

The gaze of the massive feral kept Kyo frozen in place. Facing a creature like this without his magic — was it even possible? One wrong move and it could crush him. He kept his heavy breathing as silent as possible, hoping if he didn't make any sudden moves, it would deem them insignificant and be on its way.

"Hey," he whispered. "Don't do anything crazy. We have a guest."

The others turned to follow his gaze. A leg twitched on occasion, but otherwise the centipede gave no indication it would attack.

"What do we do?" Jaune asked, keeping his voice low.

"We have what we came for. Slowly back away and hope it leaves us be." Hayner led by example, taking a deliberate step backward. The others followed, moving as a group.

It wasn't good enough for the feral. It raced down the rock formation and barreled through the group of mages, knocking them over and using its elongated body to separate them. It turned and raised its front off the ground then brought it crashing down upon them.

Kyo barely avoided the impact, keeping his buckler raised. Whether such a small shield would provide any protection against the creature was questionable. His arm would snap if he tried to block the feral's body. Kira and Roland struck the trunk with their weapons, but they couldn't damage the exoskeleton.

"Do not try to slay this thing here," Hayner called. "Our best chance is to lead it out of the bog where we can use our magic. Run!"

While the centipede took the time to turn its body, they dashed behind Hayner, rejoining each other and traveling in a group. Kyo glanced over his shoulder to see it coming after them, the movements of its many legs sending a shiver through his body.

"We're going to run all the way back with this thing chasing us?" Jaune asked in disbelief.

"It's a long shot, but it's the best chance we've got. Quit complaining and keep going," Kira spat.

They ran along the paths between pools, the feral on their heels. The occasional crocodile retreated into the water. At least they wouldn't have to worry about other ferals attacking them with this thing on their tail. Though he'd highly prefer any other creature to come at them.

"It's going for a swim," Roland called out.

No sooner had he said it than the creature burst from another pool in front of them. They leaped into adjacent pools to avoid being crushed when it came down along the path.

Kyo frantically resurfaced, Marsh doing the same a second later.

"Why is this thing so pissed at us?" Kyo pulled himself from the pool, but when he turned, Marsh hadn't done the same as the feral rose, ready to dive again. "Move, you idiot!"

Despite his own plea, Kyo didn't wait, returning to the water and grabbing Marsh by his robe, pulling him away as the creature dove again. The resulting wave washed them back onto the path. A fraction of a second longer and Marsh would have been crushed or eaten.

"Are you two okay?" Jaune shouted.

Kyo ignored him, slapping Marsh across the face. "What is wrong with you? I've had it with your carelessness with your own life." He stood, pulling Marsh up with him, gripping the collar of his robes. "I get the corruption has your head all messed up, but this isn't the answer."

"If I turn—" Marsh started.

"Then it'll be taken care of. We have the royal guard for that. But I haven't given up hope yet, and neither should you. As long as you're still you, there's a chance we can turn you back to normal."

The centipede surfaced from another pool further in the distance.

"You two, we need to go," Roland yelled. "Now!"

Kyo glared at Marsh. "You want to keep us safe? Stop putting us in situations where we have to risk ourselves to save your ass. And when that thing is dealt with," he pointed at the feral, "we'll find Sybilla and Blanq and make them cure you." He gripped Marsh's robes tighter. "My parents, Ruby, Alden—I'm not losing you too, got it?"

While Kyo could see the feral rushing toward them again, his eyes remained fixed on Marsh's, who gripped his hands and eased them off his robes.

"I am sorry. I just—" He glanced at the oncoming creature then back to Kyo. "Let us get out of here then. I will not put you at any further risk."

A relieved sigh escaped Kyo, and he grabbed Marsh, pulling him along a path around a pool as the centipede rushed through where they had been standing. They circled around and rejoined the others to continue their escape.

"This thing is determined. It needs to screw off already," Kira shouted.

"A hungry creature won't easily give up the chase," Hayner replied, glancing behind them.

"Well, I'm not about to be food for something. I say if we kill it, we eat it out of spite," Kyo suggested. As unlikely as that scenario was given their precious cargo, the fantasy alone gave Kyo motivation to be sure they slayed it. With the six of them, it wouldn't be difficult but only if they had access to their magic.

The centipede caught up again, Kyo glancing back to see it nearly close enough to touch. It lunged at him, but he was bumped out of the way and nearly fell over. When he regained his footing, the creature had Jaune in its forcipules and raised its front into the air. They pierced through the leather armor, more from Jaune's energetic struggling than anything.

"Put me down," Jaune cried, fruitlessly slashing his axe on the sharp grabbers.

"Jaune!" Kira called, charging and swinging her mace at its underbelly. The creature stirred and its legs writhed in response to each hit. The others excluding Marsh joined in, slashing and bashing with their weapons. Roland managed to pierce its skin with the sharp point of his polearm. While they struck the underside, Kyo went after its legs, able to slice off a couple thin, squirming limbs. It trembled, dropping Jaune and diving into the water.

Jaune cried out, lying on the ground and gripping his right leg. "I think it might be broken."

Panting and grunting, he tried to get up, but the slightest pressure sent him on his back again, eyes clenched.

A broken bone from that height? Kyo had underestimated how weak they were without their magic. He tightened his grip around the handle of his shield and joined the others around Jaune, keeping his eyes open, watching for signs of the feral. "Thanks, I owe you for that."

Jaune sucked in air between his teeth. "Yeah, sure. But don't let me slow you all down. That thing might not be giving up so easily."

"We're not leaving here without you, you idiot. We did some damage to it. Maybe we can kill it without our magic after all." Kira scanned the area. "If it decides to show its ugly face again."

"Let's not risk it. We continue to make for the airship," Hayner ordered.

Marsh frowned. "I would heal him if I could. But..."

"It's fine. We're all powerless at the moment. You're not the only one. But how are we getting Jaune out of here?" Kyo asked.

"I'm going to need a stronger drink after this." Roland crouched down in front of Jaune. "Grab on, I'll carry you on my back." Jaune reached up to wrap his arms around Roland's neck, pulling himself up while Roland supported him with his hands under his thighs. "I'll worry about him. It's hardly the same without my magic, but I'm used to carrying Rosette around at least. But I won't be able to do much fighting like this."

Jaune cried out again, gripping Roland's cuirass and clenching his eyes shut. "Don't worry about me. If it hurts, it hurts. Just go."

Together they took off, following Hayner's lead. The longer they went without seeing the feral, the more relief washed over Kyo. Up ahead he saw the narrow path between the large pool and cliff they'd traveled earlier. They had made the trip back much faster than he expected. He hoped this would be worth it. While Sybilla and Blanq would have at least as much trouble as them trying to retrieve the stone, he could imagine them roping in some unsuspecting people to do the dirty work for them.

"Kyo, I apologize for—" Marsh started.

"Save that crap for later," Kyo shouted.

Marsh shook his head. "I am feeling an odd shift with the corruption. As if it is becoming more natural to be within me. I cannot be sure, but it is possible I will turn sooner rather than later."

Kyo's eyes widened, his breath catching in his throat. "You're imagining things. You have to be. It hasn't even been a day." He glanced behind him. Still no sign of the feral.

"Remember what the Aurora told us. There are many factors that come into play, including will. I was a fool to underestimate it. It is possible my resignation to my fate has led to the corruption hastening my transformation," he said through panting breaths as he did his best to keep up. "I had given up hope, felt no will to fight it." Marsh glanced down at his half-corrupted body. "I do not believe I will last until we return to Alderdeem."

Kyo's breath caught in his throat. "No. It's not going to happen. We'll find a way to save you. We're not losing you." The last few words struggled to escape. He couldn't lose someone else he cared for. Family, friend, it didn't matter. There had to be a way.

"Listen. When the time comes, you must promise me you will do what is necessary. For your own sake, you cannot hesitate. And I mean before I turn completely. You will have a window of opportunity. Do not waste it." Marsh's eyes bore into Kyo's for a brief second. "Please."

How could Kyo be expected to answer? Logically, Marsh was absolutely right. Kyo swallowed hard, panting, the anxiety tightening his chest not helping his breathing as they rushed through the bog. Tears welled in his eyes, but he blinked them back.

"We've got company," Roland warned. "To the right."

Kyo glanced into the pool next to him, faintly identifying the massive body of the centipede swimming underneath. Were all the pools interconnected? If not, the ones most inconvenient to them sure were.

"We're nearly there. Keep going," Hayner ordered.

Whether it was running without magic enhancing his body, knowing what was happening with Marsh, or both, Kyo struggled to keep up the pace. It wouldn't be long before he had to stop and rest. He cursed the nixium around them.

The centipede emerged and dove for them. Marsh grabbed Kyo and jumped forward, narrowly avoiding being caught in its forcipules. Kyo pulled Marsh to his feet and continued to run but held back the faintest smile. At least Marsh hadn't willingly stood in the way this time. Though relying on his friends to kill him wasn't much better.

The feral circled a pool to continue its chase as the group entered the tall grass that led into the bog. They were out. Within seconds, Kyo could feel the suppression of his magic lifting and the weight on his chest easing. The fantasy of the centipede becoming dinner became more of a reality, and he didn't care how horrible it might taste.

"If everyone else is feeling their magic coming back, let's finally get rid of this thing," Kira suggested.

"No, keep going all the way to the airship. Something is wrong," Hayner said, keeping his eyes straight ahead.

What could be more wrong than what was on their tail? Kyo stared past the group to the airship in the distance. Nothing appeared off to him, though he did see figures standing outside. Krysta and Rosette likely got restless waiting for them, or the crew needed some fresh air.

Kyo wrapped his arm around Marsh's waist and blasted wind from his feet, taking quick leaps to further the gap between them and the centipede. Roland created barriers to make elevated steps for himself and Jaune.

Hayner used his magic to raise the ground beneath his and Kira's feet, riding it like surfers on a wave, tearing apart the earth in front of them.

As they drew closer to the airship, Kyo finally noticed what Hayner had. Though he couldn't make out more than vague shapes and colors from this distance, he hadn't remembered anyone wearing black and red. The figures became clearer the closer they got. Kyo narrowed his eyes. A man he didn't recognize stood casually outside the airship, long black hair reaching the small of his back. His clothes were all black, formalwear like he'd find someone in Alderdeem wearing. Kyo's breath caught in his throat as his eyes fixed on Sybilla and Blanq standing next to him.

Chapter 21

Confusion, anger, and even a bit of relief flooded Kyo as his eyes remained locked on the three unexpected guests standing outside the airship. How did they find them? He glanced down at the hoodie wrapped around his waist. No way would Alden use the tracking enchantment he'd placed on it to let those two know where he was, right? There had to be another explanation. The smug smirk on Sybilla's face made his lips twist in annoyance. Oh, how he wanted to punch that haughty attitude away. He glanced at Marsh. No, Kyo had to avoid upsetting them, at least until he could convince them to remove the corruption. There would be no more chances after this.

Thick vines burst from the ground all around them. Kyo jumped with wind from his feet, but they wrapped around his ankles, his legs, all the way up to his neck. He fell hard, grunting from the impact. Taking a deep breath, he used all of his physical strength to stretch the vines, to free an arm, something. The others' attempts to escape their reach were similarly futile as they all found themselves bound. All except Jaune, who kept barriers up on all sides as he lay on the ground, his face scrunched in pain.

"Well now, your reflexes are impressive," the man said, his hand raised in the air. A vine smashed into the barrier, only to bounce off with greater force than it gave. With a flick of his fingers, a new vine emerged from beneath Jaune's feet inside his barrier dome, wrapping around him. The barrier faded. "Though you are still rather green."

The massive centipede barreled toward them at full speed. The man kept his hand in the air, glowing with the crimson light of a spell, a similarly colored aura enshrouding the feral's head. It reared back, wiggling for a moment before coming back down and slowly heading for the man.

He reached out to caress the feral. "You are an incredible specimen, aren't you? I wonder what other mysteries lie in that bog?"

"Did he just tame a feral with a spell?" Kira asked in horrific disbelief, her voice shaking.

The man turned to her. "'Control' would be the more appropriate term in this case."

Domesticating a feral was one thing, something done over time with training, and often injury to the one attempting it. But to do something like this in an instant and to such a large creature...

Kyo's blood ran cold at the possibilities. "Looks like those two made a new friend," he growled through gritted teeth.

"If he's on the same level as them, we're in serious trouble." Roland tilted his head to stare at the airship. "Rosette better be okay, or I'll impale them all."

Sybilla chuckled and waved. "Hi," she called in a singsong tone. "Did you miss us?"

"Like an ulcer," Kyo grumbled.

"So, that's them? Sybilla and Blanq?" Hayner asked.

"Oh, you've heard of us? I'm so flattered. Look, Blanq, we're famous," Sybilla cried out in mock excitement, holding her hands to her chest. Blanq shrugged, and Sybilla sighed in response. "I should have known you wouldn't play along." She slapped her partner on the back hard enough to make her stumble forward. "Be more excited. We're free!"

Sybilla extended her arms, twirling in place. She paused like a statue as her gaze fell to Marsh, the flickering aura of the corruption more intense than before they entered the bog.

"And it looks like the little cleric is on his way out. What a shame. Oh! Do you think we should let him transform and watch them fight each other?" she asked, head turning between Blanq to her left and the man on her right.

"Sybilla, please. We have more pressing matters to attend to," the man said.

Sybilla released a humph and crossed her arms over her chest as he took a few steps closer. The centipede remained lying in place like an obedient saber.

"I commend you all," the man said. "No doubt you've retrieved the accrue stone, no small feat given the location. We appreciate you doing the heavy lifting. Given you've taken two of ours, it's only fitting you offer that one to us, don't you think?"

"We won't be surrendering anything to you. Don't think because you have us tied up that we won't fight back," Hayner growled with venom in each word. The ground before him trembled and cracked, splitting apart in places.

The man remained unfazed, not even a twitch in his face. "Blanq, if you'd please."

Blanq raised her hand, and her fingers waved forward. After a few seconds, Krysta stepped forward onto the deck of the airship, her arms behind her and a crew member gripping each shoulder. While Krysta held a scowl on her face, the most noticeable thing about the crew members were their glowing blue eyes.

The ground calmed and Hayner's eyes widened. "What are you doing? You dare betray Her Highness? Release her immediately!"

"Hayner. I am sorry," Marsh said, "but it is too late for them. They are already gone."

"What do you mean they're…" Hayner paused. "Necromancer." He practically spit the word. "You'll pay for their lives with your own, I swear it!"

Sybilla waved her hand dismissively. "Right, right. Should I shut him up? I could use a bit of fun."

"Behave. We're in the process of negotiations," the man warned, side-eyeing Sybilla, who rolled her eyes but didn't reply.

Kyo shivered, his gaze glued to the man. If Sybilla of all people listened to his orders without question, what did that say about his level of power? He didn't want to think about it, hoping he was overanalyzing. And there was something familiar about this man, but he couldn't figure out why.

The mysterious man bowed, his arm sliding across his stomach. "Apologies. I'm sure you—or at least three of you—are used to her eccentric ways. I admit the last time you met she had become a bit overzealous with her ambitions. But right now, it's best we all remain calm, don't you think?" He stood upright again. "Now then, let me make this clear. I am not against ending Her Highness's life. However, if you give us the stone, then we will be on our way, and we will not harm any of you. A fair trade."

"This is not good," Marsh whispered. "We cannot let anything happen to her. But giving them the stone…how many people will suffer?"

Marsh was right. The logical course of action would be to not let personal feelings get in the way of the greater good. But screw logic—when did Kyo ever let that determine his actions? In a situation like this, he didn't know what his parents might do. They always put the people first, but would they have sacrificed one of their own to do it?

"What are we supposed to do?" Jaune asked, his head turned as much to Hayner as possible. "We can't let her get hurt."

"Don't trade the stone just for me," Krysta shouted. "Who knows what they might do with it. We can't let there be another Calmarock."

For a moment no one spoke. Kyo didn't know how to resolve such a situation, and he bet no one else did either. But he did know this was an opportunity to get what he wanted and fix one problem. "Why don't you sweeten the deal a bit?" He motioned to Marsh with his head. "Cure him of the corruption. You want to talk about a life for the stone, but don't ignore all the lives that were lost during Sybilla's rampage earlier this year, including people close to us."

The man stroked his chin and narrowed his eyes. "That was then. We are speaking of here and now. Still..." He approached Marsh and crouched. "This one is a bit more important than the princess. At least he helps keep you all alive, while she, from what I hear, simply rages."

He placed his hand upon Marsh's head, and azure-and-violet streams of energy immediately escaped from the cleric's body and into the man's hand. With each passing second, the corruption faded, and Marsh's eyes drooped. The man pulled his hand away, and Marsh fell limp, not a trace of the corruption left behind.

"There we are. No more threat of a shade," the man announced. "He'll need to sleep it off but will recover in due time. Can't let the pawns be without their healer now, can we?"

Kyo released a long sigh of relief as tension left his body, despite the vines wrapped tight around him. Whatever happened to the accrue stone, at least Marsh would live. No more concern about having to put him down, no more of his attempts to end his own life prematurely. His eyes welled, but he held the tears of happiness back. There'd be time for that later. As for Krysta, he'd have to leave that to the royal guard. What happened with the stone would be up to them, though he was sure they wouldn't willingly sacrifice their princess to keep it. As incredibly annoying as she could be, he didn't want to see her dead. And with any luck, Rosette had kept herself hidden in the airship and out of harm's way.

"Two lives for the price of one stone. That's more than a fair deal, isn't it?" the man asked, making slow strides toward Hayner. When he said nothing in return, the man crouched in front of him. "Please bear in mind my patience does have its limits. I don't want to be out here all day." He stood again and spoke louder. "But if these two lives still aren't enough, Sybilla has been itching for some exercise and Ueno is barely more than a full day's walk from here. Not that the three of us need to rely on such a slow method of travel."

"Really?" Sybilla asked with glee in her voice, like a child being told she'd get her favorite treat. "Oh, please don't give him the stone yet so I can have some fun."

"Don't you dare," Krysta shouted. "You're not going to harm anyone. You try it and I'll roast you alive!"

Sybilla scoffed. "You won't be doing much of anything with those nixium cuffs on you." She gently backhanded Blanq's arm. "See, I told you we'd have a good use for those when we swiped them."

Kyo tensed and stared daggers at his captors. Of course they'd let her loose in Ueno. After Calmarock, there was no reason to doubt they'd do anything to get what they wanted. And she may not stop at half the population this time. That settled it—they couldn't keep denying them the stone. But there had to be another way. What would stop them from turning the entire town into shades immediately after they got it like she tried to do in Oasis? Ideas of how to resolve this flooded his mind, each worse than the last. He had no idea what to do, but giving in could cause a total catastrophe. Even if by some miracle the Aurora turned around and arrived, they'd be in no shape to help.

"Kira," Krysta shouted. "Just do it. Give them the stone."

All eyes turned to Kira, who released an aggravated shout then a sigh of acceptance. "Yes, Your Highness." She struggled with her bindings. "I'll need my arm free to get it."

"Of course," the man said, loosening the vines enough to allow her to reach into her enchanted pouch.

While anyone could rummage through another's pouch, they'd be reaching in blindly. Depending on how much it contained, it could take hours or even days to find what they were looking for.

Kira wiggled about, reaching into her pouch. Though it appeared to only be large enough to contain her hand, her entire forearm disappeared inside. A common and useful enchantment for travelers. A moment later, she retracted her hand, the stone gripped in her fingers. The man reached down and took the stone, examining it as the single strand of her energy floated within.

"There. You have what you want," Krysta shouted, the rage in her voice loud and clear. "Now leave, and I swear if you dare touch Ueno, or any place for that matter, you *will* regret it."

"We appreciate doing business with you." The man tucked the stone into his own pouch and made his way back to his comrades. With a flick of his wrist, the vines rebound Kira's arm. "And as promised, *we* will not harm any of you."

He placed his hand on the centipede. It squirmed and writhed, and after a few seconds, the corruption burst to life, enshrouding its body in a shadowy aura, its beady eyes glowing with a golden hue.

Kyo's jaw hung open. This man, whoever he was, had turned a feral into a shade in an instant. How? This wasn't good, not at all. Kyo put all his strength into attempting to loosen the vines, desperately trying to get into a position to defend himself, but to no avail. Despite their efforts, none of the others could seem to either as their grunts were drowned out by a high-pitched shriek from the fully corrupted feral.

Every member of the crew had left the airship and joined Blanq by her side as a white light enveloped them all.

"You said you wouldn't hurt anyone," Krysta shouted.

"We aren't. But this…" the man motioning to the feral. "Consider it a test for the little one." His eyes drifted between the bound mages. "I know you won't believe me even if I explain, but my actions are to save countless lives."

In a flash, they were gone, leaving the seven mages utterly helpless against a feral shade. Despite the man's absence, the vines held tight. Kira attempted to gnaw at them. Kyo couldn't summon his swords with his hands bound at his sides, as there'd be no room for them to appear. The same could be said for Roland's polearm. Hayner attempted to cut through them with small, jagged rock bursting from the ground, but it couldn't cut through, a testament to that man's power and the amount of magic placed into the vines.

The centipede turned toward them and shrieked, skittering forward. It would only take seconds for it to reach them. Small, jagged rocks shot from the ground and smashed into the shade's face, but it barely paused before continuing.

"Rosette!" Krysta shouted.

The young girl ran onto the deck of the airship and looked over the railing. She hopped on, launched herself as the feral reached its prey, and landed a powerful blow to the top of its head. Pushing herself off, she landed on her feet and held her fists up by her face, one leg in front of the other as the centipede fell onto its side, wiggled, then righted itself.

"Oh shit, thank the Altruists you're okay. Be careful, please," Roland pleaded, his eyes wide with concern.

While Kyo didn't stop his attempts to loosen the vines, slip his hand between them, anything he could so he'd be able to help, his eyes were fixed on Rosette. He knew she was strong and had a large magic pool, but she was still a kid. But at the moment, this eleven-year-old girl was their only defense against certain death.

Chapter 22

Kyo clenched his fists at his sides, staring at where Sybilla and her comrades had stood a moment ago. While relieved they were gone, he hated the feeling of helplessness that came with the threat they left behind. It shouldn't be up to Rosette to protect them but the other way around. Yet with that man's vines still tightly wrapped around him and the others and Krysta's wrists bound by nixium cuffs, they had no choice but to put their faith in the young girl.

"You can do this," he muttered. Though against a feral shade, he had no idea what to expect.

"Jaune, you can still cast spells, right? We'll assist her in whatever way we can," Hayner said.

The ground rumbled, and several pillars of flat earth shot up from beneath the centipede, launching it into the air. Rosette took the chance to jump and land a kick at its underbelly, sending it tumbling back to the ground.

"That's it! Aim for the underbelly when you can. It'll be weakest there," Kira shouted.

After a few seconds of writhing on its side, it returned upright and released a high-pitched screech identical to the human shades. It charged forward, ramming headfirst into a barrier summoned by Jaune.

Rosette crouched then ran with her fist clenched at her side. "Take away the barrier!"

The moment the barrier vanished, she landed a punch on the centipede's face then another and another. It raised its head to avoid her reach, its tiny front legs swiping as if to knock her away.

"Rosette, on your left," Roland cried out.

She turned too late. The rear of the centipede swung around and slammed into her hard, sending her crashing through the exterior of the airship. It rushed after her, widening the hole, wood splintering across the ground.

The sounds of shattering wood, clanging metal, and screeching could be heard from within the airship as it shook harshly from the massive creature chasing its prey. Krysta released a startled scream, leaning against the railing to brace herself as the airship rocked beneath her. No way would it be able to fly properly after this, even if the engines remained intact.

Kyo glanced to his right at Marsh's unconscious body. One mage out cold, another with a broken leg, and even if this battle ended in their favor, they'd be stranded. He clenched his teeth, mentally cursing how things went so badly so quickly. To top it off, they lost the accrue stone.

"Come on, Rosette," Kyo muttered, "give us something to be happy about."

"She'll win. My daughter isn't about to be beaten by some giant bug, corrupted or not," Roland said without a hint of uncertainty, eyes fixated on the airship.

The shade broke through the starboard side and made a wide turn, swinging its head as if to search for its target. A few seconds later, Rosette appeared on the deck next to Krysta.

"Keep it away for a few seconds," Rosette shouted.

The shade dashed forward but again rammed into a barrier, this time bouncing off and flipping onto its back. It righted itself, but any attempt to go around met with another barrier or pillar of earth jutting against its head to block its path or send it rolling on its side.

A blue glow emitted from Rosette's forehead and hands as she clasped them together in front of her chest. "Altruist Guardian, I seek thine aid. In these darkest of times when all hope fades. To protect the life which thine hath laid. In this time of need, I call you by name. Fuglavus!"

Jagged shards of ice shot up from behind Rosette and spread outward, forming the shape of a large bird with its wings outstretched. It shattered like glass, that bird becoming a living, breathing creature that took to the air with a loud chirp. Snow white and sky blue feathers reflected beautifully in the sunlight as if they were still composed of ice. Another loud chirp escaped its long, pointed beak, its tail seeming to shed ice shards that vanished before falling too far. Circling above the shade, the Altruist fired a beam of white energy from its beak, coating any part of the feral it touched with a thick layer of solid ice.

"Whoa, that's a new one," Kyo said, staring in awe.

"She hasn't only been working on her physical strength and combat these past few months. Though she had to figure that out all on her own." Roland's lips formed a small smile. "She is really something else."

"It won't matter if she can't put out enough power to break through the corruption and kill the shade. No easy feat," Hayner said.

"Then you and Jaune better keep helping how you can," Roland retorted.

Kyo tried to think of ways he might be able to help too. Controlling where spells appeared and maintaining them tended to be more difficult without use of his body. He kept his eyes focused on the fight, looking for an opportunity to lend a hand.

Rosette jumped off the side of the airship and landed a hard kick to the shade's head. It released a loud screech and wiggled violently. Fuglavus attempted another attack, but the shade shattered the ice binding it to the ground and skittered away. Rosette and her Altruist gave chase. In its attempt to escape, the shade circled around and charged right for the bound group lying helpless on the ground.

"It's going to crush us!" Kyo shouted.

A series of barriers appeared as a curved wall, redirecting the shade but not without its large body slamming against them as it turned sharply.

Kyo released a heavy sigh. "Thanks, Jaune."

"Don't worry," Jaune said. "I'll make sure we stay safe."

Fuglavus attempted to freeze the shade, each missed shot leaving clumps of jagged ice behind or for the centipede to ram through. It turned its head and spit out a gelatinous green goop, which the Altruist barely avoided. It landed close to Rosette, who squeaked and stopped in her tracks. The substance ate away at the grass beneath it and slowly sank into the ground.

"It looks acidic," Kira said.

"It can do that? Even while it's a shade? Oh great." Kyo raised his head. "Rosette, don't let that stuff touch you!"

"I won't," Rosette shouted and ran after the shade. The Altruist and the centipede were locked in an exchange of firing and avoiding each other's attacks. A large rock popped out of the earth and slammed into the shade's head, distracting it long enough for it to be struck by Fuglavus's beam, freezing many of the legs on its left side to the ground. Rosette closed the distance and kicked upward, making its head snap back.

"There are apparently differences between a shade formed from a feral and one formed from a human. That does not bode well, especially if that man can corrupt humans and ferals alike on a whim." While Hayner spoke, his eyes remained fixed on the battle. "This adds a whole new level of complication."

"Alternatively, that thing's acidic spit might not be related to magic at all but a natural ability that comes from its biology. Since the corruption is an infection of the magic, it wouldn't affect something like that," Kira suggested.

"I hope you're right. We don't need shades that can use magic," Hayner said.

Jaune grunted as he shifted within the vines. "That man is more dangerous than Sybilla or Blanq. We'll need to let the Aurora and His Majesty know as soon as possible,"

The shade released an ear-piercing shriek. Kyo groaned and clenched his eyes shut, unable to cover his ears. He peeked one eye open, watching Fuglavus crash to the ground. Rosette crouched, hands covering her ears. Kyo's hearing faded in and out, his eardrums vibrating.

With a shout from Hayner, a pillar of earth knocked against the bottom of the shade's head, interrupting the sonic attack. Kyo lay there panting, his ears ringing, sounds fading in and out. He spotted Krysta hanging over the airship's railing, barely moving.

Fuglavus attempted to stand, but the shade crawled over and curled its body around it, squeezing tight. The Altruist released a shriek of pain then blasted the shade in the face, coating it in ice. Yet it didn't let up, gripping like a serpent. The shade reared its head back then headbutted Fuglavus, the Altruist's body going limp.

Rosette jumped expertly atop the segments of the shade's body and delivered a swift punch to its exposed underbelly close to its head. Hayner caused rocks to rise from beneath the ground and launch at the centipede, continuously pelting it, not shy about reusing the same rocks continuously. Despite continued attacks from the two mages, its grip held steady.

"You have to protect that Altruist," Roland demanded. "Rosette needs all the help she can get."

"We're trying," Hayner said, keeping a stern focus on the shade and casting his spells. "That feral turning into a shade makes it difficult to injure."

The shade's upper segments dodged and weaved, attempting to avoid incoming rocks, occasionally spitting acid at them.

Rosette screamed, gripping her arm.

"What happened? Are you okay?" Roland shouted.

Hayner clicked his tongue. "Spitting its acid on the flying rocks is causing some to splash everywhere. If I keep it up, I might harm her further."

"If only I could help," Kira grumbled, glaring at the shade. "I want to beat on that damn thing so badly."

"Hayner, keep doing what you're doing. I have an idea," Jaune said.

Kyo glanced at Jaune, the grimace on his face showing his leg still caused him pain. The vines must have been squeezing it. While the guy might be timid at times, Kyo understood why Jaune was among the royal guard. He gave it his all when it counted.

"If it won't hurt Rosette, then do whatever you can to help," Kyo said. "Otherwise, I can try to use wind to keep the splash back away from her."

The rocks continued to rise from the ground, pelting the shade in the face. It slightly reared its head, and as it spit out another glob of acid, a curved barrier appeared, coating its head like a mask. The barrier formed in such close proximity the acid splashed back toward the centipede, a thick layer coating its face. It immediately released Fuglavus and dug into the ground.

Rosette ran to the Altruist as it lay on its side, panting heavily. "Are you okay? You have to get up before it comes back."

"Do you think it's dead?" Kira asked.

"They never die. The avatar returns to where it came from. But no, if it was defeated, its body would disappear." Roland grunted, wiggling and attempting to slip through the vines. "It's still got some fight in it, but it'll need time to recover."

"Let's hope the shade gives them that time. At least you're all able to hurt it. Last time I fought a shade, I couldn't do a damn thing." Kyo knew they'd grown stronger since then, but it was nice to see the results play out before him. He watched as Rosette rubbed her arm, and even from this distance, he could see her chest rising and falling at a quickened pace.

Fuglavus stirred, releasing a weak cry. One massive wing rose and fell.

At this, Rosette perked up. "Are you feeling better? That thing might come back." She reached out to gently pet the Altruist's beak. "Can you still fight?"

At first it lay there, breathing heavily. The ground trembled, calmed, then trembled again. The shade was on the move. Fuglavus stumbled onto its talons, spread its wings, and released a loud caw.

Rosette punched her fist into her palm. "Okay, let's kick its butt."

Fuglavus dipped its body, allowing Rosette to climb onto its back. With her as its passenger, it took to the air and circled overhead.

"At least she learned how to make barriers like the rest of us. Otherwise, I'd be a nervous wreck about her falling." Roland groaned. "Still, I might pass out from stress if this drags on any longer, She's strong but she's a kid."

"Yeah, she is. But from what I've seen since meeting you two, she can do this. You said so yourself, right?" Kyo asked.

Roland's lips tightened and his eyes narrowed. "Yeah. I did."

"Be careful, Rosette," Krysta called from the airship.

The shade erupted from the ground, its body rising into the air like the stem of a plant, spitting acid upward. Fuglavus dodged and descended, spewing its magical energy, coating a large section of the centipede's body in ice. The shade slammed against the ground, shattering the ice, then skittered away from the airship. Whenever it turned, it took the chance to launch more acid at its target while avoiding Fuglavus' attacks.

"Hayner," Rosette called from the air. "Can you keep it on its back?"

"That's a tall order," Hayner grumbled. "Especially from this distance."

The shade and Altruist continued to exchange attacks. As requested, Hayner gave it something else to dodge. Wide pillars of earth shot upward in the shade's path. It maneuvered between them, narrowly avoiding a few. Fuglavus fired a burst of energy in front of the shade and right next to a pillar, causing it to pause. In that half second, another column of earth launched the shade's front half from the ground. More followed, spell after spell until its entire body flailed in the air. As it came back down, more dirt and solid rock rose like tendrils, wrapping around the shade. They both flipped its body and bound it to the ground.

The shade wiggled and screeched, releasing another sonic assault to the ears. Hayner grunted and kept his eyes focused. One more tendril of earth appeared, this one entering the shade's open mouth, silencing it.

"Thank you," Kyo said, panting and clenching his eyes shut for a second.

Fuglavus flew in a tight circle, spewing more magical energy from its beak until the ice formed a gigantic icicle floating in the air.

"Jaune, launch it down," Rosette shouted.

A reflective barrier appeared above the icicle and rammed into it. The icicle launched at high speed, piercing the shade's underbelly. Its desperate writhing became wilder, the earth binding it falling apart piece by piece.

Fuglavus dove straight down. The earth bindings attempted to reform to keep the shade in place. As the Altruist neared its enemy, Rosette let go, free falling.

Kyo—and he was sure everyone else—held their breath as they watched their young friend descend. When she met the icicle, the impact of her fist against it reverberated, the force pushing the icicle's tip through the shade's body. In that moment, its body stiffened then fell limp, the corruption fading away. Cracks formed through the ice then shattered into countless shards.

Rosette fell, but Fuglavus swooped in to catch her, swerving, then landing in front of the others.

"Rosette, are you okay?" Roland asked quickly, eyes wide and desperate. "Did you hurt yourself? Can you walk? What about your arm?"

"That was so damn incredible." Kyo smiled wide, his heart filled with pride for her. He wasn't even upset that, in his mind, she was a better Aurora candidate than himself. "Marsh isn't going to believe what he missed, that was Aurora level awesome."

Rosette climbed off Fuglavus and stumbled toward the group, falling onto her knees in front of Roland. Her eyes were half-lidded and her breathing heavy, but she wore a proud smile. "That was crazy," she said, giggling weakly. She leaned forward to show Roland her arm, her bicep red and with some layers of skin burned away. "It hurts, but I'll be okay."

Roland frowned as he stared at her arm but then glanced at her face. "I am so proud of you, kiddo. So, so proud."

Her smile brightened as she hugged her bound father the best she could.

"That really was something. We can put in a good word for you if you want to join the royal guard when you're older," Kira suggested. "But for now, do you think you have enough strength to get us out of these vines?"

Rosette nodded. Starting with Roland, she tore at the vines while Fuglavus carefully coated them in ice to weaken them.

Kyo couldn't wait to move freely. Witnessing such a spectacle had put him in a better mood. They may have lost the accrue stone, but somehow, they'd all survived, and Marsh was back to normal. For the moment, he resisted the urge to think of what Sybilla and her comrades would do with the stone and focus on the positives.

But one thing stuck in his mind. The possible implications of that man calling them pawns, hoping it meant nothing more than this moment of doing the hard work of retrieving the stone.

Chapter 23

The bindings fell away, Kyo's joints popping as he stretched his limbs. Even with no interference, freeing Marsh was no quick task. The amount of magic contained within the vines must have been immense. Rosette tugged at them while Kyo summoned one of his swords. He cast the spell on his blade to make it sharper, emitting that deep cerulean glow, to have any effect on the vines. One by one, they freed the others, all of whom stood except Jaune, who remained seated and kept his broken leg outstretched, and Marsh, still unconscious.

"Is everyone okay?" Krysta asked, approaching the group with her wrists still bound behind her back.

"Yeah, fantastic." Kyo gripped his hair and grunted in frustration. "If you ignore the accrue stone being taken and our favorite duo now being a trio."

Sybilla and Blanq were bad enough on their own, but this new addition, and one powerful enough to keep Sybilla under control, made his head spin. They would not be able to handle this without the Aurora. If Alden didn't find a way to destroy the accrue stones soon, Kyo didn't want to think about what could happen. Alden probably didn't know about any of this. With any luck, he could remain hidden from both the Aurora and the psychotic trio until he succeeded.

"On that note, we won't want to be here when they come back, so we'd better get our asses moving. We're clearly not flying anywhere, so hiking to Ueno is our best bet," Kira said as she hurried toward a piece of broken wood from the airship and brought it to Jaune. She then grabbed some of the discarded vine and made a splint for his leg.

"You think they're coming back?" Rosette asked, leaning against Fuglavus and running her fingers through its feathers.

Kira paused her work and reached into her pouch. She pulled out the accrue stone and looked at the group with a mischievous grin. It shifted into the appearance of a light pink rubber ball, the kind kids used to throw against a wall for a variety of games, then back into its original form. "Proficient might be a stretch, but I have a little skill in illusion spells. What they took was a round rock from the pile we found the accrue stone in." She frowned and sighed. "Shame, it was such a nice smooth rock too."

Kyo's eyes widened. He couldn't believe it. She held the stone in her hand. It hadn't been taken. His legs almost gave out from the relief that washed over him.

"Kira, I could kiss you," he exclaimed, bouncing on the balls of his feet.

"Try it and this stone is going up your ass," Kira warned with a sharp glare.

"I was hoping you had something to trade it off with," Krysta said.

"It was a gamble, Your Highness, but it worked out. Good thinking." Kira tightened the vines around Jaune's leg, who grunted in response.

"So, we still have the stone. Okay, that's great. Let's hurry up and get going," Roland approached Fuglavus and pet its beak. "Thanks for helping Rosette," he said in a gentle voice.

Fuglavus chirped and rubbed its beak against Roland's hand. From its talons upward, it disappeared, blue and white sparkles rose into the air in its wake.

Kyo ceased any movement as a thought occurred. "It *is* great, but why do we still have it? Blanq is basically a master of illusion spells. She should have seen through it, right?"

"Maybe she wasn't thinking about looking for illusion spells in the moment." Hayner tapped his finger on his cheek. "Though that's a stretch. Based on what I've heard of her, she should have noticed signs, especially from an amateur caster like Kira." Kira shouted a protest, but he ignored it. "Regardless, let's not poke the treasure, as they say. Your Highness, were there any survivors among the crew?"

Krysta frowned and shook her head. "No. I'm sorry. I tried to protect them, but Sybilla snuck the cuffs on me. Not that it would have mattered. I'm still drained from venting. All I could do was tell Rosette to stay hidden unless I specifically told her to come out."

"I see," Hayner said in a quiet voice. He picked up Jaune's axe and used it to snap the chains of Krysta's cuffs. "Bend forward and extend your arms behind you as best you can please."

Krysta reluctantly complied. He brought the axe down on one cuff as she screamed.

"Trust me," he said, his gaze meeting hers.

After several more strikes, the cuff was damaged enough that he and Roland could pry it open. They repeated the process with the other cuff. Krysta breathed deeply as she rubbed one wrist with her hand.

Hayner smirked. "I hope I didn't frighten you." His face turned serious again. "We won't reach Ueno before nightfall. We'll travel west during what daylight we have then camp for the night. We should get there sometime late tomorrow. Kira, Your Highness, let's gather food and anything useful from the airship and do so quickly. If anyone wishes to discard their armor, they can do so now and place it in the airship. It won't be much use anymore."

Kyo was more than happy to oblige. While the three of them headed for the airship, he removed his leather armor.

Roland sauntered to Jaune and cast a barrier beneath him, raising it slightly off the ground. "I'll carry him for a while."

"I got the bedhead," Kyo said, doing the same for Marsh. He stared at his friend for a moment, a smile forming on his lips. While Kyo wouldn't go so far as to thank the mysterious man, he could breathe easy knowing Marsh was no longer under threat of becoming a shade.

They left the broken airship behind, following Hayner's lead on their journey toward Ueno. It'd take time for Jaune's leg to be healed and for another airship to pick them up. Maybe Kyo would get to do a bit of sightseeing after all, explore his father's home for the first time. Some good local food would take his mind off things for a while.

During their travel, a few ferals approached them with hostility but were chased off without having to be slain. It was for the best. They were large, furred rodents that brought a pungent odor wherever they went. According to Roland, their flesh wasn't any better.

Several hours into their trip, Kyo felt the barrier shift. He turned to find Marsh running his hand over his face as he groaned.

"Hey, look who's awake. Good, I was getting a bit sick of carrying you," Kyo said with a smirk. The group stopped and Kyo crouched beside Marsh. "How do you feel?"

"I feel weak," Marsh groaned barely above a whisper. "But good."

"Well, a bit of good news, you're not corrupted anymore," Kyo declared.

Marsh stared at Kyo and blinked a few times then looked over his own body. He peeked under his robe for good measure. "Oh, thank Tutelvus."

Kyo narrowed his eyes. "So, no more attempts to end yourself, right? You're done with that?"

Marsh frowned and nodded. "Yes. I am so sorry. I was a fool and put you all in additional danger. I felt so hopeless. I could not bear waiting for the inevitable. It was—"

"It's fine," Roland assured. "Something like that, we can't pretend to know how it feels. And hopefully we'll never find out."

Marsh stumbled, but Kyo caught him and helped him to stand. "In retrospect," the cleric started, "it would have been best to accept my fate, keep you all out of danger, and accept that you would have to end me. But in the moment, I was so afraid."

Krysta embraced him. "We know. And we're so glad that you're okay now."

Rosette grabbed his hand and jumped up and down. "Yeah, you're all better, and once you get your magic back you can help us kick their butts."

Marsh smiled and nodded, pulling away from the hug. "I intend to. I will not let this scare me away from doing what I said I would. I plan on helping you all until the end, especially now that Sybilla and Blanq are free again." His eyes widened and he gasped. "The accrue stone. Did they take it?"

"Take it easy." Kyo patted his back. "I'll catch you up on what happened."

As they continued their trek, Kyo recounted what had happened after Marsh had passed out, going into exceptional detail about Rosette's fight. Each time he praised her, she smiled wide and giggled.

"I am sorry I do not have my magic back yet to help with your injury, Rosette," Marsh said.

"It's okay. If I don't touch it, it's not too bad."

"My girl is a tough one," Roland said with a proud smirk. "We'll get it checked out at the clinic once we get to Ueno."

"While I am glad I was cured and we retained possession of the accrue stone, that encounter brings a number of questions and concerns," Marsh said, walking with his arms crossed over his chest. "Top among them, that unknown man. We already know Sybilla's power is on the level of an Aurora, and though Blanq is not one for direct combat, we can make the same assumption for her. From what you tell me, this man must be at least on that same level."

"It's possible they met him while in Spellnix Hold and escaped together," Hayner mused. "Once we're back in Alderdeem, I'll put forth a query with whoever is left there to confirm his identity. We'll need to let the Aurora know what happened as well." He glanced at Jaune. "How are you holding up?"

Kira grunted, having taken charge of carrying him via a barrier when Marsh awakened. "Oh, you don't have to ask him. He's doing just fine. Lying back, relaxing, carried like he is the one with royal blood."

"My leg is *broken*," Jaune shot back. "I'd prefer it to be fine and I walk on my own. But I don't have that choice right now. And can you try to keep it steady? It hurts when it—" A stern look from Kira silenced him.

"A lot of things don't make sense, but right now all we have to worry about is getting the stone back to Alderdeem and letting the Aurora handle those three." Every time Kyo saw them, he hoped it'd be the last time. Yet they kept popping up like weeds.

"Or maybe those four," Krysta hissed. "Now that they're free, they might grab their good friend Alden to join them again."

Kyo clenched his jaw and stared daggers at her. "They are *not* friends. He was forced to help them, and right now there are three accrue stones not protected by enchantments, so they wouldn't need him."

Krysta huffed. "As of now, he is still considered a cooperator in their actions. And I believe he should be punished the same as them. You're just biased because he's your family."

"He's trying to find a way to destroy the accrue stones," Kyo retorted. "Even Cedric couldn't manage it. Destroying them will be the best for everyone."

"It would be," Krysta agreed. "But he could have easily lied to your face, and your dense head wouldn't realize it. The only way we ensure tragedies like Calmarock never happen again is to be rid of everyone involved."

"Both of you, enough," Roland barked. "Like Kyo said, we'll let the Aurora handle it, and whatever happens, happens. Who is punished and how is out of our hands, so there's no point in debating it."

Rosette scrunched her face and stomped her foot, forming a small crater in the dirt. "Besides, you promised you wouldn't fight like this anymore."

That promise had slipped Kyo's mind. He stared at Krysta, certain she was trying to will a hole in his head with her eyes the same as he was doing to her. She didn't know Alden like he did.

"Alden told me…" He got firm glares from Krysta and Roland, but he continued. "The accrue stones were part of the reason why my parents were killed." Their faces softened. "Whatever it was they were trying to stop involved those stones. Alden was their best friend, and their deaths hit him hard. That's why I believe him when he says he wants them destroyed."

Silence fell over the group, and he hoped it stayed that way for a while. The day's events wore on him, his legs feeling like they had weights attached to them. The horizon nearly hid the sun completely, so they'd need to find a place to camp shortly. The land offered no shortage of hills and cliffs to take advantage of.

* * *

A crackling campfire lit the faces of the group as they ate. Snake meat was hardly Kyo's preferred meal, but when a massive python came at them thinking they are easy targets, why say no? Roland and Hayner worked together to skin and debone it then placed the meat on sticks for them to cook over the fire. It tasted a lot like a cockatrice and should keep him full for the night.

After the day's events, Jaune had reservations about being out in the open where a fire could be seen from far away. Even tucked under a curved cliffside, they were fully exposed, should Sybilla and her comrades come looking for them. So, they agreed the fire would remain lit for as long as they needed it for cooking and no longer.

After taking the final bite of her dinner, Krysta tossed the stick to the ground and grunted. "I don't like this." She hunched forward, face buried in her hands. "They threatened Ueno, then we gave them a fake stone. There's no reason to believe they won't make good on their threat once they find out. It was a decision in the heat of the moment, but what are we supposed to do?"

"There isn't much we *can* do," Kira said before tearing off a piece of meat with her teeth.

"Ueno might end up like Calmarock, or worse, and you're saying we can't do anything? We already know from Aquarin Port that Sybilla can make people more susceptible to the corruption, and now this new friend of theirs can corrupt people directly," Krysta growled through clenched teeth, struggling to keep her voice low.

"I do not like it either," Marsh said. "However, for the life of me, I cannot think of a valid course of action."

"Besides, it was your idea to give them a fake by calling out Kira, wasn't it?" Kyo asked. "Why are you complaining now?"

Krysta clicked her tongue. "I thought we'd at least try to protect Ueno, keep them safe."

Hayner gestured to the campfire, dirt and rock rising from the ground to smother it. Krysta followed by creating a block of ice and placing it atop the new dirt mound.

"Your Highness, what happens to Ueno isn't our responsibility," Hayner said.

"Excuse me?" Krysta asked slowly with wide, angry eyes.

"Our duty is to Alderdeem and its people. To that end, we absolutely could not allow them to have the stone." Hayner kept his eyes firmly on Krysta. "Ueno is a small town that would unfortunately be easy for those three to wipe out, given what we know of their power. Alderdeem, however, would be much more difficult so long as they are without an accrue stone."

Krysta shot to her feet. "So you're saying we let whatever happens happen and forget about it? It would be our fault."

"Your Highness," Jaune started, seated against the cliffside with his broken leg outstretched, "sometimes there is no right or wrong decision. Sometimes, there are just decisions. Alderdeem is on high alert since Sybilla and Blanq escaped. Every enforcer and member of the royal guard is ready in case they decide to do something. By now, word will have spread to many towns across the continent. Ueno's leadership should be aware of what could happen."

Kira nodded. "We have two accrue stones in Alderdeem after all, and they have none. I bet those three aren't going to let them go. Giving them one would make it far easier for them to get the other two."

After a few seconds of silence, Krysta sat and punched the ground beside her.

Roland reached into his enchanted pouch, grunting as he pulled a sleeping bag from the too-small opening. "I can't say I want to leave the people of Ueno in harm's way. But wouldn't giving them the real stone mean a better reason to repeat the events of Calmarock there? They'd need to fill the stone with magic before they used it."

Rosette ran her hands over the ground, tossing any rocks she found. "I don't want anyone to get hurt though." She placed the sleeping bag flat on the ground. "Can't the Aurora go and protect them?"

"Maybe. But they'd need to know to come here first, kiddo." Roland pulled another sleeping bag from his pouch. "They might not be somewhere immediately reachable. "

Kyo did the same. He'd packed it when he left Mistwell over six months ago. Funny he hadn't needed to use it before tonight.

"When we reach Ueno and get Jaune settled into the clinic, I will go to the chancellor and contact His Majesty," Hayner said. "That or Spellnix Hold would be the best places to start. I will also let her know of the threat and what to expect. The best we can do is provide them with information." He shifted his attention to Krysta. "Does that sit well with you, Your Highness?"

Krysta took slow, deep breaths before nodding. "That's better than nothing."

"The longer we stay, the better chance those three have of taking the stone from us," Hayner said.

Kira stretched her arms above her head and yawned. "And while you're at it, make sure His Majesty sends us another airship so we can get home."

"Not like we can trust anything those three say. What was that crap about doing what they're doing to save lives?" Kyo spat. "All they've done so far is end them. So even if they said they'd leave Ueno alone if we gave them the stone, I don't believe them."

As everyone settled down for the night, Kyo lay in his sleeping bag and stared at the night sky. Out here, there were so many sparkling stars to get lost in. His thoughts turned to his parents and the nights they'd spent stargazing on the roof. If only they were here, they'd be an enormous help. The image of either or both of them beating the crap out of Sybilla, Blanq, and that mystery man brought a brief smile to his lips. But as quickly as it appeared, it faded as the thought of Ueno becoming another Calmarock filled his mind. Like Krysta, he didn't like the idea of not ensuring the town's safety, but against those three, they didn't have much choice. They had been allowed to live, but their patience, especially Sybilla's, was limited.

Chapter 24

Nestled in a cozy patch of land at a lower elevation than its surroundings sat a humble town. Most homes lacked a second story but seemed to all be made of the same material given their matching chestnut coloring. Roads were wide, with trees and tall grass filling the excess space. Despite its small size compared to Mistwell, it still reminded Kyo of home, simple and peaceful. To their right and up a gradual hill stood a tall, proud marble building of completely different architecture with soaring, white columns lining the front.

"I think I found the Pantheon's Library," Kyo said, staring at the massive four-story structure.

"Can we go see?" Rosette asked.

"We're going to the clinic to get you and Jaune patched up before anything else. We'll see how long we have to wait for an airship to come get us." Roland placed his hand on Rosette's back to guide her along.

Krysta's eyes lingered on the library. "I wouldn't mind visiting it myself. It's far larger than the library in the palace."

The group made their way into Ueno. The roads, which were more dirt paths than anything, could hardly be considered busy even by Mistwell's standards. But given the size of the town, they could be considered full of its citizens, some watering flowers outside their homes, others carrying bags of groceries. Everyone they passed had deep black hair and monolid eyes, much like his dad. Hayner broke away to approach a woman. Kyo couldn't hear the conversation, but she pointed down the road then swished her hand as if giving directions.

Minutes later, they found themselves entering a clinic, the only other person in the waiting room an old man seated in the corner.

"Welcome," the woman behind the counter said in a cheery voice as she bowed at the waist, each syllable drawn out and separated.

Once Hayner explained about the injured, a man in a white robe appeared from the back and helped Jaune onto his good leg and guided him in for treatment. The rest took seats in the waiting area. Eventually, the old man was called back, then a few minutes later, it was Rosette's turn, escorted by Roland.

"Jaune is going to owe me big for carrying his ass so much," Kira grumbled.

"Didn't you insist, saying anyone else would probably drop him?" Krysta asked with a smirk on her lips.

Kira's face began forming an angry glare, but she caught herself, groaning and slumping in her chair instead. "I just got used to how he moves while on the barrier, that's all."

Kyo chuckled then asked Marsh, "How's your magic feeling?"

"After twenty-four hours, I would say it is less than a quarter replenished. I suspect it takes longer to recover when it is forcibly removed." Marsh leaned forward to look at Krysta. "How is yours fairing after venting?"

"Hmm." She paused. "Maybe three-fourths if I had to estimate."

On average, the time for magic to fully recover after venting was about three days. So, her answer sounded about right. Kyo focused his senses on the magical energy flowing within him. With less magic came less warmth with cool gaps in spaces, like holes punched into a sheet of paper. This gave him an estimate of how much magic he had remaining.

He stared out the window at an empty stall used to sell goods across the street. He'd never trade Mistwell for anything, but he couldn't help but wonder what it would have been like to grow up here. Was it something his parents considered before they had him? Though if he had, he may not have known Alden. That alone made him glad they decided to live in Mistwell.

Some time later, Rosette emerged with a bandage wrapped around her bicep, Roland beside her. "I'm done. It's mostly fine, but they put on an ointment to help with the rest of the healing." She scrunched her nose. "It kind of stinks though."

"Bear with it, kiddo. Cleric's orders." Roland pulled his flask from his coat and took a drink. "So, we're just waiting on Jaune?"

Hayner stood. "Yes, and a broken leg will surely take longer to mend. I'm going to visit the chancellor and get in contact with His Majesty. If you all want to visit the Pantheon's Library, feel free. But either be there or be here so it's easy to find you."

Rosette gasped, bouncing on the balls of her feet. "Let's go! Let's go!"

"Only for a little bit. Anyone else coming?" Roland asked.

"I'll stay here until the klutz comes out," Kira said.

"I'll check it out, even if it is a library." Kyo rose from the chair to join them.

Marsh and Krysta agreed, and together the five left the clinic. While Kyo wished to explore more of his dad's birthplace, the visit came at a terrible time. Sybilla and her comrades were bound to discover the stone they took was a fake if they hadn't already. He wouldn't be surprised if they turned up here looking for them. As they strolled through town, his body remained tense as he kept his eyes open for any signs of them.

Roland paused mid-step. "Do you hear that?"

Kyo strained his ears, listening for anything out of the ordinary. Seconds passed, and as he was about to speak, he heard it. A high-pitched voice, a scream carried on the wind. "I think it's coming from over there." He pointed southwest toward the woods in the distance.

"Do you think someone's in trouble?" Rosette asked.

"I am days from recovering my magic, but I still say we investigate," Marsh suggested, staring in the direction of the distant scream.

"Stay behind us," Kyo said to Marsh. Roland led the group, running between two homes and weaving between the water pools in the paddy fields where rice grew, filling in the space between the town and the tree line.

The farther they ran from the town, the louder the screams became. Or more accurately, screeches. Multiple high-pitched screeches that made Kyo's blood run cold.

"Those sounds don't belong to a person," he cautioned in a shaky voice. "At least not anymore."

Roland stopped and held his right arm out to signal the others to do the same. "They're close. It doesn't sound like they're coming from the woods."

They took careful steps, scanning all directions.

The overlapping screeches sent a vibration through Kyo's head, and he rubbed his ears. "I hope Ueno's enforcers can hear this."

Rosette stumbled, catching herself and glancing behind her. A patch of fake grass and dirt folded over. She crouched and pulled at it, exposing a large metal door in the ground.

"It's coming from down here," she said.

"I'm not sure we should touch it," Krysta warned.

Kyo had to know what lay beneath them. He pulled the handle, lifting the door that stood taller than himself, revealing thick metal bars beneath it. "Krysta, can you send some lights down there?"

"What did I just say?" Krysta asked, groaning. She complied, however, sending several fireballs through the bars to illuminate the pit.

Shades stood, stumbled, and sat within the pit, which stretched farther than they could see. Some were unmoving, reminiscent of the "statue" in Calmarock, the shade that had been coated in molten metal. Those that were still alive joined the others that were already screeching.

"How many do you think there are?" Marsh asked in a raised voice, covering his ears.

Kyo swiftly shut the metal door to muffle the screeching. "Ten or fifteen maybe? Why are they even down there?"

"Where else would they be?" an accented voice asked from behind, similar to the woman in the clinic.

They turned to find a woman with straight, coal-black hair reaching her hips, wearing violet enforcer robes embroidered with golden flowers. Her eyes were narrowed at them with suspicion.

Roland cleared his throat. "Sorry. We heard the screeching from town and thought someone needed help. But then we found this," he said, motioning to the door.

The enforcer took hold of the fake patch of grass and spread it neatly over the door. "Noble of you. But do not judge us for how we deal with shades," she said, speaking in firm, short sentences. "We could not transport them to Spellnix Hold before they turned. I should suggest we deal with those currently down there. They've grown too many in number."

"Judging by the still ones, I take it you use molten metal?" Krysta asked.

The woman nodded. "Astute of you. Yes, our chancellor learned of the method from Chancellor Barion of Calmarock. Our resource of spare metal is slim, so we wait. When their numbers grow, we deal with them together."

"I am sorry. Dealing with shades is no easy task," Marsh said.

"No, it's not. Especially when families and friends refuse to accept the truth. Sometimes to their own peril. Now, come. And do not open this door again. They get loud." The enforcer motioned for them to follow.

They obliged, heading back to town, where they went their separate ways after receiving another warning about the door.

"I don't like knowing there are that many shades so close to us," Kyo said.

Krysta shook her head. "Neither do I. But what else can they do? Their enforcers might lack the power to slay them."

Kyo thought back to Milo, the enforcer from Aquarin who struggled as much as them to do damage to the shades there. As frustrating as the man was, he hoped he and Karu were doing okay and no major outbreaks had hit the town since then.

"Come on, let's head to the library," Krysta said.

"So, why did they build such a huge library out here of all places?" Kyo asked. "I'd figure something like this would be put in Alderdeem." He expected Roland or Krysta to give an answer, but to his surprise, it was Rosette who chimed in.

"When it was built, people hated summoners a lot more. So, it was a safe place for them to go and learn from each other. Some came here to commune with the Altruists. Then, when people started accepting summoners more…well, some people…it was more than just them who started visiting." Rosette rubbed the back of her hand with the other through her gloves. "People started donating all kinds of books and tomes. So many that they had to build more floors underground."

"From what I've heard, it quickly became less about sharing knowledge or helping summoners and more about the goal of making it the largest public library in the world." Roland stared at the massive building in the distance. "They succeeded."

They climbed the stairs of the library and approached the massive white metal doors with deep engravings of the pantheon as a family was leaving. When they entered, Kyo paused and stared with wide eyes. It was like the palace's library, multiplied several-fold, not including the additional floors below he couldn't see. Towering bookshelves stood against the walls, tables and chairs positioned next to railings stopping anyone from falling to the lower floors. Ahead of them, a massive, curved bookshelf stretched to the ceiling.

"How is anyone supposed to reach even half of these books?" Kyo asked. As if to answer his question, a woman pushed a step ladder on wheels in front of a shelf and climbed to take a book. "Oh. Well, seems like a hassle."

Sauntering deeper into the library, Kyo eyed the many people browsing shelves, sitting and reading, or having quiet conversations at a table. So many people in such a rural place, their skin tones and clothing styles hinting at them being from all over the continent. How many of them were summoners?

"I want to find books on the Altruists," Rosette shouted. Roland hushed her and she covered her mouth.

"I would be interested in that as well, though where to begin searching is the question," Marsh said.

"Looking for something?" a gravelly voice asked. An old woman supported by a cane approached them.

Each tap of the cane against the floor appeared forceful, but no sound emitted from the impact.

"Uh huh. I want to read more about the Altruists," Rosette declared with a beaming smile.

The old woman narrowed her eyes and gave Rosette a once-over then raised her cane to tap the young girl's hands. The end of the cane had a patch of bright green cloth attached to it. "Is that so? You're the youngest summoner I've seen in a long while."

Rosette frowned. "Is that okay?"

The old woman smirked and held out her hand so they all could see the symbol etched in the back of it, a double helix with a filled circle in the center. "If I wasn't, that would make me quite the hypocrite, now, wouldn't it?"

Rosette's eyes lit up, and she rushed to embrace the old woman. "I've never met another summoner before."

The woman's eyes widened in shock, but when Roland attempted to pull Rosette away, she waved her hand dismissively. "Never? Well then, you've come to the right place. You can call me Murielle."

"I'm Rosette."

"It's nice to meet you. I think I know just where to take you for what you're looking for. You and your friends…family…whatever, can follow me. And don't fall behind." Murielle turned and led the way.

She moved at a faster pace than Kyo expected. In that way, she reminded him of Chancellor Demaskus. Did it really matter if they fell behind though? Her vibrant violet shawl over a white dress reaching her ankles made her hard to miss. She and Rosette chatted, a few Altruist names spoken on occasion. Even Roland couldn't insert himself into their discussion. It was like they belonged to a completely different world from the rest of them.

They remained on the main floor, brought toward the back of the library, though no less crowded.

A place like this must have been paradise for intellectuals. Kyo preferred an open, outside space with a single tome to practice his spells.

"You'll find mentions of the pantheon in many books within this library, but if you want books with them as the primary subject matter, you'll want to stick to these last few shelves on your left and right." Murielle gently tapped Rosette's head with her cane. "Even so, don't take everything you read as fact. It's been a very long time since humans and the pantheon were in this world at the same time. So, you can damn well bet that much of the information is conjecture at best. Even the ones written by fellow summoners."

"I'm surprised that those who can summon the pantheon could know so little about them," Krysta said.

"They are quite tight-lipped when it comes to many things. And what they are willing to reveal to those who commune with them can come muddled and vague." Murielle turned to Rosette. "Have you ever communed with an Altruist?"

"I tried. I don't get much of a response though, maybe a greeting if I'm lucky," Rosette said sadly.

"May I ask, what is the difference between summoning and communing?" Marsh asked.

"Summoning is calling an avatar of a pantheon into this world. Communing is attempting to communicate with them while they are in theirs. It's really hard to get them to talk about anything." Rosette smiled. "But that's okay, they don't have to if they don't want to."

Murielle hobbled toward a set of curved stairs leading to the next floor. "Who would have thought they'd be shy? Oh well. You enjoy reading and behave yourselves. I need to keep an eye on a few troublemakers."

Rosette scanned the books on the nearest shelf then pulled one out and set it on the table. She flipped through the pages, stopping on one that had a detailed sketch of what looked like a gorilla with tree bark skin, mossy fur, and flowers sprouting from its back. "This one is Florlantvus. It's a Relinquished though. It stinks that they would be violent if we summoned them. All because the Altruists wanted to teach us magic."

"It does sound like a dumb reason to hate us. But as long as they do, they can stay in their own world and leave us alone," Kyo said. Irrational hatred like that was a reason he never bothered worshipping any of the pantheon. He'd rather go through life not worrying about any of that.

"Let's not think about that, kiddo. Focus on the Altruists instead." Roland leaned over and flipped through a few pages, stopping on a less detailed drawing of Duxvita. "Now this one is worth looking at." Duxvita was depicted as a massive serpent-like dragon similar to a Leviathan, its entire being composed purely of a pitch-black flame.

"Well, yeah. The one who created humanity and all," Kyo mumbled.

"I doubt you would have such an attitude toward it if Rosette summoned it," Marsh said with a grin.

Rosette shook her head. "I don't know if I could. The Prime Altruist and Relinquished are very picky about who can summon them. And you need to have a lot of magic to do it."

"You're only eleven and already powerful. I bet when you're an adult you'd be able to summon it without a problem," Krysta assured.

The sound of someone clearing their throat came from above.

"Excuse me," came a voice. A frighteningly familiar voice. They gazed up, staring at Sybilla leaning over the railing on the above floor. "Would you brats mind keeping it down? Some people are trying to read."

Chapter 25

A harsh chill ran through Kyo's body as he stared at Sybilla, her upper half casually leaning over the railing. Of course they were here. They must have already discovered the stone was a fake. Did this mean they were going to attack the town in retaliation? If they weren't careful, the people in the library would get caught up in their troubles and end up as shades or mindless undead. And those in town were sure to follow.

"Tell you what, you go back to what you were doing, and we'll keep it to a whisper," Kyo said, trying to hide the shakiness in his voice.

Sybilla tapped her chin, staring up as if considering his words. "Mmm no. The other two might be fine with their noses in books, but honestly, I find it exceptionally boring."

"You're not wrong," Kyo mumbled under his breath.

"Our friends are here," Sybilla called to her unseen comrades before sitting on the railing to the stairs and sliding down with her arms in the air.

Blanq came into sight, the undead members of the airship crew close behind. Unlike the previous undead he'd seen, Kyo noticed they kept a more upright posture. Their movements were still a bit jerky, but their glowing blue eyes were the only clear indication something was wrong.

"How dare she," Krysta whispered through a clenched jaw. "They were just doing their jobs managing the airship." Her fists were clenched, and her eyes wide with fury. Yet she, like the rest of them, could do nothing but stand by as people they saw alive yesterday and casually chatted with during their trip had their bodies manipulated like puppets.

One of the crew stumbled upon reaching the bottom of the stairs, bumping into Sybilla.

"Hey, watch it," Sybilla complained. "Blanq, I thought they were better at walking now."

"So…rry," the crew member struggled to say in a raspy but still feminine voice.

"Did she speak?" Marsh asked in a horrified voice. "But they are dead, correct?"

Roland placed a hand on Rosette's back and kept her against him. "I don't like that one bit."

"It is a little unsettling at first, isn't it?" Sybilla asked, stepping behind Blanq and placing her hands upon the necromancer's shoulders, shaking them lightly. "But she's really advancing her practice with the undead. I'm so proud of her. Oh! Watch this." She turned to the same undead. "What's your name?"

For a moment, silence followed. The undead gazed around before looking down at herself. Sybilla sighed, shaking her head.

But then the undead opened her mouth again. "My...ra."

Krysta covered her mouth with her hands. "Oh no. No, no. She remembers? She's aware?"

"So, she knows she's dead?" Rosette asked. "But then, is she actually dead? I don't get it."

"How could you do something so cruel to them?" Marsh asked. "This is absolutely unforgivable, an afront to life itself."

Kyo found himself in the same boat as Rosette. The horror on display made his blood run cold and brought forth so many questions. Questions Blanq appeared ready to answer, given her body language from beneath her hooded robe, fidgeting and rubbing her hands together.

"While Blanq is the only one capable of answering that, we have more important matters to discuss." The mysterious man descended the stairs to join his comrades. "I figured you would make your way to Ueno, though I hadn't expected to find you all so easily. They haven't truly made good on our previous deal, have they, Blanq?" he asked, adding an extra bite to her name. When she didn't respond, he tightened his lips and sighed. "Please try to be more vigilant in the future. We rely on you for more than your personal experiments."

"Did you expect us to simply hand it over, after the things you all have done? How many more people need to die, and for what?" Krysta shouted. Her words echoed off the high walls, gaining the attention of others nearby who paused to look their way.

"Was that not made clear in Oasis?" Sybilla asked.

"But why? What's even the point?" Roland asked, narrowing his eyes. "For fun? I'm not about to let my little girl grow up in a world filled with shades."

The man shook his head. "For a much greater purpose. Though as I said previously, one you are unlikely to accept."

"Don't give us that bovine crap. You think you're so high and mighty, but you're just full of yourself. Who even are you, anyway?" Krysta asked.

The man's eyes widened, and his mouth opened silently for a second before speaking. "Oh, I was so fixated on the stone I hadn't realized I failed to introduce myself. My sincere apologies. Allow me to rectify that." He took a few steps forward, then bowed at the waist, an arm over his stomach. "I am Zeshin Valeheart, formally of the Aurora. A pleasure to officially make your acquaintance."

Others spoke. Said…something. But the words didn't register with Kyo. Time slowed; any words spoken were nothing but muffled background noise. The only thing filling his mind was that man's name, repeating itself over and over.

Zeshin.

Their eyes met, Kyo's heart pounding in his ears. His breath hitched with each inhale and exhale, his face burning.

This man. Cedric's words in Aquarin. So many emotions flooded Kyo they threatened to collapse his mind. His eyes widened, and his teeth clenched so hard he thought they might break but didn't care. Every muscle in his body tightened as one emotion overcame all the others.

Unbridled, unyielding rage.

Wind formed above his palm, rotating into a drill. He released a guttural scream unlike any he'd emitted in his entire life as he launched himself forward and thrust his spell into Zeshin's chest. Grunting, pushing, Kyo's body shook as much from fury as the power behind his attack. His shout echoed throughout the library as his spell compressed then exploded, launching Zeshin through a bookcase and the wall it stood against, books and broken wood flying in all directions.

Frightened shouts erupted from others in the library and their frantic footsteps headed for the door. Murmurs came from behind him, though he didn't bother looking at those too curious to leave with the rest of the fleeing patrons.

No. Only this man mattered. This man and ending his life.

Kyo panted, grunted like an enraged beast. One attack wasn't enough—he needed more, needed to release his rage until he was too exhausted to move. Friends and enemies both released words and sounds of surprise, but he didn't care about them or their thoughts. Destruction of property, consequences—it didn't matter.

Wind burst from his feet, launching him forward. But he barely left the ground when vines emerged from the hole in the wall and wrapped tightly around his body before he had a chance to react. They kept him upright, covering him from the neck down.

"Let me go! Let me go so I can kill you!" he shouted at the top of his lungs.

"Kid, I don't think this is a good idea right now," Roland warned.

"He's right. Do you not remember what happened yesterday? What's gotten into you?" Krysta asked, her voice laced with a mixture of panic and anger.

Kyo attempted to slip through the vines by stretching them with his wind, the excess seeping through whatever gaps it could. The narrow bursts of escaping air toppled chairs, flung books off tables, and violently rattled the chandelier above them.

"It's him," he shouted. After several heavy pants, he put more power behind his wind, allowing his rage to fuel his spell in a fruitless attempt to free himself. "He killed my parents!"

"What?" Krysta asked in a low tone. Her sharp gaze shifted to the hole in the wall, flames engulfing her hands.

Roland summoned his polearm, Rosette clenched her fists by her face, and Marsh extended his hand as if ready to cast a spell. His friends' support should have relieved him, brought some peace of mind. But at the moment, it only encouraged the violent fantasies overtaking his mind.

Zeshin emerged from the hole in the wall, brushing dust off his suit and the section of bare chest where Kyo's spell had torn through his clothes. "It was an unfortunate circumstance, but Kei and Iris shouldn't have stuck their noses into my business. They attempted to stop me from doing what was best for all."

"Shut up. You took away my family. You murdered them! I swear I'm going to cut your damn head off!" Kyo screamed, fighting against the vines that bound him. No matter how much muscle or magic he exerted, they hardly budged.

"I swear his yelling is making my brain vibrate in my head," Sybilla grumbled, wiggling a finger inside her ear. "I'm going to shut him up."

When Kyo glared at her, he found Blanq approaching him instead. His friends attempted to rush to his side, but a wall of poison gas erupted from the ground, blocking their path. That was fine. At the moment, Kyo felt as though he could take on all three of them with his bare hands. If Blanq dared to touch him, he'd bite her fingers off. No way was he letting her turn him into one of her undead.

"Don't even try it," he bit out.

Blanq stared at him from beneath her dark hood for a few seconds. Raw magical energy engulfed her hand, then she swung it and slapped him across the face.

Kyo's vision flashed from the impact. He clenched his eyes for a second, his sight clearing when he opened them again, but the ringing in his ears remained a bit longer. Of all the things she could have done to him, he hadn't expected that. For a few passing seconds, the shock overtook his anger. But that faded as quickly as it came, clenching his teeth, glaring at her like a saber ready to pounce.

"Enough. Control yourself," Blanq insisted in a soft but firm voice. "If you can't control your emotions, you *will* die."

"He murdered my mom and dad. I'll use every ounce of power I have to stab him until he's nothing but a pile of mutilated meat! Don't you *dare* tell me to calm down. I'll do the same to you too." Kyo lunged his head forward but not far enough to headbutt her like he wanted.

Blanq pulled back her hood, for the second time exposing her young face and disheveled, dirty blond hair. But she didn't stop there. She lifted her robe over her head, tossing it to the floor, leaving herself in a black shirt and pants. Without breaking eye contact, she rolled up her sleeves and the legs of her pants as high as she could, then raised her shirt to expose her stomach.

Kyo's grunts and panting ceased, his breath catching as he took in her exposed skin. He heard at least one other gasp from his friends but didn't know who it came from. All he could see were blemishes and scars, hardly a trace of smooth, untouched skin. Deep cuts and stab wounds that had healed over time, burns, welts, among others.

"You are not the only one who has lost their parents. Mine were slain before my eyes when I was young. A random attack from a group of thugs. Despite my age, it wasn't fear that took me but anger. During the confrontation, my father dropped a glass bottle. I took a broken shard and attempted to stab one of their killers. If I were smart, in control of my emotions, perhaps I would have thought to run instead." Blanq absentmindedly ran her thumb and index finger over a long scar that ran across her throat. "They easily subdued me and took me with them. I was held as their prisoner for months, and they delighted in torturing every part of my body. All except my face. They said it was too cute to touch."

Kyo couldn't stop analyzing her scars. What must it have been like for a child to be in such a situation? The pain, the screams. He shuddered at the images running through his mind. The longer she spoke, the more his body slumped.

"I eventually escaped. But this," Blanq said, motioning to her body, "was my punishment for allowing my emotions to run wild and overtake logic. And if you allow that to happen here, against Zeshin, you will face a worse fate. If you wish to take that risk, Kyo Sonata, then be prepared for your journey to end here."

After a few seconds of silence, Sybilla huffed. "My way would have been a lot more fun. You could have at least turned him into an undead or something."

Kyo stared into Blanq's eyes. Was it sympathy that looked back? Understanding? He didn't know, but something about her gaze seemed off. Like he saw no hint of villainous intent. He shifted his attention to Zeshin, and though his anger returned immediately, the adrenaline it gave him before hadn't. Blanq was right. He hated that with every fiber of his being. Here stood the man who murdered his parents, yet he was powerless to do anything about it. If he tried, he would be easily overpowered or killed. A new rage gnawed at him directed toward himself. He'd improved quite a bit over the past six months, but he was still too weak to avenge their deaths. Tears trickled down his cheeks, not from sadness but frustration.

Zeshin picked up Blanq's robes and handed them to her. "Please put these back on. It's a chilly day." Without a word, Blanq complied. "Still, thank you. While I would prefer not to kill him at present, it's certainly not off the table. I suppose your situations were too similar for you to remain silent, hm?" he asked, though got no response as she lifted her hood, shadow covering her face again. "Now then, I'd think it's fair to say the accrue stone wouldn't be left with you all. I suppose we'll have to go search for those members of Alderdeem's best, won't we?"

The vines removed themselves, snaking back into Zeshin's hand. Kyo fell to his knees, unwilling to move, even as his friends rushed to his side.

"If you truly wish to fight us, we can oblige. But I think you know how that will turn out for you. Besides, there is still more work for you to do, and I am not inclined to start over." Zeshin turned to the second story balcony. "We're leaving," he shouted.

Who else could he be speaking to? Maybe ensuring Muriel there would be no more trouble? Kyo raised his head as he heard footsteps descending the stairs.

"No," he whispered, eyes glued to Alden with the book from Alderdeem's library in his hand, eyes downcast. "You can't. There's no way."

Alden still refused to look at him as he joined Zeshin and the others and walked toward the door.

"What are you doing with *him*?" Kyo asked.

No answer came. There had to be a mistake, something he wasn't understanding. They had to be forcing him to help again, blackmailing him. But even if that were true, how could he stomach being anywhere near Zeshin? Everything was wrong. Kyo could feel his friends staring at his back, but he dared not look, especially at Krysta.

His eyes shifted to Zeshin as he walked away. The view of him from behind, his hair, his clothes. Kyo had seen him before. A flash of realization struck him like a lightning bolt.

"Alden didn't become corrupted by chance, did he?" Kyo asked, choking out his words.

Zeshin didn't stop as he glanced over his shoulder. "I tried to make things easier and create an alibi for him."

It had all been a lie. Alden had never been in any real danger. No anger. No tears. His mind blanked as he watched his godfather disappear around a corner with his parents' killer.

Chapter 26

Kyo kept his eyes firmly focused on the tiled floor as his mind struggled to process what had happened. His parents' killer was alive and well. Alden knew and even worked alongside him. Even if Alden intended to undermine Zeshin, how could he stand to be around that man? Kyo's body tensed, both desiring to unleash his pent-up frustration and lacking the energy to do so.

He felt Krysta's stare boring into him. Normally, he'd defend Alden, come up with some reason, repeat what he'd said previously. But seeing him walk side by side with Zeshin—could it be that Krysta was right? Could Alden have been lying about his goals? Had Alden lied to Kyo's parents? But then why spend all that time raising him? So many conflicting thoughts and ideas swirled in his mind like a maelstrom. He wished someone would knock him unconscious and silence them.

"Kyo, is there anything you know that you haven't told us?" Roland asked in a parental tone.

The words registered in Kyo's mind, but his body wouldn't respond in any way. No action, no voice, only dreaded thoughts consuming his mind.

Roland sighed. "This isn't good. But what are we supposed to do? We got lucky last time we fought Sybilla. Even with Hayner and the others, if it comes to a fight, I'm not confident we'll win."

"We need to warn them," Krysta said in a panicked voice. "Especially Kira. So long as she has the stone, she needs to stay hidden."

"I agree." Marsh paced as he spoke. "However, before we rush off, I would like to see if they left anything behind. We know they want the stones and wish to turn others into shades, but to what end? Simply to do it? And if so, why seek information here? We are missing something."

"I knew they were no good." Murielle's voice echoed from the upper floor. "No manners, scaring off the other guests. Though, I suppose that last bit is more thanks to your silver-haired friend, isn't it?"

Kyo tore his eyes from the ground, glancing at the stairs as Murielle carefully descended, her cane supporting her on each step. As if he was supposed to care about scaring a few people or knocking over a bookshelf.

"It sounds like you all know quite a bit more than I do. So, how about this? You tell me what you know, and I tell you what they were so interested in."

Kyo didn't bother opening his mouth, allowing the others to explain, with an emphasis on the events of Calmarock and Oasis. While they spoke, he wondered if it would have been possible to gather enough magic to kill Zeshin with his previous attack. His wind ripping through Sh Zeshin's flesh, his cry of agony. Kyo wanted it to happen so badly, but knowing he couldn't filled him with such self-hatred. He clenched his fists until his knuckles ached.

"Well, that's a frightening prospect," Murielle said, shaking her cane as she spoke. "And it's you yolks who are dealing with this? There should be a much greater effort from the chancellors and Aurora to put an end to them. I swear, you can never trust the people in charge."

"The king and royal guard of Alderdeem are doing the best they can," Krysta argued.

"And look what good that's done," Murielle countered. "They're free from Spellnix Hold, walking out in the open like they don't have a care in the world."

"So, what were they looking for in the books?" Rosette asked.

Murielle glanced at Rosette then sighed, her face softening. "They had gathered literature about the Relinquished. It seems they had a specific interest in the Prime Relinquished, Magistquerat."

"As if their known intentions weren't disturbing enough. But why Magistquerat?" Roland asked.

"Whatever the reason, it cannot be good," Marsh said, lightly snapping his fingers. "As far as we know, none of them are summoners. Since they have such a strong interest in the corruption, perhaps there is a connection between Magistquerat and…what was the name you heard, Kyo? Mordibrae?"

Murielle's eyes narrowed. "And how do *you* know that name?"

Kyo perked and stared at Murielle. Did this old hag know about whatever was beneath Crossroads?

"It sounds like we should be asking you the same thing," Krysta said, crossing her arms over her chest. "Given how we learned of that name, I can't imagine how you came across it."

"If the name is familiar to Murielle, I guess that proves Kyo wasn't just hallucinating back then. There really is something to what he said." Roland rubbed his eyes with his thumb and index finger. "This shit keeps getting more complicated."

Rosette stepped in front of Murielle. "Kyo heard the name when we were underground. We think it's the source of the corruption."

Murielle released a light laugh, though it was hard to tell if she found something humorous, or disturbing. "Well, I don't know how on Feracael you came to that conclusion, but based on what I've learned over the years, you'd be correct."

"Wait, you already knew this? Did you bother to tell anyone?" Krysta asked, her voice raising.

Murielle waved her off. "Of course I did. What do you take me for? But I was ignored. The problem is, to understand that information, you'd also have to accept a reality that challenges what people think they know about the pantheon. And in case you haven't noticed, people can be quite stubborn and stuck in their ways. Imagine walking up to someone and telling them Tutelvus used to be human until he hid in a box for a hundred years and became an Altruist. Obviously, that's not real, but to most people the truth may as well be just as absurd."

"Please, tell us what you know. It could be vital to stopping them and maybe ending the corruption for good." Krysta grabbed one of Murielle's hands, cupping it between both of hers. "Anything might be helpful."

Murielle yanked her hand away. "Fine but only if you promise to clean up the mess you made." She pointed to the bookshelf that lay on its side and the scattered books strewn across the floor. "I don't expect you to be able to fix the hole in the wall, but you can at least pick up after yourselves. Now, let's make this simple. Gather around." She lightly smacked Kyo on the head with her cane. "And get up. I heard everything. We all have problems. Don't tell me you're going to fight with magic and not with your head. Figure it out and get over it."

Kyo narrowed his eyes at the old woman. While he'd love to assume she didn't know what she was talking about, Blanq had already shown him the mistake of that mindset. He stood and joined his friends while Murielle sat in a plush maroon armchair.

"Why is this like story time for kids?" he mumbled.

"Because it is," Murielle said, raising her hands, palms up. "But with more of a visual aid. Don't get your undergarments in a bunch. It's only an illusion spell. But I figure it'll make for easier storytelling. Besides, I rarely get to do this, so I'm taking the opportunity."

A blanket of white overtook the library, leaving them in a bright void. Seconds later, like unveiling a painting, they found themselves surrounded by lush trees and rolling hills, as if they were out in the wilderness. One by one, ferals of all types appeared around them—wolves, blobs, giant wasps. A massive zu flew across the sky.

Kyo's eyes widened as he took in the new surroundings. "This is a whole different level of illusion." He took a deep breath, reminding himself it was just that, swearing he could reach out and touch a boar that wandered by.

"Wow." Rosette's voice trailed off as she took a few steps away from the group and gazed around in awe.

"As I've mentioned before, communing with the pantheon is difficult, and their messages can be rather vague." Murielle's voice echoed around them. "So, what I am going to show you is what I've managed to piece together over decades. While it does rely on my own interpretation, I'm confident that it's a more accurate telling of humanity's beginning than anything you've heard."

Before them appeared a group of unusual creatures, nine in total. Kyo didn't need to be told they were the pantheon, already recognizing Ignivus and Tutelvus among their number. Though the one that captured his eye the most was Duxvita, the Prime Altruist depicted on his parents' shrine in his living room.

"Five Altruists, four Relinquished. We all know that. And why are they separated into two groups?" Murielle asked.

"Because there were disagreements among them about teaching humans how to use magic and leaving Feracael to them," Rosette answered, her hand raised as if she were in a classroom.

"That is only partially correct," Murielle stated. "There is a massive detail that is missing. But let's start from the beginning."

The pantheon and ferals all vanished, leaving nothing but empty wilderness.

"This is incredible. To use illusion magic to such a degree—I never knew it was possible," Krysta said, her eyes wide and voice filled with awe.

"You'd be surprised what old people can do. Now then, it's common knowledge that the pantheon are the reason life exists on Feracael." A stream of multicolored magical energy seeped from the ground, floating through the air like a gentle river. Natural magic that ferals could harness but humans could not. "They used the planet's natural magic to do so."

Kyo cringed as Saecluvus appeared, a Relinquished resembling a wolf, if that wolf's body were comprised entirely of writhing tentacles. That was not a Relinquished he'd want to see summoned. Saecluvus closed its eyes and stuck a paw into the energy floating about. The scene around it sped up, the energy flowing rapidly, the light in the sky dimming, turning to night then day again. After the seventh new day, a creature appeared that Kyo had never seen, leaving him wondering if it truly existed or was made up for the illusion. A tiny ball of cedar-colored fur with large eyes glanced around, no taller than Kyo's shin.

"I can't say how long it took to create many of the species that exist, but this process occurred all over the world," Murielle said. "While individual trees, bodies of water, rocks, whatever you see have some of this magic within them, there are masses of natural magic which run like a collection of underground rivers within the planet. Of course, there are places where they do not reach."

The illusion shifted to a desolate wasteland, the ground dehydrated and cracking. Within this place, Ignivus stood alone. Kyo inhaled sharply when he noticed what the Altruist held.

"That's not something I expected to see," Roland said.

"Is it holding an accrue stone?" Krysta asked.

"I didn't expect the stones from your story to be the same, but those were the tools they'd use to bring life to places out of reach of the flow of natural magic. They'd draw the magic into the stone for storage and use at a later time and different location," Murielle explained.

Marsh ran his hands over his face. "The accrue stones were tools of the pantheon. I never would have imagined. And that makes it all the more frightening that Sybilla and her comrades are looking to use them."

"It does help explain why they're so hard to destroy. They must have been left behind after the pantheon fled Feracael. Any chance you can summon one to take them back, kiddo?" Roland asked. Rosette shrugged.

A towering dragon with golden scales appeared next to Ignivus before the scene shifted again.

"Now, here is where people throw doubt into my interpretation of things," Murielle said. "This is my understanding of events significant to our current situation."

They found themselves in a grassy plain stretching into the distance. The sky brightened, and a massive fireball crashed into the ground. Kyo raised his arms to shield himself, before remembering it was an illusion. He glanced at the others, glad he hadn't been the only one to react that way. Instead of the impact creating a crater, a wide hole with smooth, melted edges was left behind. Kyo stared at the hole identical to the one he'd found beneath Crossroads.

Once again, the sun rose and fell in rapid succession, indicating the passing of countless days. Then Magistquerat, the Prime Relinquished, appeared, approaching the pit. It seemed as though the Relinquished couldn't decide what it wanted to look like and took aspects from various creatures: the body and head of a lion, draconic wings and claws, horns of a ram, and a living snake as a tail.

"Whatever it was that fell from the stars, Magistquerat communicated with it. With it came the name Mordibrae. While I don't know the details of their communication or what lies within the pit, I do know the end result," Murielle said.

Magistquerat stood before a stream of natural magic like they'd been shown twice before. This time, the creature that had been formed from its efforts was undoubtedly a human.

"Okay, hold on," Kyo said. "You're telling me it was the *Prime Relinquished* that made humans and not the Prime Altruist? How does that make any sense?"

"It's no wonder people don't take your version of events seriously," Roland muttered, his own tone disbelieving.

"You'll understand better if you hush and watch," Murielle snapped. "As humans began to multiply and spread, Magistquerat became prouder of its creation, to the point it altered its form. What had previously been the body and head of a lion changed to that of a human, though retaining the other feral-like properties."

More humans populated the scene, and with them were the pantheon.

"Humans of course had the capacity for higher thinking, and so it was decided to guide them into forming societies and learning magic. And this is where the disagreement we all know about occurred. While Magistquerat created humans, it disagreed with this idea. What no one else understands is the reason why. You might want to brace yourselves for this next part," Murielle warned. "There was a specific reason why Magistquerat decided to create humanity. We can surmise that it was at the guidance of Mordibrae, and that purpose was…well…"

Magistquerat stood before a group of humans. It extended its hand, engulfed in what appeared to be a black shadowy aura. It shot forth and consumed the group. Where they stood a second ago were now frighteningly familiar creatures of shadow. Shades.

"No, no, no. There is no way this can be true," Kyo said, pacing, his voice growing louder with each word. "You want us to believe that our whole purpose in existing was to become shades?"

"Nuh uh." Rosette shook her head. "We were made to populate the planet after the pantheon left."

"And now you yolks understand why when I got to this all-important part of my explanation, I wasn't taken seriously," Murielle said. "It was too drastic a change from what people believe to be true. While I did say some of this is left to my own interpretation, some of it was too clear to be denied. And this is one such example. I have no doubt in my mind this is the truth."

"But—" Kyo started.

Roland clapped loudly. "Kyo, quiet for a moment." He cupped his hand over his mouth, eyes narrowed. "I don't like the sound of it either, but it fits, doesn't it? You described finding a pit like the one we were just shown while beneath Crossroads. The vision you saw also depicted shades. And what happened after that explosion of force that knocked you down? You found Marsh corrupted."

Krysta groaned. "I really hate to admit it, but when we put both stories together, they complement each other too well to be a coincidence."

"So, the reason the pantheon split into two groups was because one group wanted us to become shades and the other didn't?" Rosette asked.

"That seems to be the case, yes. You'll need to tell me more about what you saw near that pit. And if you know where it is, even better. Maybe now my warning won't go unheeded, for all the good it'll do for those already affected." The illusion vanished, Murielle staring at them from her armchair. "Once the other pantheon found out about Magistquerat turning humans into shades, those we know as the Altruists forced the others out into another plane of existence. But not before Magistquerat cast a spell upon all humans, blocking them from harnessing natural magic. I can't say it was necessarily a bad choice, seeing what some choose to do with their own magic reserves."

Kyo glanced around the library and again his heart ached. With the fascination of Murielle's illusion gone, the memory of Alden working alongside Zeshin rushed back. Maybe getting Alden that tome from the palace library wasn't a great idea after all.

"At least the Aurora know about the pit and Kyo's vision. And they do intend to investigate further. That'll be difficult though with so many active shades," Krysta said. "Do you think Zeshin knows about Mordibrae? Or is he like Sybilla and just wants to create chaos?"

"Regardless, the objective remains the same," Roland said. "If possible, destroy the accrue stones and put a stop to those three. Hopefully that all can be handled by the Aurora."

Marsh nodded. "We will also have to inform them about what Murielle showed us, hopefully putting a priority on that pit and what lies within. Murielle, thank you very much. This information may be invaluable. However, we must hurry and warn our friends about the presence of Zeshin and the others."

"We've waited too long already. Let's go." Krysta ordered, rushing toward the library entrance.

"You said you'd clean up after yourselves," Murielle shouted after them.

Kyo rushed to follow. The faint sound of a high-pitched screech reached his ears. "I can even hear the shades from here. They need to soundproof their shade pit better."

"No, that sounded too close," Roland said.

They pushed the front doors open and paused, staring in horror at Ueno. Fires burned, screams echoed in the air, accompanying the screech of shades that ran rampant, their dark figures visible even from such a distance. And somewhere among the chaos were Zeshin, Sybilla, and Blanq, hunting for the stone.

Chapter 27

Which way should he go? The people of Ueno were helpless against the shades, Jaune remained vulnerable at the clinic, and Kira had the accrue stone. Kyo's chest heaved as he struggled to make a decision.

Roland summoned his polearm. "Our top priority needs to be Kira. We need to keep the stone safe."

"Knowing her, she's out there fighting," Krysta said. "I really hope Hayner is with her."

"Then we look for her and help anyone we can along the way." Roland took off down the hill, Rosette on his heel.

Kyo and the others followed. Leave it to the oldest among them to keep his head together and know what to do. It showed Kyo still had a lot to learn. Keeping cool under pressure—or most circumstances, for that matter—had never been his strong suit, but it must have come second nature to his parents in situations like these.

A shade stopped mid crawl atop a roof of the closest home, turning its head toward them, releasing a loud screech. It leaped from the house and charged.

Rosette ran past Roland and met the shade head on, kicking upwards into its chin before it could slash at her with its claws. While the shade was in the air from the powerful punt, Roland jumped and swung his polearm, creating an arc of magical energy and knocking it back to the ground.

"Move," Krysta shouted. She threw nearly a dozen palm-sized fireballs at the shade, each exploding seconds later, its screech piercing through the explosions.

Kyo gathered wind above his palm, forming his favored wind drill spell. He hopped between barriers under his feet until he was above the shade then launched himself downward, thrusting the drill against the shadowy aura. Kyo grunted and pushed with every bit of muscle he had, and the drill condensed, the aura giving way to the attack. Then it exploded, sending him hurtling through the air. With the shade's body already against the ground, it took the full force of the blow, releasing a pained hack. Kyo corrected himself midair, summoned his swords, and launched himself back against the shade. The blades glowed as he thrust them against the shade's chest, piercing through the aura and the body underneath. Panting, Kyo retracted his blades, the aura fading, revealing the body of a middle-aged woman.

Don't write their eulogy. Marsh's words echoed in Kyo's mind as he stared down at her.

This corruption. Mordibrae. They'd taken so many people, and more would follow before all was said and done. The thought of this occurring due to some cosmic deity made his blood run cold. If the Aurora were to do anything, if they were capable, it'd better be soon.

"That's one down. It's nice to know we're capable of this much when we work together," Krysta said.

Her voice snapped Kyo back to reality. "Yeah, glad those last six months weren't for nothing. Though it's taking more magic per spell than I would like."

While a sense of pride filled him for being able to slay a shade without the help of enforcers, royal guard, or Aurora, they couldn't do this for every shade they came across. Not with Sybilla, Zeshin, and Blanq to contend with.

"That was excellent work. I apologize for being unable to help," Marsh said, his eyes downcast.

"You were corrupted only yesterday. Naturally, you need time to recover," Roland assured him.

"Of course." Marsh flexed his fingers, staring at his palm. "Though I can likely cast a few spells before my magic is depleted. I think I may be better off at the clinic, doing what I can to help the injured. While magic is nice, I can attend to injuries without it."

Krysta grabbed Marsh's hand and pulled him along. "Then let's go. We'll check on Jaune while we're there and see if Kira is with him. If not, he might know where she is."

The moment they reached the outermost homes, a woman's scream pulled Kyo's attention. Behind the house to his left, a shade leaped at a woman, but she managed to trip it with a water whip spell.

"You all keep going, I'll catch up," Kyo said, running toward the woman.

As the shade rose to its feet, he launched himself forward, slashing a sword at its neck. Though the blade glowed again, it barely pushed past the aura enough to nick the skin. Like before, he had to pour more magic into the spell than usual to manage even that much.

The shade slashed at Kyo as he leaped back, its claws tearing his hoodie and scraping the skin of his left arm. He cringed, blood dripping from the wound. A quick glance revealed it wasn't deep enough to be concerning, but it still stung.

"You should run," Kyo suggested to the woman.

She shook her head. "My children are hiding inside. I will not go anywhere."

Of course they were. Why shouldn't this situation become more complicated? The shade charged at the woman again, but Kyo launched himself forward, slamming his shoulder into its chest and knocking it onto its back. Maybe it wasn't a good idea to split from the group after all. He might be able to defeat the shade with the woman's help, but it would significantly drain him.

She stretched her arm forward, whips of water extending from each finger. They wrapped around the shade, raised it into the air, and hurled it into the nearby rice fields. "Someone released them from their underground cell. We should put them back."

Work smarter, not harder. He liked it, even if he wasn't always good at the first part.

Kyo gazed past the rice fields, knowing it was down there somewhere. "Do you know exactly where it is?"

The woman nodded. "The responsibility to eliminate them falls on everyone, not only the enforcers. I was with the latest group."

Kyo kept his eyes fixed on the shade but couldn't help questioning her. "How do you deal with them?"

"It depends on what resources are available. Once, we poured liquid metal into the pit. Though most commonly, we gather a mixture of enforcers and citizens and vent our magic to destroy them."

Effective, but he hoped no one had to do it too frequently. Anyone who learned how to vent was taught that doing so too frequently could have long-lasting effects, like persistent fatigue or issues harnessing magic down the line.

The shade screeched loudly, running on all fours toward them. Kyo gathered air to circulate on the ground between him and the shade and, at the right moment, released it to hurl the shade into the air and farther from the town. They chased it, and when they caught up, the woman once more used water tendrils to toss it across the ground.

Sure enough, the door to their prison had been left wide open, the metal bars bent downward and broken. It didn't take more than one guess to determine who'd caused this mayhem.

Each time the shade rose to its feet, they made sure it tripped or was thrown, not letting up. With one last effort, the woman whipped the shade into the pit, and Kyo rushed to close the hatch and lock it.

The woman panted, hunched over, hands on her knees.

Kyo had to take a few heavy breaths himself, but he smiled. "Good job. Your kids are lucky to have a brave mom like you."

She offered a weak smile before standing upright. "I have to be. I'm all they have, since their father…"

Frowning, she glanced at the hatch in the ground, telling Kyo all he needed to know.

"Come on, let's get you back to them." Kyo led the way, doing his best to ignore the screeches and shouts of terror in the distance. He couldn't save everyone. He knew that. But that didn't make it any less painful knowing there were people crying out for help who wouldn't receive it.

Once they reached her home, she opened a closet door and pulled her children out, embracing them. They cried in their mother's arms, the oldest no more than seven or eight.

"Thank you," she said, glancing over her shoulder.

"Sure thing. But you need to leave."

She nodded, and he took that as his cue to move on. He had to rejoin the search for Kira.

Leaving the house, he headed deeper into town, coming across the occasional body lying on the road or in front of a home. He tried to keep his eyes away from them, hoping at least one of them had been a shade that Hayner or Kira had dealt with.

In the distance, a shade burst through a home with a man, limp and bloody, in its claws. Kyo clicked his tongue and dashed forward. His eyes widened when Blanq approached the shade first. Its aggressive screech was interrupted by a blast of raw magical energy from Blanq, creating a shockwave that stopped Kyo in his tracks and flung the creature through the air and onto its back. From that single blast, the dark aura faded, leaving behind the corpse of a young woman, a chilling reminder how much power Blanq had, despite her calm and quiet demeanor.

But why would she take out a shade? Didn't they want as many as possible roaming around? Seemingly oblivious to his presence, Blanq knelt beside the man, a deep cerulean glow surrounding his body. A moment later, he rose again, the glow in his eyes noticeable even from a distance.

"Turning more people into your undead toys?" Kyo cried out.

Blanq glanced his way then approached the woman who had been a shade a few seconds ago, casting the same spell upon her. She rose to her feet, glancing around and taking in her surroundings. Would these two speak like the ones in the library? The memory sent a chill down his spine. Dead people who could talk, the uncanniness of it set off all sorts of alarms in his mind.

The two undead stared at one another for a long moment. Without any coaxing or instruction, the woman reached out her hand. The man returned the gesture until their fingers interlocked.

Staring in awe, Kyo walked slowly over to them. "What did you do?"

"Though unintentional, it would seem they have been reunited." Blanq circled the pair, analyzing them. She reached into the woman's shirt, pulling out a locket connected to a chain around her neck. After opening it, she studied their faces. "As I thought. It seems they were married in life and now recognize each other even in undeath." She bounced on her heels. "Wonderful. Such amazing progress." Mumbling to herself, she paced. "Now I can attempt the next step."

Kyo tore his gaze away from the undead couple to see a shade rushing toward them. Instinctively, he gathered the magic for his drill spell again and managed to leap and thrust it at the shade before it could reach Blanq. She swiftly turned her head and shuffled back as he pressed his spell against the shade, digging through the aura that protected it. The spell exploded, sending the shade hurtling across the ground, raising dust clouds from the dirt path. He took a deep breath and shook his trembling hand.

Why did he do that? While he doubted the shade would have been able to kill Blanq with a single blow, why bother stopping it from trying?

"Thank you," Blanq said. Though her face remained hidden beneath her hood, her words sounded sincere.

Kyo shook his head. "Don't thank me. I shouldn't care if you two try and kill each other." His instinct to protect others might have been getting in the way of common sense. "It'd just be cruel to have this guy be killed by a shade twice in the span of a minute."

The shade rose and charged at them, but Blanq blasted it with raw magic like before, enough to slay the creature, leaving the body of an old man behind. "Zeshin will not be happy if I keep doing that."

Kyo glanced back at the undead couple, the man holding the woman protectively in his arms. Their actions really did reflect consciousness. He found it equal parts incredible and terrifying.

"Blanq," he started in a deep, accusing tone. "What are you trying to do here?"

Blanq motioned with her hand. And after a moment's hesitation, the couple approached her.

"You've just witnessed it for yourself. Or do you not trust your own eyes?" As they casually walked away, she called out. "I know you will ask, as you always do. Alden has left Ueno. He would be in danger if he stayed."

Maybe he was a bit predictable when it came to Alden. But at least he'd be safe wherever he was. As angry as he was that he willingly worked alongside Zeshin, he didn't want his only remaining family harmed. For now, Kyo shouldn't linger. It'd take too much effort to try to kill Blanq, and one hit from that magic blast of hers would likely be his end. But besides that, the desire to do so simply wasn't there. While he felt incredible rage toward Zeshin and Sybilla, he hardly felt a hint of that toward Blanq, and he didn't know why.

Kyo grumbled and took off in a different direction. He had to find Kira. But even if he had, what then? If they all worked together, would they be able to take on Zeshin and Sybilla? Remembering how easily Zeshin kept them bound after escaping the bog was enough reason to doubt it. But they couldn't run and leave Ueno to the hands of the shades either.

One thing at a time. Kyo hopped onto a rooftop and crouched, surveying the area. He spied a man and a child huddled together, hiding behind a thick bush on the side of a house as a shade skulked by. He held his breath as it paused and shifted its gaze.

"Just keep going," Kyo whispered.

A screech in the distance pulled the shade's attention, and it took off down the road. He released a heavy sigh of relief. Thank goodness. He mentally wished the two luck in remaining hidden and unharmed.

Kyo headed toward the clinic, keeping a close eye on his surroundings to make sure he didn't run into any more shades. When the clinic came into view, Sybilla stood outside, her hand outstretched toward a barrier protecting a group of clerics, Marsh among them.

Chapter 28

Kyo ground his teeth, tightening his grip on his swords. Leave it to a monster like Sybilla to target clerics during a time like this. He flung the sword from his right hand. Guided by an air current, it flew with the tip of the blade headed for her neck, but she noticed at the last second and swatted it away with an arm covered in stone. Before the blade could hit the ground, it vanished and reappeared in his hand.

"Oh goodie, it's Alden's brat again." Sybilla said, waving her hand dismissively. "Why don't you go play with a shade?"

Kyo lips twisted into a mocking smirk. "What's wrong? You don't want to fight one of your pawns? That's what Zeshin called us, right? I bet he'd be pretty upset if you killed me, wouldn't he?"

"Don't misunderstand." Sybilla turned to fully face him, the clerics taking the opportunity to pull an injured man and child into the clinic, keeping a barrier erected in front of the doorway. "If you die, he'll be upset, sure." She clenched her fingers layered in stone, sharp claws forming. "But that doesn't mean we can't get what we want. None of you are immune to being killed if you cause too much trouble. We're merely trying to avoid inconveniences."

Kyo sucked in a breath, turning his body to have his side facing Sybilla to give her less of a target. His heart pounded as he steadied himself as best he could to keep his legs from shaking. At this point, it'd be possible to defeat her, maybe, *if* the other four were with him and all at full power. But his instinct to protect others had lured him into a battle he couldn't hope to win. With Ueno being such a small town, hopefully the others would notice their spells going off from a distance.

Kyo didn't need to win. He needed time.

"So, what is it you want?" Kyo asked. He ran through the information he'd learned over the past few days, trying to put the pieces together. "You want to turn people into shades, right? But this has to go beyond what you said in Oasis, about having people's outside reflect the inside or whatever."

Sybilla strolled toward him. "Naturally. But me, I'm just along for the chaotic ride until I reach my inevitable end. I don't envy the rest of you, having to be around for what's to come."

"A world full of shades. That's what you all want?" Kyo asked. "What Mordibrae wants?"

Sybilla froze mid step, her eyes widening, digging into him. The two stared at each other for a long, silent moment.

"You've been going places you shouldn't be, haven't you?" After a tense moment, she shrugged. "Well, whatever. That *thing* can have its little war. I'm more interested in the battle happening here and now." With a wicked smirk, she dashed forward.

The word *war* stuck in Kyo's mind, but he'd have to think more about it later. He jumped onto a nearby roof, but she crouched, her legs condensing and stretching like rubber, and leaped after him. Dismissing his swords, he stretched out his hands, blasting her with a torrent of wind, sending her crashing into the ground with a shriek.

"Want to try that again?" Kyo shouted. "I can do that all day." Knocking her to the ground brought a satisfied grin to his lips, and it didn't take too much magic. Surely someone like Hayner or Kira would come by before he ran dry.

Sybilla rose, dusting off her dress. "That's fine. Stay up there all you want until a shade spots you. I have an appointment with a few clerics."

Shit. Of course she'd use them against him. With no other options, he jumped to the ground to face her head on. He released a slow breath, letting the muscles in his body relax. Though unseen with the naked eye, strands of air stretched from his body in all directions. No better time to try the spell that made his dad known as Kei the Untouchable.

The spell stretched far enough to reach Sybilla and the homes at his sides. As she shifted her body weight, her dress brushed against a few tendrils of air, which sent a vibration through the strands back to him.

Sybilla charged forward, attempting to slash him with her stone claws, but a burst of air from his feet allowed him to leap to the side and avoid it. She didn't slow down, charging from behind him. He didn't bother to turn, feeling her every movement as they sent signals through the air like an invader to a skitter's web. He bent forward to dodge a strike aimed for the back of his head and flipped the sword in his left hand so the blade faced Sybilla and thrust it toward where he knew her neck to be.

She yelped as he felt the blade come in contact with soft flesh before she retreated. Once he turned to face her, he saw no blood and clicked his tongue. Perhaps if he put magic into his blade like he had with the shade… But keeping his current spell active took too much focus. He could already feel it wavering.

"Well, well. I guess you've gotten better in these past few months. Good for you." Sybilla licked her lips, her eyes wide and wild. "But don't think it means you stand a chance against me alone. Out of everyone, I'm most eager to tear *you* to shreds."

The look on her face chilled him to the bone. He remembered Blanq's words about Sybilla being unstable, already proven in multiple cases.

"How come? Isn't it a little pathetic for a grown woman to let a sixteen-year-old get under her skin so much?" Kyo let the spell fade with a heavy sigh, and it was as though a pressure had been released from his head. It still required far more practice. If he couldn't concentrate on using offensive spells at the same time, there was no point.

Sybilla laughed, laced with more madness than humor. "You get under my skin because you remind me too much of my old self. Young, stupid, naïve. And much like I eliminated the old version of me, I want to do the same to you."

A screech tore his attention away from Sybilla. A shade sat crouched on a nearby roof, eyeing both of them.

The shade released another, more powerful shriek. Kyo pressed his palms against his ears and crouched. Sybilla did no such thing, but her grimace showed it affected her in some way. The creature jumped from the roof and charged toward him.

"Aren't you unlucky?" Sybilla cried out, raising a hand in the air. Moss green gas formed and grew around her like a whirling tornado.

Panicked, Kyo jumped high into the air until he was well out of reach. A barrier appeared beneath him, where he crouched and kept an eye on his enemies. The shade stared up for a second then turned its sights on Sybilla.

The shadowy creature leaped for her, her body further coating in a layer of rock before being knocked down. They wrestled on the ground, the shade viciously clawing at her but unable to break through her defenses.

"Stupid thing!" Sybilla rotated them so she had the shade pinned beneath her. "I'm not supposed to kill you, but I'm caring less by the second."

It screeched in her face. This time she covered her ears and stumbled back.

Kyo kept his palms to his ears but watched the fight play out with a slight smile. While he had no hope the shade would kill her, any magic she used to fend it off would be a benefit to him. Another screech pulled his attention. Two more shades approached from the nearby intersection and a third from between two homes, all with their sights on Sybilla.

"Forget this." Sybilla released a frustrated grunt and ran, with the shades giving chase.

"Have fun, Sybilla," Kyo called, suppressing a laugh. That filled him with a much-needed dose of dopamine, and he couldn't wait to recall that story with the others later. Once he surveyed the area and saw no other nearby shades, he descended and rushed into the clinic.

Cots had been brought into the waiting room, with the pained groans and sobs of half a dozen victims and who knew how many more in the back. Marsh knelt wrapping gauze around a deep gash on a young boy's arm. Other clerics worked to help seal wounds with magic.

Any happiness Kyo felt from seconds ago vanished. With so many people gathered in one place, it was a miracle no shades had broken in. It'd only take one to slaughter everyone here. And Sybilla wanted to do so herself. It'd be poetic if those shades managed to rip her apart. It took too long to notice Jaune sitting in the chair closest to the door, an injured woman with a bandage around her head next to him with her eyes closed.

"Jaune," Kyo said. "Glad to see you're okay. How's your leg?"

Jaune gazed up with sad eyes. "They started working on it but didn't get far before everything went crazy. So, I still can't walk on it. Sorry. I was going to help you with my barriers from in here, but you apparently had it under control. With a lot of luck."

"Yeah, at least something decided to go my way for once." Kyo searched the room. "I'm going to guess Kira isn't still here?"

"No, as soon as the shades started entering town, she left. You can't keep her from a good fight. I hope she's okay."

"Does she still have the stone?"

Jaune nodded. "As far as I know. She left before we could think things through. Always so darn hasty. If you find her, tell her to hide her pouch. Somewhere, anywhere. It'd be a lot harder to find the stone that way."

"Yeah, I'll tell her."

"The others might beat you to it. They were here earlier, before Sybilla showed up. But the more people we have searching for her, the better."

Marsh spoke quiet words to the young boy then rose and approached Kyo. "Where is Sybilla?"

"Gone, for now. A group of shades appeared and came after her," Kyo said. "It was funny. You would have enjoyed seeing it. I guess Zeshin has a rule about not letting her kill shades."

"In this case, it was to our benefit. However, it is concerning someone like her does not wish to go against Zeshin's words. But that is beside the point. Thank you, Kyo. If you had not shown up when you did…well, we know what would have happened." Marsh glanced around the room, his eyes filled with concern. "I feel so helpless. Even if I could cast spells easily, there are so many out there beyond help." His fist shook at his side. "And all for what?"

Kyo's lips twisted. "I don't know. Sybilla mentioned something about a war related to Mordibrae, but we can think about that later."

"Have you made any progress on finding Hayner or Kira?" Marsh asked.

"No. I'm hoping the others will have better luck. Maybe I should stay here with you to make sure you're safe." Kyo focused on a cleric woman working to heal a deep gash in a man's chest. He swore he saw a hint of an exposed rib, causing him to cringe. "With a whole town to heal, they won't be left with much magic to defend themselves."

Marsh gently shoved Kyo toward the door. "While your assistance would be greatly appreciated, I must insist otherwise."

"What do you mean? If I leave—"

"Then I'll protect this place," Jaune said. "I don't need to move to cast barriers. I'll make sure nothing gets in here. At least for a while."

Kyo groaned. Jaune wouldn't be able to keep Zeshin or Sybilla out for long. Then again, neither would Kyo.

"Fine. I'll find Kira and hopefully the others. Maybe they've already found her." Kyo reared back to peek out the front door. "Stay safe."

He leaped atop the clinic's roof and searched for any sign of the others. Down beyond the rice fields, a trio was being chased by a shade as they headed for the underground cell. At least others had the same idea. Kyo's breath caught in his throat as the shade caught up to one of the runners and took them down with a single swipe of its claws to their back. His legs tensed, ready to rush to help, but he didn't move. Yes, his parents would have done so and had a much easier time than him. But like Roland said, his individual choices could make all the difference. He couldn't delay finding Kira any longer.

"Good luck," he mumbled, turning his back to them.

A pillar of fire, an echoing incantation—he hoped for some sign of his friends. He heard rumbles and crashes but saw no sign of where they came from. By the sound of it, he needed to go deeper into town to the west.

Kyo hopped between rooftops and over narrow streets, knowing it risked him being spotted, but the vantage point was his best bet of finding them. If only the homes were two stories like most other places.

Every few roofs, he paused, listening for the sounds of battles and keeping a cautious eye out for nearby shades. Maybe Hayner and Kira were making quick work of them.

A shout echoed through the air, down a tight path between the backs of two homes. In the lot, Kira used the shadows near her to tangle around a shade. They squeezed and beat against the creature, keeping a wrap over its mouth. Then a shadow stabbed it through the chest. The aura faded, and the body of an elderly man was laid gently on the ground. A sad thing to see but one less shade to worry about.

Kyo jumped to the ground and raised his hand. "Kira."

She turned and smiled, returning his wave. His smile faded, and his face stiffened as his eyes locked with Zeshin's appearing behind her from the corner of a home. Before Kyo could find his voice, a pair of thick, sharp vines twisted together plunged into her back and burst from her stomach, blood splattering onto the ground as he raised her body into the air.

Kira's eyes widened, and her jaw hung in a silent cry.

"Found you."

Chapter 29

Blood flowed from Kira's wound, soaking her robe. Her gasps for air came out as pained gurgles, her body stiffening, unable to do anything as she dangled in the air. What organs might he have struck? Liver? Kidney? Was her spine still intact? Kyo didn't know anatomy well; these were questions for Marsh. All that aside, the blood loss would kill her if not handled quickly, but he could do nothing to help.

Zeshin reached beneath Kira's robe and retrieved her enchanted leather pouch. "I'm assuming the stone is in here?"

He flung Kira to the side, leaving her bleeding, curled up and unmoving against a wall.

"Zeshin! How many more people do you have to hurt before you're satisfied? All of this for one stone?" The rage that had consumed Kyo in the library returned in full force, his fists squeezing tight at his sides, ready to be buried in Zeshin's face. Yet Blanq's words kept him at bay. He knew full well he was no match for Zeshin, for his parents' murderer. Tears of frustration welled in Kyo's eyes, knowing he couldn't claim the opportunity to avenge them by himself.

"Preferably, none." Zeshin rummaged through the pouch, tossing aside any item that wasn't the stone. "However, that's a fool's dream. I know full well many will be against what I'm trying to accomplish, despite it being for the greater good."

"Greater good, my ass," Kyo said through clenched teeth. His gaze drifted to Kira. No time to argue, he needed to help her, but how? If only he'd learned a healing spell from Marsh over the past six months like he initially intended to.

Zeshin felt around within the pouch again. Kyo thrust his fist forward, launching a gust of wind at his face. While the force caused his head to jerk back, it didn't so much as pause his search or gain a reaction.

After a deep breath, Kyo extended his hands, palms facing out. Wind rotated in a circular motion around Zeshin, picking up dirt, a bucket, a bed sheet that had been hanging on a clothesline, anything light that wasn't nailed down. The wind formed a twister that rose well above the surrounding homes. Hopefully, his friends would investigate. Though the shades might keep them busy. While the spell itself hadn't deterred Zeshin's search, the bedsheet wrapping around his head and upper body did, at least long enough for him to tear it off.

"You truly have your parent's determination," Zeshin said loudly through the whirling wind. His eyes met Kyo's. "I never hated them, you know. In fact, I admired them. But I couldn't allow them to get in the way."

Kyo's face grew hot, the urge to thrust a sword at the man's face growing by the second. But he had to focus, not only on maintaining the spell but ensuring it didn't cause any harm to Kira. "Right, this grand plan of yours. Turn everyone into mindless shades. I don't care what your reason is—it's not happening."

Zeshin pulled a tome from the pouch and released it into the torrent of wind that surrounded him.

"It *must* happen. The very idea of free will is at stake. To preserve the freedom of all life, I will assist Mordibrae."

It all came back to that being, that deity Kyo had seen below Crossroads. Why would anyone think turning all humans into ravenous beasts was a good thing? "Preserve freedom? Becoming a shade rips that away from us."

The ground around Zeshin rose like thick worms, each battering against him, knocking him back and forth like a ball between rackets before a final strike sent him crashing against the exterior of a house. Hayner leaped from a rooftop and landed in a crouch. The pillars of rock chased Zeshin through the home and crashed into him all at once. With a sigh, Kyo dismissed his spell, and the various items that had been floating about crashed to the ground.

"Thank goodness this town is so small. Kira needs help!" He pointed to where she lay motionless.

Hayner searched before locking his sights on Kira, but before he could move, Krysta dashed between two homes and knelt by her side. "Kira! No, no, no. Please hang in there."

Roland and Rosette came up behind her but could do nothing but stare helplessly.

"We need a cleric," Roland shouted.

The rock around Zeshin shattered, revealing him standing with a tall shield made of hardened tree bark attached to his right arm. He rotated his opposite shoulder. "That hurt."

Kyo stepped closer to Hayner, summoning his swords. "He has Kira's pouch. We have to get it back."

"We will," Hayner said. "Your Highness, go get a cleric, quickly!"

Krysta rose and waved her hands around Kira. A combination of ice and barrier surrounded her in the vague shape of an igloo, entrance included.

"Roland, Rosette, protect her. I'm going." She ran for the alleyway leading to the main road then propelled herself forward with fire bursting from her hands.

Zeshin eyed them for a second then glanced at the pouch in his hand. "I suppose there is no guarantee the stone is with her, is there? It could have easily changed hands. I'd much rather avoid a repeat of what happened at the bog."

"We will make damn sure you don't get your hands on it," Hayner growled, unable to help a glance to where Kira lay.

"Your compliance is hardly necessary. You are an impressive mage. But you are no Aurora," Zeshin taunted.

A giggle came from above. "Oh, this looks like fun. Can I join?" Sybilla asked, sitting on a rooftop, feet dangling off the edge.

Kyo froze upon hearing her voice. One of them would be difficult enough to deal with, but if they fought together, they had no chance of winning.

"Please let me. As a reward for being good and not killing any shades like you asked." Her face scrunched in annoyance. "I sure had reason to."

Zeshin shook his head. "Leave this to me. You can find Blanq and leave for now. I have a little test to perform, but I have a feeling we'll want to start getting ready for the next step."

"Ugh, and here I was hoping to get a bit of payback for Oasis. Fine." Sybilla stood and dropped off the other side of the roof.

Kyo released a silent sigh of relief. At least death wasn't guaranteed, only highly likely. What an improvement. If they all worked together, they might squeeze out a win.

"This is bad," Hayner whispered. "I hate to say this, but I'm not confident in our chances."

"Hey, Roland, Rosette…"

"Don't worry, we'll keep a close eye on Kira, but we'll back you up as best we can," Roland said.

That provided Kyo some comfort, and Krysta would surely join in as soon as she returned. Even so, that left a gloomy prospect for victory. The way Sybilla took orders from Zeshin and his overwhelming confidence strongly hinted at him being a more horrifying opponent.

Zeshin raised his hand, vines bursting from the ground, stretching to wrap around them. But Hayner acted first, surrounding himself and Kyo in a wall of rock. Grunting heavily, Hayner motioned with his hands for the rock to spread, stretching the vines until they snapped.

"It won't be that easy this time." Hayner raised a boulder about half his height from the ground, sharp bits flinging off as projectiles.

Zeshin raised his shield to protect himself, the bark reforming as quickly as the rock chipped away at it. Kyo raced forward, gripping the hilts of his swords, but had to dodge to the side to avoid a flurry of sharp thorns shot from Zeshin's hand.

When the next wave came, Kyo blasted them away with a burst of wind. He had to keep up the pressure. The blade of his sword emitted a deep azure glow. He flung it toward Zeshin, whirling through the air like a buzzsaw. Though Zeshin was able to knock it away, Kyo kept it spinning in the air to assault him no matter how many times he deflected it.

The ground rumbled, a thick jagged rock shooting out toward Zeshin's legs, but a shield of bark formed around his shin, though the force slid him backward and nearly made him fall.

Kyo slid to a stop at Zeshin's right side, thrusting his swords toward his neck, but Zeshin formed another shield, small like the buckler Kyo had used in the bog and parried the strikes. As much as Kyo would love to pierce through his defenses and secure a kill, he kept his main focus on distracting Zeshin enough to allow Hayner to land a decisive blow. Thrust after thrust toward the neck, chest, and stomach were all blocked or batted away while Zeshin continued to use his larger shield to block Hayner's projectiles and shift his body to avoid larger oncoming attacks from above and below.

Kyo struck faster with precision. It was all Zeshin could do to keep their attacks at bay. A bit longer and…

No.

His heart jumped when his eyes met Zeshin's. The emotionless look on his face and the lack of tension in his muscles sent a chill down Kyo's spine. Despite the relentless assault against him, there appeared no sign of struggle. Zeshin was bored.

This both horrified and enraged Kyo. He dismissed his swords and created a wind drill in his right hand, launching himself forward, and thrust it toward Zeshin's face. Much like Sybilla, Zeshin coated the skin of his hand in armor, though made of tree bark instead of rock or metal, and caught the drill. Kyo pushed with all his might, grunting as more magic flowed from his core down his arm and into the spell in hopes of chipping away at the armor.

As the spell condensed and readied to explode, Zeshin gripped Kyo's fingers with his own and flung it to the side. The condensed spell erupted and blasted a large hole in the wall of a hopefully empty home.

Before Kyo could react, Zeshin summoned a green bo staff resembling a thick thorny rose stem and thrust the end into Kyo's gut, knocking the air from his lungs and sending him tumbling backward. He scrambled to his hands and knees, his chest burning with each cough, pain radiating from the impact point.

With a single push of his foot, Zeshin closed the distance to Hayner, sidestepping the rocks and bashing him in the head with his shield. Hayner stumbled but regained his balance. He created a large hammer out of rock and swung it at Zeshin's head. A single thrust from the bo staff shattered the hammer, showing a massive difference in the magic behind both weapons, and followed up with several more slams to the head with the jagged shield.

Rosette leaped in the way and parried another attempted blow to Hayner with a powerful kick. As soon as her feet touched the ground, she punched Zeshin's stomach, the force pushing him back. Roland joined, wielding his polearm, standing protectively in front of Hayner, who swayed.

Kyo rose and took a deep breath, heart pounding at seeing Hayner struggle to right himself and the blood trickling down the side of his head. From this angle he could see Kira's pouch, gripped in the hand connected to Zeshin's shield. They didn't have to defeat him, just grab the pouch and escape. Much easier said than done.

"I truly do admire you all," Zeshin said. "A band of strangers coming together, forming a family of sorts, and fighting alongside one another. Not so different from the Aurora when I was a member. Unfortunately, you misunderstand what's at stake. Mordibrae's war is our war, whether we like it or not."

Kyo narrowed his eyes. "We understand enough. We'll fight to keep more people from becoming shades and go back to living peacefully."

"Even if you succeeded, that peace would be shattered eventually," Zeshin said. "This is bigger than any one race, any one world. If Mordibrae fails, all worlds will be lost, our freedoms stripped away."

Zipping among the stars, landing on another world to see a waging battle. Whatever the golden light in the vision represented must have been Mordibrae's enemy. Combining this with Murielle's interpretation and Zeshin's explanation, Kyo couldn't accuse him of being a liar. But even if all of that were true, turning humanity into mindless soldiers couldn't be the only way to deal with it.

Krysta returned to the alleyway, Marsh and another cleric in tow. The two slipped directly into the igloo.

"Hayner, are you okay?" Krysta joined Roland and Rosette, fire engulfing her hands.

He blinked hard. "Yes, Your Highness. I won't let you fight without my aid."

Roland charged forward and thrust the tip of his polearm at Zeshin's chest. Zeshin parried the strike then swung the same end of his staff across Roland's face, a thorn slicing into his cheek, followed by a swift jab to the chest.

Rosette jumped and swung her leg at Zeshin's head but was gently parried with the staff. Each punch and kick that followed, he either dodged completely, blocked with the staff, or finally met by tripping her. He stepped on her back, and with a swift fling of his staff, a thorn cut the tie of her pouch and flung it into the air for him to catch.

Grunting, Rosette pushed herself up with her hands, grabbed Zeshin's foot, and tossed him into the air. Before he could land, she hopped to her feet and side-kicked him through a nearby wall.

Krysta raised her hands, building more fire around them.

But Roland grabbed her wrist. "Stop. We don't know if there are people hiding in there."

With a frustrated grunt, she relented.

Zeshin stepped out of the hole, tilting his head to crack his neck. "I forget how strong you can be. It's highly impressive. And I must commend you on taking on the feral I corrupted and winning." His gaze shifted to the entrance to the igloo.

Vines stretched from his hand and flew inside. They pulled Marsh out from his ankle. As he dangled helplessly, Zeshin snatched his pouch and tossed him to the ground.

"There we are. How many more?" Zeshin asked, glancing between them.

Marsh paused for a moment, blood on his hands and some on his robe. His eyes fell on Krysta before silently scrambling back into the igloo.

Kyo charged, swinging his swords at Zeshin's head, but instead met his staff. "You have no idea how badly I want to kill you."

"I know. But you're simply too weak." Zeshin swung his staff at Kyo's arm. The strike was blocked, but he followed up by swinging it upward, a thorn slicing his chin.

The deep cut sent a pained shiver through Kyo's body. His eyes fell on the staff, trying to keep his focus on it to avoid further harm, and noticed whenever Zeshin's hands shifted, the thorns retracted where appropriate to keep from harming him and protruded from where his hands had previously been. The next strike hit Kyo's right thigh then another on the left side of his head, dizzying his vision. The flurry left cuts and gashes wherever they touched, coming too quickly to block or avoid and easily bypassing his magic defenses. Blood dribbled down his face, limbs, and torso, staining his clothes.

Kyo swayed, vision hazy and body twitching. Through occasional flashes, he registered attacks from Krysta's flame and Roland's polearm, both effortlessly blocked with Zeshin's tree bark shield. Like the others, he sliced the pouch from Kyo's hip and claimed it. A boulder fell from the air, but Zeshin shattered it with his staff before it could land on him. Roland and Krysta had to cease their attacks when vines shot from the ground and threatened to bind them, putting distance between themselves and Zeshin.

Kyo fell back, struggling to control his own body. His arms and legs shivered, he couldn't see straight, and sharp pain assaulted him from head to toe.

Weak. That had been proven time and time again.

Whatever power he'd gained over the past six months hadn't been nearly enough. Of course not. In the big picture, it was such a short time, especially if he hoped to match an ex-Aurora. That would easily take years. A sixteen-year-old expecting to match a man like that, laughable. But he couldn't afford to lay there and lament his sadness. He had to get up, had to do everything in his power to stop him, no matter how small his chances of victory.

Rosette began her incantation to summon an Altruist, but a vine shot forth from Zeshin's hand, wrapping around her mouth and head to keep her from speaking.

Even through his daze, Kyo's eyes widened as Zeshin's hand became engulfed in a shadowy aura, the same one used to corrupt the centipede.

"I was initially against this," Zeshin said, "but I suppose turning one or two of you into shades wouldn't hurt."

Breath hitching, Kyo couldn't move, couldn't avoid Zeshin's hand reaching for him. Would he become corrupted or go straight to being a shade? His body refused to listen, words wouldn't come. Someone's voice, he wasn't sure who's, cried his name.

A barrier appeared before Kyo. Zeshin's eyes narrowed, and he struck at the barrier. Though cracks formed, it held strong.

Rosette pulled Kyo away and leaned him against a wall.

Kyo glanced to his side, seeing Jaune supported by a crutch, his other hand outstretched. "I'll provide what support I can, Your Highness."

More fighting commenced while Kyo attempted to regain himself.

"Shit," he mumbled, attempting to blink away the pain.

"Are you okay?" Rosette asked, lightly shaking him.

"Stop shaking me and I might be." She stopped and Kyo's vision came into focus. Hayner, Roland, and Krysta engaged with Zeshin, Jaune creating barriers here and there to protect them from blows or bounce attacks away from them.

The Aurora, Blanq, Zeshin, Jaune—they all had something in common that set them apart, and he felt like an idiot for not realizing it earlier. The way they're able to focus their minds and spells were on a whole different level. It wasn't about power alone. While he proved he could focus to some degree when he fought Sybilla earlier, it was nothing compared to them.

Taking a deep breath, Kyo rose, ignoring the sharp pain from the deep gashes in his body. "Rosette, go help them, but be careful. I'll be okay."

She gazed at him hesitantly then nodded, rushing to punch Zeshin from behind. The surprise strike allowed the others to land several attacks of their own. Even when his hand became engulfed in the corruption, Jaune's barriers managed to keep it from touching them.

One by one, Zeshin blocked or parried attacks and took the opportunity to claim more of their enchanted pouches, Roland's after keeping his polearm pinned with his foot, Krysta's and Hayner's stolen from vines stealthily sprouting behind them.

Kyo's eyes widened when Zeshin turned toward Jaune. Not from fear but renewed confidence. Though slight, a trickle of blood slid down the side of Zeshin's head.

He was not invincible.

Powerful, yes, but human like the rest of them.

When Zeshin charged at Jaune, Kyo threw both his swords, the blades glowing and spinning rapidly, forcing him to stop and parry them with his staff. Using wind to control the rotation and direction, Kyo continued to assault him, aiming everywhere from his head to his ankles. Zeshin expertly blocked as many strikes as possible but couldn't avoid them all. Kyo had the swords spin faster than he could keep track of, moving up and down so as not to be predictable. A slice to his arm, another to his back.

Krysta shouted, engulfing Zeshin in a wave of blue flame that charred the ground and radiated heat throughout the entire lot. Barriers with spikes surrounded him from multiple directions, keeping him encased.

"Rosette, Roland," Jaune called.

Needing no further instruction, the two struck the barriers repeatedly to sandwich Zeshin between the spikes.

Kyo's swords reappeared in his hands as he watched the attacks come to a halt. Silence fell. No one moved. As the flames cleared, they were greeted to what looked like a giant walnut shell. A crack formed along the side, and the second it split open, Zeshin crashed through the barrier in front of him, striking Jaune's broken leg.

Jaune fell with a cry that echoed beyond the lot. Zeshin yanked the pouch from his side and reached for him with a hand engulfed in the corruption, and fresh trickles of blood running down his head and torso.

Kyo shot his hands forward, blasting Zeshin away and sending him tumbling across the ground. Zeshin quickly righted himself and gazed between them, a smirk crossing his lips.

"Not bad. I thought we'd have to wait a bit longer, but I believe you're at the level we need." He brushed his fingers over the side of his head, wiping away some blood. "Thank you for showing me."

A wall of vines burst from the ground, stretching across the gap between the two homes Zeshin stood between. From the other side, a bright white light shone through.

"He's getting away," Hayner called.

While the others attacked the vines, Kyo jumped onto the nearest rooftop, tensing his shaky limbs and clenching his teeth through the pain. But the vines stretched with his every movement to keep him away. With a burst of air, he leaped over the vines. He pointed his swords downward, and he closed in on Zeshin.

The strike met nothing but dirt. He'd vanished.

Kyo stared at the spot Zeshin had been a second ago, body stiff. They'd lost the accrue stone, and Ueno remained in shambles with who knew how many dead. He couldn't even take comfort in knowing none of his party had been killed while Kira remained in her current condition. His swords fell from his hands. He sat on the dirt, unmoving. They had failed.

Chapter 30

A fireball burst through the wall of vines, and though the heat engulfed Kyo like a wave, he didn't move, not even to shield himself with his arms. The weight of their failure pressed on him, as well as the question of what to do next. Were they really so helpless without the Aurora? Though this had never been a situation people like them could handle in the first place.

"He escaped, didn't he?" Krysta asked.

Kyo glanced through the hole in the vines. Roland, Rosette, and Krysta stood together. Next to them, Hayner supported Jaune. All of them except Rosette had shed at least some blood during the fight.

"Yeah. By a fraction of a second." Taking a deep breath, he stood, his swords vanishing from the ground.

Krysta gritted her teeth, but her anger subsided as she rushed back toward the igloo. Waving her hands, she dismantled it block by block to expose Marsh and the other cleric working on Kira. The wound was deep and bloody but no longer a gaping hole within her body.

"Please tell me she'll make it," Krysta pled.

The cleric shook her head. "Too early to tell," she said. "The focus is mending the wound enough to move her." Panting and beads of sweat dripping from her brow, a pale green glow emitted from her hands, carefully binding flesh together while Marsh absorbed any excess blood with cloth.

"She will need a blood transfusion as soon as possible. When it is safe to move her, we will take her back to the clinic," Marsh assured her.

Krysta hid her face in her hands, and Roland patted her back. Rosette paced impatiently, occasionally glancing at Kira.

"She'll make it," Hayner said. "She's strong."

Jaune stared at his friend lying on the ground, tears trickling down his cheeks. "She'd better. My siblings wouldn't ever forgive me if I couldn't protect her."

"Did she still have the stone?" Kyo asked, unable to help but ask the burning question.

"No, she didn't." Krysta lowered her hands. "She passed it on to Hayner, then I suggested Hayner give it to me. They didn't even try to search us in the library, so I figured they'd be satisfied assuming one of the royal guard had it."

He didn't know what had made them change their minds about assuming the stone had to be with a member of the royal guard, but he wished they hadn't. So much happened so quickly, if only they'd stopped to think for a moment, think to hide the pouch somewhere it wouldn't be found. The library, a random home, anywhere would have kept it out of their hands. He pinched the bridge of his nose, clenching his eyes and wishing he could go back in time instead of facing the consequences of their failure.

* * *

Night had fallen and stars consumed the sky. Usually a welcome sight to Kyo, but though beautiful, they were a contrast to the tragedy that had occurred.

The screeches of shades were absent, thank goodness, leaving him and the others confident it'd be safe to remain outside the clinic. Most had been slain in one way or another. The few that had been led back to the underground cell were finished off by Hayner, who needed something to do besides sit and wait for an update on Kira's condition.

Kyo ran his fingers over the various bandages that covered his injuries. While the gashes had been closed, a few left scars behind, most notably one across his left cheek and one down his forehead. He'd been marked by his parents' killer and had not been able to return the favor.

"I wish we could stay and help," Rosette said quietly.

Roland placed a hand on her head. "I know, kiddo. But we need to get back to Alderdeem. There isn't much we'd be able to do here anyway."

Unfortunately, Kyo agreed. The sights that greeted them after exiting the lot were terrible. Broken, sometimes destroyed homes, blood splattered here and there, and survivors unsure how to handle the deaths of loved ones, emotionally or otherwise. Despite their best efforts, Ueno became a repeat of Calmarock.

He glanced at Krysta, who had remained silent since they'd returned to the clinic. Her uncle lecturing her was undoubtedly the least of her concerns. First Layla, now Kira. Leaning his head against the wall, he stared up at the stars. There was no point in wondering what his parents would do in this situation. Even if he knew, he wasn't strong enough to do the same. Only the Aurora could handle this, yet now he had doubts about that. Unless they brought in more members to help, the three he'd known might not be enough. They were on a fast track to a future where everyone became shades or undead, all because of a few maniacal mages, some mysterious entity, and those damn stones. And they were helpless to stop it.

The door to the clinic opened, drawing everyone's attention.

Marsh stepped outside, glancing between them with heavy eyes. "Kira is finally stable. We are keeping as close an eye on her as we can while also seeing to everyone else."

Krysta rushed to hug Marsh, releasing sobs into his shoulder. "Thank you."

He returned the embrace. "I did very little. You should thank Mai. She saved Kira's life."

"Don't sell yourself short, kid," Roland said. "You were there the whole time, doing the best you could. I'm sure you played a damn important role in saving her."

A slight smile crossed Marsh's lips. "Either way, she has not regained consciousness yet. You should get some rest for the night." His eyes turned to the Pantheon's Library in the distance. "Those who no longer have a home are taking refuge in the library. Given the size, it should accommodate everyone who needs a place to sleep. I am sure you will have no problem finding space there."

"What about you?" Kyo asked.

"A cleric's work is never done. I will stay here and help how I can and rest when a moment allows." Marsh stared at his hand and flexed his fingers. "My magic is slowly returning. So, if there is a need for me to cast a spell, I should be able to do so."

"I'm sure they're grateful to have your help. And even if you didn't use magic, you still helped patch me up. I didn't get a chance to say thanks before you got pulled away." Kyo placed his fist over his heart and bowed at the waist. "So, thanks, bedhead."

Marsh smirked. "It is the least I could do after what you have done for me."

"Wow, what's that?" Rosette asked, staring into the distance.

Kyo and the others turned to see what must have been over a hundred streams of azure-and-violet energy flying above their heads from all over town, the glow illuminating their faces. They raced for the tree line well past the shade pit and converged onto one spot.

Memories of Calmarock returned to Kyo, when Sybilla had drained the magic from her many victims into the accrue stone to much the same effect. He knew he should follow the trail, attack whichever of the three was responsible, but his legs wouldn't move. What was the point? He'd arrive, be beaten down or worse, and they'd escape.

"They found the stone," Krysta growled through a clenched jaw. "That was quicker than I would have liked."

"So, they can drain magic from people just like that? Without touching them?" Roland asked.

"As long as the people are dead, it apparently makes the process a lot easier for them," Kyo snarled in a low voice. "At least that's what Sybilla said in Calmarock."

Rosette stomped her foot on the ground several times, creating a deep footprint in the grass. "I want to punch them so hard."

Seconds after the energy stopped flowing, a white light shined from within the trees. Kyo glared, his eyes focused on the spot, knowing whichever of them stood out there was about to teleport away again. They were lucky to have such a skill to make things easier for them. He doubted they'd be so bold without it. The light vanished, leaving them with the knowledge a stone had been filled with stolen magic, ready to be used for who knew what.

"Any news?" Jaune asked, approaching with a limp beside Hayner.

"Kira is going to recover," Krysta said, her face softening.

Jaune sighed and pinched the bridge of his nose. "Thank Tutelvus." After a few seconds, he took a deep breath. "We just finished speaking to His Majesty. An airship should arrive by late tomorrow to bring us home."

"I'm ashamed to have to keep relying on his airships. But I'm grateful to have access to them. Was he upset?" Krysta asked.

"He was more concerned than anything. For you, for the stone, and whatever they have planned next. Word will be spread to other chancellors around Feracael so they can prepare as best they can." Hayner peered through the window of the clinic. "We should go see her."

"I will not say no," Marsh said, "but only for a moment. And if an airship is coming tomorrow, she will be in no condition to travel. She will have to stay here for the time being to recover."

Jaune turned to Hayner. "Permission to stay here with her until she recovers?"

After a moment of silence, Hayner shook his head. "Denied. We are needed back in Alderdeem." He placed a hand on Jaune's shoulder. "She'll understand."

Silently, Jaune nodded then stepped into the clinic.

"There is not enough room for us all to see her," Marsh warned.

Roland gently nudged Krysta. "Go ahead. You three go in with Marsh. I'll stay out here with Rosette and Kyo."

Krysta smiled and headed inside.

"If what Murielle said about the accrue stones being left here by the Pantheon is true, it'd sure be nice if they came by to pick them up, clean up after themselves, and end this mess," Kyo grumbled.

"I wish they could too. But they can't come and go as they please, only when they are summoned. And I don't know if they can take anything back with them."

Rosette stepped in front of Kyo and stared up at him. "Isn't your godfather trying to destroy the stones?"

Roland glanced at them both. "I wanted to ask, now that Krysta isn't here to get all uppity. Where do you stand on all of that? You obviously have a bias, but do you trust him?"

Kyo remained silent, a thousand thoughts flooding his mind. Each time he'd seen Alden since his "kidnapping," he'd acted like himself, spoken like himself. His words sounded genuine, and how could he doubt his desire to avenge his friends after Zeshin killed them? Which brought up the question of how he could stand being around that man, even if it was to get close to the stones. Seeing Alden walk beside Zeshin had broken Kyo's heart, filled him with rage, the shock too much to process at the time. But as he ran through everything in his mind, from his childhood to the events of the past six months and today, he could only come to one conclusion.

"Yeah, I do." Kyo locked eyes with Roland. "I really believe he's trying to find a way to destroy the stones and avenge my parents. The way he's going about it is risky, but I guess it's the only way he'd be able to. He isn't a fighter, but he is smart and very good at what he does."

"You mean enchanting?" Rosette asked.

Kyo nodded. "Yep. Not even Cedric could destroy the stones with raw power. So, Alden is looking for a workaround. I doubt they think he is loyal to their cause, given they use me to blackmail him. But it feels like the closer they get to winning, the more willing they are to kill me. If they're keeping him around, there must be at least one more stone that they need him to get. But after that, I sure hope he has a plan to get away from them."

"And I hope you're right about him. We need all the help we can get. If he can figure out a way to destroy the stones, I'm all for it. But that's a big 'if'." Roland took

Rosette's hand. "It's getting chilly. Let's stay in the waiting room for now."

Kyo couldn't blame Roland for his doubts. They were talking about tools belonging to deities. Destroying them might be entirely impossible. But if there was even the slightest chance, Kyo had to hope for the best and let Alden try. He followed them inside, standing against a wall so he wouldn't be in the way. Though some of the faces had changed, there were no fewer injured people than earlier that day. The clerics had their work cut out for them, but they deserved an enormous amount of respect for sacrificing sleep to help those who needed it. More than anything, everyone in Ueno needed rest. And for his group, time to think, to plan for a way to get the stone back and deal with Zeshin, Sybilla, and Blanq, before they gathered enough magic to turn all of Feracael into shades.